ISBN: 978-1-64456-378-6 [Paperback]
ISBN: 978-1-64456-379-3 [Mobi]
ISBN: 978-1-64456-380-9 [ePub]
ISBN: 978-1-64456-381-6 [Audiobook]

Library of Congress Control Number: 2021944904

INDIES UNITED PUBLISHING HOUSE, LLC
P.O. BOX 3071
QUINCY, IL 62305-3071
www.indiesunited.net

Also by Glenda Carroll

Dead in the Water

"**DEAD IN THE WATER** is....so well written you just can't put it down...If you're like me, you'll be trying to figure out who committed the murder while you're working out." - *Lynne Cox, NY Times Bestselling author, "Swimming to Antarctica," "Open Water Swimming Manual," "Swimming in the Sink: An Episode of the Heart."*

"Carroll combines a skill for mystery writing...with her sports journalism and Masters swimming background by nailing the details of what it's like to race in open water...I liked Carroll's characters immensely, but it was the story that kept me up late reading." - *Swimmer Magazine*

"(**DEAD IN THE WATER**) is a swim-centric mystery that will keep you turning pages while you think about your strokes. It's the first open-water-detective-novel that I know of, and it's great fun to read." - *Lynn Sherr. Sherr was a broadcast journalist and writer for more than thirty years at ABC News. Author of "Swim: Why We Love the Water."*

Drop Dead Red

"A smart, steadfast gumshoe who, in her second book, continues to flourish...Carroll's writing bounces off the page." - *Kirkus Reviews*

"Glenda Carroll, in her new novel, **Drop Dead Red** leads us through the nooks and crannies she knows so well in San Francisco and its neighbor, Marin County. Her heroine, Trish Carson, a sports swimmer, has intimate knowledge of those hearty souls who swim in icy cold lakes. Put these elements together with an unusual murder of ... swim leader, Shari Grantner, a beautiful, complex redhead, and the suspects around her, you have a mystery worth reading." - *Rita Lakin, author of the "Getting Old is Murder "series.*

To Joseph, Carolina, Caden, and Eddie, Jr.

A Trisha Carson Mystery

DEAD CODE

Glenda Carroll

INDIES UNITED PUBLISHING HOUSE, LLC

CHAPTER 1

"I can't go into this lake by myself. I just can't. Lena? Are you listening to me? I can't do this. I'll die if I do."

I stood on a pebbly beach behind a circle of excited swimmers that curled ten deep around a tall lifeguard podium. Next to me was my younger sister, Lena, the one who'd pushed me into aquatic sports and its Zen-like subsection, open water swimming. The other athletes laughed and chattered nervously, waiting to hear the race instructions for the one-mile swim. Napa County's largest lake, a glorious blue body of water with small islands in the distance, stretched out behind the lifeguard chair. A mild breeze barely made a ripple on its glassy surface, the air warm, against my increasingly clammy skin.

It should be inviting, welcoming, appealing. Not for me. My heart was racing. My stomach muscles tightened and cramped while the wide lake in front of me narrowed. The swimmers faded into the background until they disappeared altogether, leaving a chilling silence. I knew if I stepped into the water, I wouldn't come out.

More than a year ago, after months of Lena urging me to 'do something' about my excess pounds, I stuffed myself into one of her much-smaller swimsuits, borrowed goggles and a cap and slipped into the water. My haphazard training turned out to be a lifesaver. Literally. Not long before, I'd been forced to swim down the shore of a lake much like this one, to escape a maniac murderer. The emotional effects of that swim lingered in the background. But now, with another body of water in front of me, they marched front and center.

I leaned over and put my hands on my knees, trying to catch my breath. I stared at my feet, wondering if they belonged to me.

"Trisha? Hello. What's the big deal? There will be 150 people swimming around you," said Lena. I turned my head and tried to fix my attention on her mouth. It moved, but her voice was indistinct. She smiled. "Let's make that swimming in front of you. Just follow them. You'll be fine."

She put her hand on my back and gave me a little push forward, closer to the pack. The tiny rocks hurt my feet as I shifted my weight back and forth. I squeezed my swim cap between my hands. I dropped it. Picked it up. Dropped it again. Picked it up again. *Did the temperature drop?* I stood there shivering, watching goosebumps grow on my arms and legs.

"You promised," I said a little louder than I expected. A few swimmers glanced in my direction, but I ignored them. "You promised that when I finally believed I could get back in the water, you'd be swimming next to me."

"Last year, you swam the entire length of a lake a lot longer than this, totally by yourself. You even swam around a point in San Francisco Bay, albeit to rescue me. This is nothing."

"That was different. Someone wanted to kill me. It was the only way I could get away and it was the only way I could get to you. That was a necessity. This is a stupid choice."

I bit my bottom lip so hard I tasted blood.

"I planned on swimming with you, you know that. But I couldn't find a babysitter for Little T."

Six-month-old Timmy, or "Little T," was Lena's adorable son. He slept in the baby backpack, his head resting on her shoulder.

"What am I supposed to do? Leave him on the beach?"

"Well," I started to say.

"You're not serious?"

"No. Just. . . I don't know. I've been anxious before, but never like this. I've got to get away from this lake." The swimmers lining the beach chatted, smiled and laughed. Me? I could barely breathe. "Nope. I'm not ready. Not yet. You swim. I'll watch the baby." I reached for Little T. Lena shook her head.

"Move up a little closer or you'll miss the instructions for the swim."

She reached over, grabbed the strap of my swimsuit and dragged me forward into the crowd.

"Didn't you hear me? I'm not swimming."

A tall guy in black jammers inched closer as we talked, clearly eavesdropping but trying to look like he wasn't. He took a few steps in our direction.

"Swim with me," he said. He stuck out his hand. "I'm Burk."

"I don't think . . . I . . . I'm not very fast."

He shrugged his shoulders.

"I'll do breaststroke or fly."

"For a mile?"

He shrugged his shoulders again and smiled. "I can try."

"Great. Problem solved," said Lena.

Timmy woke up and started to fuss.

"Need to go feed him or change diapers or something," said Lena.

Lena smiled at Burk. "This is my sister Trisha. Trisha Carson. This is her first open water race.

She's swum in lakes and rivers before, but not competitively."

He fastened his eyes on mine. "Nice to meet you, Trisha. I'll see you at the water's edge as soon as the instructions are done. You'll be there."

I didn't know what to say.

"That's not a question. Be there. We'll swim together," he said, placing his hand on my arm. "Need to tell some friends what I'm doing."

I turned to talk to Lena, but she and Timmy had already made a beeline for some shade. I watched her in disbelief, tiptoeing over the hot rocky beach toward the picnic table where we'd dropped our backpacks and towels. This Burk guy could be the equivalent of a swimming axe murderer, for all she knew. And why would he give up this race to swim with someone he'd never met before? If my open water anxiety hadn't already been at full throttle, I might have given this particular point more thought.

I watched Burk as he walked a little north on the beach, zigzagging between groups of swimmers. Then, he turned around, caught me looking, and pointed to the shoreline, then at me, then back at the shoreline. I nodded. I was going in the water. For some reason, I felt like I didn't have a choice.

The race directions began, and I tried to listen. I heard individual words and phrases like "course," "starting waves," and "countdown." But then everything became crystal clear. "If you are in trouble anywhere along the course, wave your hand and someone in a kayak or paddleboard will come to get you," said the event director.

There it was. My way out.

The directions over, the faster swimmers in the first wave rushed the water, dove in, and swam out to the starting line between two round yellow buoys, about 300 yards away. The next fastest wave followed them five minutes later. I stood with the third group, eyeing the crowd for Burk. He came up behind me.

"Ready?" asked Burk.

"No."

"Come on. We're next."

I inched my way into the lake. The muddy bottom oozed between my toes and over my feet. I stopped when the water lapped around my knees. It had a crisp chill to it. A curtain of calm rippled across my body. My breathing steadied.

"Okay. Okay. Guess I'm doing this," I said to no one in particular.

I inhaled, ready to belly flop into the lake and take a stroke toward the starting line when Burk caught my arm.

"Might want to put on your cap and goggles."

CHAPTER 2

Once the horn blasted, signaling the start of our wave, the water erupted. Splashing, arms and legs everywhere, bumping into me, kicking me. One swimmer pushed me underwater and swam across my back. Burk took my arm and guided me to the side of the frenzied pack.

"I'm ready to get out," I announced, spitting out lake water.

"Take a breath and exhale slowly."

I did.

"Again."

I sputtered but managed to control my breathing.

Burk said, "Let's get going." And off we went. From then on, every time I turned my head to breathe, there was Burk, smiling, swimming, and cheering me on.

"You're doing great. Keep going."

That's all the encouragement I needed. Thoughts about quitting drifted away as I settled into a rhythm. I concentrated on my stroke, watching my arms stretch out in front of me in the murky water. I wouldn't say the mile flew by, but surprisingly, I realized I was enjoying myself. When I saw the finish arch ahead, I came to a dead stop and started to tread water.

"Everything okay?" asked Burk, stopping beside me, water splashing around his neck.

"Yes. Better than ok. Thank you. I mean it."

"Wait until you finish. Then you can thank me." He laughed. "Now go. Sprint to the end. Go! Go!" And I did, arms and legs churning through the water.

When I stood up and jogged through the finish arch, I threw my arms toward the sky, smiled gloriously, and let out a huge whoop. I turned around to thank Burk but didn't see him. I scanned the crowd, but he wasn't there, either. I would have to find him later.

I ran past the other swimmers, up the hill, anxious to find Lena. She sat at the picnic table, pawing through her swim backpack.

"Can't find my tinted goggles. Do you know where they are?"

"I did it," I proclaimed, my big smile still on my face. "Not only did I start the race, but I finished it."

"I knew you could. Do you feel better now?"

"Mostly relieved, but I feel quite proud of myself."

Lena smiled. "I converted my big sister to the joys of open water swimming. Congratulations!"

She continued to rummage through her backpack. "Where are they? Ah, here they are." She slipped on her cap, fitted the goggles to her face and stood up.

I gave her an exceptionally soggy hug. "Thank you. Thank you. Thank you for pushing me. No way I would have been brave enough to do it without your support."

"Good job. I mean it. Tell me all about your swim when I get back. My heat is going to start in about fifteen minutes. I'm so nervous I'm going to throw up. I haven't raced in... I don't know how long. Keep an eye on Timmy, ok?"

"What a happy baby," I said, glancing over at Little T jiggling his plastic keys. I picked up a huge beach towel and wrapped it around my shoulders.

"Did that guy Burk stay with you?"

"Every time I took a breath, there he was, gliding along beside me. You know that he—"

"Trish, not now. No time. Tell me later."

Lena started down the hill to the lake and then stopped halfway, turned around and yelled, "Everything okay? Does he need me?"

"Everything is fine." *First time moms. Always so paranoid.* "Relax. He's incredibly happy with me. Go. You'll miss the start."

She nodded, hesitated for another moment, then trotted across the stubby grass and onto the beach, heading for the group of swimmers waiting for the next race, a two-mile swim.

"Your mother is gonna kick some butt," I told the chubby baby still completely preoccupied with his keys. He shook them and giggled at the rattling sound they made.

"You'll be out there soon, Little T," I said with a smile.

Tired but exhilarated, a pleasant sense of accomplishment spread through my whole body. I'd finished the swim. The black cloud hanging over me before the start had faded away with each stroke. I wrapped myself in the towel and shrugged off my wet swimsuit underneath, replacing it with a pair of shorts and a San Francisco Giants tee shirt.

"Come on, Tim, let's get some food. I'll introduce you to my swim partner. I need to thank him again," I said.

I carried the baby on my hip across the pebbly beach, walking from one end to the other, scanning the crowd. I couldn't find Burk. Maybe he left as soon as he dried off.

"That's too bad," I said, squeezing my eyes shut for a moment. *Shake it off, Trish. The swim was a big deal to you. For him, not so much.*

Just to make sure, I surveyed the swimmers one more time. Still no Burk, so Little T and I plunged into the crowd at the food tables. Swimmers lined up three deep, grabbing slices of oranges, bananas, and chocolate chip cookies. With a secure grip on the baby, I slathered a bagel with cream cheese. Then I grabbed a handful of grapes, carefully balanced everything, and walked back toward the picnic table, scanning the clumps of swimmers and friends spread out along the beach.

"Hey, to squ Trisha, good to see you," said a woman that I couldn't quite place. "I'm a friend of your sister's. Did you swim?"

I nodded.

"Sorry to hear about Shari. She was a good friend of Lena's, right?"

"Best friend. They grew up together. I drove them to swim meets all the time," I said.

"I joined the last open water clinic she ran before she was. . . you know. So sad," the woman said.

I squirmed and mumbled something like, 'Gotta go.'

"Hope the bad guys leave us swimmers alone," she said. "But we have you to keep us safe."

I groaned internally and felt my face flush. Over the past few years, I'd solved a few murders in the open water community, including the drowning of Shari Grantner, Lena's oldest friend. But that didn't mean I liked talking about it.

"Nice to see you," I remarked as I moved past her, tightening my grip on Little T and the sagging plate of food. *Time to think about something pleasant. Where did Burk go?* He had been right behind me at the end, or so I thought. He must have jogged to another part of the beach once he ran through the finish gate.

A wave of fatigue swept through my body, from my wet head to my wobbly knees as I carried the baby back to the picnic table. The plan to connect with the swimmer drifted away. The need for food took precedence.

I put Timmy in his stroller, sat down on the blanket beside him, and devoured the food in front of me. The bagel and fruit gone, I pulled out two energy bars from my swim bag and ate them, too. Out in the water, the swimmers stroked their way to the large triangular orange buoy floating in the distance. Beads of crystal spray shot off the water-borne athletes and glittered in the sunshine. I glanced at my watch. Lena would be back in less than an hour. I stretched out on the blanket, plugged earphones into my cell phone and searched until I found KSPT, the local sports radio station. Had the SF Giants made a much-needed trade for a power hitter? I listened for the deep voice of the jock broadcaster who specialized in baseball, Tyler Stockton. But it wasn't Tyler giving his opinion about why the trade hadn't happened and why it no doubt wouldn't happen. A different radio personality, Jan Johnson, had the microphone instead. She was a well-known baseball fanatic who knew the game's stats like she knew her home address. When she lamented that the power hitter had been scooped up by the Florida Marlins, her call-in fans went ballistic. No doubt about it, she kept the unruly callers under control. But Tyler … his irresistible chuckle, his knowledge of the game, its history, his close contact with the team … the boy hit it out of the park every time he hosted a show. I muted the broadcast, pulled out the earphones, propped myself up on my elbows and gazed at the calm lake as the last of the swimmers disappeared behind a spindly point of land.

I'd seen Tyler just the day before as I finished my shift at Oracle Park, the home of the San Francisco Giants.

He had walked by me and waved before he disappeared beneath the bleachers. "Hey, Trish, I'll see you later. I'm stopping by Pearl's house to pick up The Babe and take him for a walk."

"I'll be asleep," I said. Tyler called his grandfather Pearl, a contraction of Grandpa Earl. As a baby, he'd mashed the words together and came up with Pearl. He still called him that after all these years.

I lived in Earl's house now. A well-known architect constructed the beautiful estate in Kentfield north of the Golden Gate Bridge, on the edge of La Cruz Canyon. Earl had been my father's friend for years and Dad lives there, too. Last year, I moved out of my sister's extra bedroom in San Rafael when I found out she was expecting the plump little guy passed out in the stroller next to me. Earl had offered me his extra room, which turned out to be an elaborate suite built to be maid's quarters.

Basically, I now resided in a small apartment, complete with a kitchen that included a smart refrigerator that answered my many ridiculous questions on a daily basis.

I unmuted the radio show only to hear Jan break for a commercial. Jan was great, but I missed hearing the smile in Tyler's rich voice. I'd heard him, at least I thought I had, open the front door last night around ten, calling for The Babe. In response, The Babe, Earl's boxer—sixty pounds of sniffling, snorting sweetness—had whined and danced in circles, his way of greeting his loved ones.

I rested in a happy relaxed bubble for at least forty-five minutes, until I heard Lena's whoop as she ran up the hill toward me and Little T.

"I won my age group," she exclaimed, grabbing Timmy out of the stroller and twirling him around. "First time in, oh, I don't know, three years."

She pulled off her cap and shook her mop of curls like a wet dog. Timmy laughed and covered his face with his chubby hands.

"I was right in there with the women I used to compete against. We were swimming almost shoulder to shoulder. On the last leg, I just ignited and pulled away from them. One swimmer was so close behind me, I felt her fingers brush my toes with each stroke. But, after a few minutes, she dropped back, couldn't keep it up. I finished ahead of all four of them. I almost tripped running out of the water and up the beach. But I won. I can't believe it. So excited. And very tired."

She plunked down on the wooden bench connected to the picnic table bench and put Timmy on her lap.

"How did it go? Did he cry? Did he miss me?" she asked.

"He napped the whole time. He didn't miss you one bit."

Lena brushed a wisp of hair away from Timmy's face. "Do you work this evening?"

"No, the Giants are out of town."

"Is Jon coming over?"

"He's busy."

"Please tell me you're still seeing him. Finding you another boyfriend would be exhausting."

"We're okay. He has something to do and it's hard to connect during the baseball season."

"Trisha."

"We're okay. Really."

Lena said. "Maybe you need one of these."

"No babies for me. Anyway, I'm too old."

"Mid-forties is not too old."

"Right. My job with the Giants is seasonal and part-time. I live with my father and his friend. Nothing feels permanent. A baby is *exactly* what I need."

"You don't need to be sarcastic," she said. "Gonna get some food and change. Then we can start home."

Lena and Little T moved out of the shade, trotting down the hill toward the food table.

My phone vibrated in my pocket. Earl.

"Hey, there. How are you this beautiful day?" I asked.

"How come you left The Babe out all night?" The question was direct, if not startling.

"Not me. Tyler said he planned to take him for a walk. That's what he told me at the ballpark. I heard him come into the house last night and call for the dog. He woke me up."

"I'll have to talk to that young man. This morning, there was no dog sleeping at the end of my bed. Instead, The Babe was sacked out in a lounge chair on the deck."

"The deck? What was he doing out there?"

"I don't know. I thought you would."

"I'd suggest calling the radio station and talking to him, but he's not on," I said.

"No?"

"Nope. Jan took over his spot for the afternoon. She's pretty good. Don't worry about Tyler. He'll show up."

Earl let out a big breath. "I'm going over to China Camp for my volunteer stint. If he's there when you get home, tell him I want to talk to him."

He hung up. Although Ty could be flaky, he was devoted to his grandfather and would never renege on an obligation to Earl or The Babe. A chill passed through my body and I pulled a damp towel over my shoulders.

Two minutes later, Terrel Robinson, MD, called. He couldn't reach Lena and wanted to know how the swim went and if Little T had enjoyed himself. Terrel, or "Dr. T," is Lena's live-in boyfriend and the baby's father. If anyone needed a live-in doctor, it was Lena. Since my sister can be over the top on a good day and had spent much of her time in orbit since becoming a mom, she needed someone like Dr. T. A voice of reason, he calmed her down like a warm bath. As an Emergency Room physician in San Francisco, he dealt more with gunshot wounds than pediatrics. But that didn't matter. He watched out for his son and my sister, and he took exceptionally good care of both of them. I genuinely liked the guy.

The swimmers had begun to trickle out of the venue and head for the parking lot. They carried deck chairs, small coolers, and their ever-present swim backpacks. I glanced at a group of athletes standing around the results board. I recognized a few of them, thanks to my sister. Unable to help myself, I searched the crowd again for my floating security blanket and personal cheerleader. Without him, I never would have finished the race, or started it, for that matter. *Where did he go?* Instead of Burk, I spotted Lena with a group of women in their thirties, strong, tan and ready to swim another two miles. As I folded up the towel and cleaned the area around the picnic table, my phone buzzed with a notification from my bank. I get them all the time, yet another annoyance of modern technology. I deleted it and headed over to meet my sister, pushing the stroller. Our little extended family of three moved down a path bordered by huge maple trees, away from the serene lake and into the sunny, almost-empty parking lot.

CHAPTER 3

Later that evening, I sat on the deck at Earl's house feeling extremely pleased with myself for finishing the one-miler. La Cruz Canyon stretched below. Mt. Tamalpais, Marin County's 2,500 foot mini mountain, climbed above. Dark shadows crept in my direction, turning the redwoods, oaks and the bushy, low chaparrals shades of black.

Strangely, the little trio of me, Dad, and Earl co-existed in this lovely house much better than I had expected. It was Earl who had come to my father's rescue when he resurfaced in Marin, broken down, sad, and homeless a year ago. That's when Dad stepped back into my sister's and my life following a twenty-five-year absence with no contact. Nothing. Zip. Nada. He'd left not long after our mom died of cancer. Said he couldn't handle us. At least he had waited until I graduated from high school. According to him, I had developed into a capable young woman who could sufficiently care for my little sister. So, I became the one in charge. "Large and in charge," as Lena used to say. I struggled during this changing of the guard, as any 18-year-old would, but I worked my ass off to keep my sister and I together. And out of the Marin County social welfare system.

If someone told me then that I would complete a one-mile swim in a lake, in my forties no less, I would have laughed in their face.

My swim buddy preyed on my mind. I pulled out my phone and brought up the open water swim app. After finding the day's event, I browsed the preliminary results. First, the overall results, then by age group. No Burk. Could it be a nickname? Had someone contested the results and his name had been pulled? If he wasn't listed as a racer, I didn't know how to track him down and tell him how much I appreciated his help.

"Hey, Trisha." I jumped. I hadn't heard Earl come in.

"Sorry, didn't mean to startle you." After hours of working on the ancient 300-foot fishing pier at China Camp State Park, sawdust covered every inch of his body, from his hair to his work shoes.

"Need a shower," he said as he climbed the stairs to his suite of rooms. Thirty minutes later, I heard him in the kitchen. He ambled out to the deck holding a beer and wearing a Rolling Stones tee shirt and faded Levi's. With a full head of gray hair pulled back in a ponytail, he reminded me of an aging rock star, not a retired, multi-millionaire computer genius. In his other hand, he carried the case that held his favorite drone, Black Betty.

"Did you talk to Tyler?" I asked.

"Couldn't reach him," Earl said. He moved over to the edge of the deck, unpacked the drone and sent it flying out across the dirt trail by the house and then up until it hovered over the canyon. I watched the video display of the treetops as it went.

"There she is," he whispered. A spotted owl twisted her head upwards and I found myself gazing at huge dark eyes outlined in yellow and a sharp, hooked beak in a heart-shaped face.

"I wonder if... oh, there are her babies." One branch down was her nest and inside, barely visible, were two chicks- little blobs of whitish-gray fluff with small heads and dark eyes.

"We have a front-row seat to Marin's wildlife," I laughed in amazement, watching the screen in Earl's hands.

"Don't want to bother the little family," said Earl. "Momma might pack them up and move to another tree if I overdo it."

He flew the drone back in our direction, circled The Babe's head and landed it safely on the deck. The dog had never been impressed with this flying thing of his owner's and started barking, but he immediately settled down after a stern glance from Earl.

"Didn't you have something to do with drones back in the day?" I asked.

"I'm not that old," he laughed. "The first ones were built during World War I. But I did work on them for a while."

He sat down on one of the patterned lounge chairs, put his feet up on a small glass table, and picked up his beer. Besides being a drone flyer and a volunteer at China Camp State Park, he followed the locally brewed beer scene. He'd even financed a brewery started by friends of his grandson. He took a sip of their latest creation, Coyote Ridge. He studied the bottle as he contemplated the taste. With a grimace, he spat it out.

"Awful. They need to tweak their recipe," he said and put the bottle down.

I wasn't offended when Earl didn't offer me one. He knew better. My background included a few DUIs, a stint in jail and AA. This all happened when I was living in Colorado with Brad, my husband. We'd been married fifteen years and then he walked out the door. Just like that. I didn't know where he went. Still don't. Trying to understand what had happened led to sitting in my dark kitchen, eating ice cream and cookies, and washing them down with gin and coconut water, which morphed into straight gin. When I couldn't stand myself anymore, I moved back to Marin and took up residence in my younger sister's house. I ached even now, thinking about it. My sister emerged as the successful one; my "large and in charge" status evaporating like San Francisco fog on a sunny day. And my sense of failure remained.

"So, nothing from Tyler or his friends?" I tried again.

"Not yet. His buddy Jason stopped by to drop off these samples," he said lifting the brown bottle of beer.

"He hadn't seen him," Earl added. There was a long pause.

Earl took another sip from the craft beer and shook his head. "Too yeasty."

"I'm going to call Ty," I said, picking up my phone.

"Maybe you'll have better luck than me," said Earl.

No answer. I left a message. Then I texted him.

"Did anyone go to his house?" I asked.

"Yup. Even checked with one of his neighbors," said Earl. "They haven't seen him all day. What bothers me is not that I haven't heard from him, but that he's missed work. The station even called me to see where he was. He never showed up and didn't contact them. That boy might be a scatterbrain sometimes, but he would never jeopardize his job at the station."

Earl understood his grandson. Working at KSPT, K-Sport to the locals, consumed Tyler. When he left his parent's home in Oregon, he lived with his grandfather for a few years while he laid the groundwork for his career. He did anything the station asked: swept the floors, made coffee, helped on the night shifts after ballgames. Slowly but surely, he'd moved up the broadcasting ladder because of his limitless knowledge of sports stats, goofy sense of humor, contagious laugh, and uncanny ability to handle the weirdest of fans calling into the station. On the short side, stick thin with wild black hair, he possessed a deep, mellow voice made for radio.

I heard Dad's car pull up outside. He walked in while Earl talked and sat down next to him. He patted Earl's arm. "Don't worry. That loony grandson of yours will show up."

"Should I call the police? His parents, maybe?" asked Earl.

"Might be a little soon, don't you think? Why worry them?" asked Dad. "Give it another day or two."

"Want me to make a few phone calls? See what I can find out?" I asked.

"No!" they both said in unison.

I scrutinized one man, then the other. "Ok. I get it. Stay out of it. Right?"

Earl smiled and stood. "No offense, Trisha, but I think we're good here. Tyler will turn up."

With that, he walked up the stairs to his spacious suite of rooms.

"Trish?" said my father.

"Hmm."

"You heard Earl?"

"Hmm."

"Trish?"

"What?"

"Let things play out, so we know what we're dealing with."

"Sure. Absolutely."

He watched me closely and shook his finger at me.

"Got it, Dad. I know."

He walked into the kitchen. I heard him talking to the refrigerator and the refrigerator talked back, something about half a carton of milk. Then he wandered down the hall.

"Night, sweetheart."

"You talking to me or the fridge?"

"You."

"Goodnight, Dad."

I waited until I heard his bedroom door slam. Then I texted my sister. *Wanna help me find someone?*

She didn't. Her reasoning went something like "He's young and probably holed up with a cute little Giants fan he met at the ballpark." Not to mention that new mom duties took all of her free time. And a company that manufactured aerodynamic swim fins wanted her to design a new website for them. She couldn't possibly help me out. My sister had developed into *the* designer for many companies in the aquatics field. I was proud of her.

I walked up to my suite of rooms—more like a small apartment—tossed the phone on my bed, and turned into the bathroom. This Tyler thing was strange. He didn't know how to be abstract or evasive. He was not into intrigue. I'd call him the epitome of "What you see is what you get."

I heard my phone ding in the distance. On my way to find it, I stopped in front of my talking fridge, Frida, the friendly refrigerator that sat at one end of my bedroom. She was just one perk of living in a house designed by a well-heeled retired entrepreneur of the computer field. When I walked in the front door, the fridge's AI turned on the lights next to my bed, adjusted the air conditioning, and gave my room a spritz of sweet lavender oil. Earl mentioned that I could change the scent to pumpkin and cinnamon for the fall, if I wanted. As much as I enjoyed the technology, it made me uneasy at times. It was like having a roommate that never left.

"Frida, do I have any oranges?"

"No, Trisha, you do not. You do have one peach."

"Thank you."

"You are welcome."

I didn't know why I always felt obligated to thank this chatty kitchen appliance, but I did. Maybe something to do with my mother's coaching on the importance of being polite. I opened the fridge door, grabbed the peach and a napkin, and sat down on my bed. My bank had sent me another alert. Something about my credit card, this time. Curious, I clicked on it and saw that more than $500 of baby clothes from Rodeo Drive Baby in Beverly Hills, California had been charged to my account.

What? I reread the senseless email. Then I read it again, this time word by word and out loud. I hadn't bought any baby clothes, certainly not from *Rodeo Drive*. It had to be Lena. She had my credit card information. She had copies of all my bank cards, health care info, car insurance papers ... everything, for emergency purposes. If anyone knew about my feeble financial situation, she did.

"Call Lena," I directed my phone. She answered.

"Sorry, Trisha, I can't get involved with one of your 'Where in the world is... fill in the blank' right now."

"That's not why I'm calling. Why didn't you ask before you used my credit card?"

"What?"

"The baby clothes. Really? Does Little T need fancy-dancy duds from Rodeo Drive?"

"What are you talking about?"

"That charge on my credit card."

My phone pinged again. It was another alert from my bank.

"Wait a minute." I read the alert. "You're not in a club in Las Vegas called Druids, are you?"

"It's finally happened. You've lost your mind."

There was a long pause.

"These charges, $400 at Druids on the Strip and $500 at Rodeo Drive Baby, aren't yours?"

"Are you on drugs?"

"Of course not. Someone's been using my credit card. I thought it was you."

"Maybe Little T deserves designer baby clothes, and maybe your life would improve if you *did* go to some club in Las Vegas… but I had nothing to do with it. Call your bank."

She hung up.

I checked my phone again, willing it to tell me who made the purchases and how they managed to unearth my credit card information. But no information magically appeared. Thankfully, it only took a few minutes to clear things up with Western Mutual, my bank. They apologized, canceled my account, and said that they would send me a new credit card.

"That's it?" I asked.

"Yes. You're not financially responsible for these charges. We apologize for the inconvenience. Goodbye."

Well, the bank had made it easy, at least, but who had my credit card information? Locating Tyler would be simpler than digging up this culprit. So, tomorrow I'd direct my attention to the missing grandson.

CHAPTER 4

It turned out I was the last person to see Tyler, Friday night at the ballpark. When he was still unaccounted for by Monday morning, Earl and Dad went to the local police station. They called in the Marin County Parks Department, who began a thorough search of La Cruz Canyon since I'd mentioned I heard him pick up the dog for a walk after the game. Earl did reach out to Tyler's parents. They wanted to fly down. But Earl convinced them to put it off for a few more days until the police had a chance to find their son. Dad agreed. He kept an eye on his friend and knew the added stress of his son and daughter-in-law wouldn't help the situation. Let's just say that Earl had been very generous to them over the years and now, their expectations of him were out of line. Or so Dad thought. I kind of agreed.

To make things easier on Earl, I volunteered to walk The Babe on nights I didn't have a game. When I had to work, Dad filled in as my backup, but he'd promised to babysit little Timmy and I had a game. That left the backup to my backup; my quasi-boyfriend, Jon Angel, a strapping brown-hair security guard at Fort Mason in San Francisco. We'd met there a few years ago when I worked in one of the buildings he patrolled along the waterfront. Jon arrived early and walked out onto the deck, peering out at La Cruz Canyon while he waited for me.

"Well, don't you look stylish," he grinned when I walked out to join him in my Guest Services uniform.

"Only you and the fans who drink too much think so," I said with a chuckle.

"I was being sarcastic."

"Yeah, well, they do the job. So where are you taking The Babe?"

"The Canyon. Maybe he can pick up Tyler's scent."

"The police and the Marin County rangers are combing those hills."

"I have the super sniffer with me," he answered.

I gave him a kiss on the cheek and laid my head against his shoulder. "See you after the game?"

"Hope so. Not sure. I'll let you know."

To everyone's surprise, I had ended up with a legitimate boyfriend, somehow. After returning to Marin, I'd developed an obsessive crush on a psychopathic swimmer and sports drink entrepreneur, which didn't end well, to say the least. In the middle of that strange relationship, I met Jon. More than once I tried to push him away or so says my sister. But he hung in there. For all his endurance and compassion, he was now the backup dog walker.

CHAPTER 5

Normally, I carpooled to work, but this evening I planned to drive into San Francisco alone. By the time the Golden Gate Bridge came into view, traffic had slowed. Almost stopped. On my right was the Pacific Ocean, with an impenetrable layer of cool fog advancing toward the span. The wind swirled around the cars inching across the iconic landmark. A quick glance in the opposite direction showed the city in full afternoon sunlight, washing everything with a smoldering glow. I knew that when the sun set, the fog would tumble into the city, sprawling until it reached the ball field and making for a damp night.

I reached the parking lot an hour early. I usually catch up with the other employees walking toward the ballpark and chit chat about the upcoming game. But this time, I wasn't in the mood. The last time someone disappeared in my world, they turned up dead. Then thugs harassed me in this very parking lot. I didn't want a repeat of the experience.

A loud, long clanging tore me out of my daydreams. The Lefty O'Doul Bridge (better known as the Third Street Bridge) was about to open. I stopped on one side while a deep siren blasted through the early evening air. Traffic halted; the long span of the bridge moved in an upwards arc, reaching for the sky as one lonely sailboat motored out of China Basin. The arm went down, and traffic and pedestrians scooted back on their way. A lot of effort for one boat. The solitary craft reminded me of Jon, who occasionally moved boats from one side of the Bay to the other. He'd turned it into a lucrative side gig. I took out my phone and texted him.

Enjoying your walk with TB?

I had no reason to worry when he didn't respond. Reception could be spotty in La Cruz Canyon.

Once inside the tall, cavernous hallways of the ballpark, I bolted down the halls into the fan area, headed for the small radio studio that housed KSPT. Jan, the woman who'd been filling in for Tyler, sat at the console.

She was of average size, but that's where the average part of Jan ended. She wore her dark hair short, spiky and tinged with bright purple. Her hoop earrings were the size of silver dollar pancakes and her lips blazed with bright red lipstick. She punched buttons on the large control board in front of her, then glanced up and smiled at me through the glass window. I motioned for her to come closer. A puzzled expression flitted across her face. She flipped a few switches on the board and came over.

"Make it quick," she said when she opened the door. "Only have thirty seconds."   "Tyler," I said. "You took his place on the air the other day. Do you know why he wasn't there?"

"I know you, don't I?"

"We met once. Tyler introduced us. I live in his grandfather's house. We can't locate him. Earl, his grandfather, is worried. Have you heard from him?"

"Can't talk right now but stop by after the game. I might be able to help," she said, closing the door and sprinting to her board. Behind me, a supervisor walked by.

"You know you aren't supposed to talk to the broadcasters."

"Yeah, I know. Sorry. But it's kind of a family emergency and I thought she might be able to help. She knows my—"

"Talking to the ballplayers, broadcasters, or famous guests should not take place."

I didn't say anything else, just nodded, then turned and scooted in the opposite direction. Just my luck to have someone in charge spot me. I had a feeling I would hear about it later.

I pulled open the door to the wardrobe department and a stream of employees walked out, talking, laughing, and zipping up parkas as they moved on to their evening's assignment. I slipped into the lady's locker room.

Sitting down on the wooden bench, I leaned over to open my locker. My friend Charlee Ann walked in. She pulled off her Giants beanie. "Child, I don't know if I have enough clothes stashed in my locker to keep me warm."

I smiled but didn't answer.

"You okay?"

I shrugged.

"Not feeling so fine, are you?"

"We have a missing grandson in our house."

"A what?"

"Earl … you know the friend of my dad's? I'm staying at his house? Well, his grandson went missing. He works here."

"The radio sports guy?"

"That's the one."

"And you're about to stick your nose where it doesn't belong. Am I right?"

"I have to go," I said, closing my locker.

"You know, a cat only has nine lives. What's left for you? Two? Three?"

"More than that," I corrected, wrapping my orange and black scarf around my neck and tucking it into my oversized parka. I slipped on my beanie and twirled around.

"How do I look?"

"Like you always do." Charlee Ann said. "Those lives are disappearing real fast. And once they're gone, they're gone."

"If you don't hurry, this game will start and you'll still be sitting here," I said, walking out the door. I heard her giggle behind me.

I had been assigned to the Garden, which is an actual garden right outside the centerfield wall. Although the fans inside couldn't see the field, except through the slats at either end of the wall, there were at least six televisions broadcasting the game. A crowd-pleasing bar held court in the middle. Two vendors used the vegetables and fruits grown in the planters to concoct organic and veggie-oriented dishes. To some fans, the Garden bordered on sacrilegious. This was a ballpark, after all. Others loved the place, especially before games.

A mom and her seven-year-old daughter stopped and asked for directions to the ladies' room.

"I'll walk you there," I said and led them into the women's bathroom. I went into a different stall and pulled out my phone and texted Jon again.

Find anything?

No response. About forty-five minutes before the game, the Garden filled up with enthusiastic fans. A girls' choir from San Francisco sang the national anthem and ten minutes later, the first pitch was thrown, right on schedule, 7:15 p.m.

The baseball game took three and a half hours, and the Giants had a much-needed win. As the fans left the bleachers, hundreds of seagulls streaked across the sky, dive-bombing for leftover hotdogs, popcorn, garlic fries and whatever else had missed the mouth. The first set of glaring stadium lights switched off. My co-workers waited until the second set of ballpark lights went dark and then began shooing the rest of the fans through the Marina entrance. Once the last fan reluctantly left and security locked the gate behind him, I rushed down the hall, clocked out, and speed-walked to the small broadcast booth. It was empty. No Jan. My shoulders sagged as I placed my forehead against the radio studio glass window. I had hoped to learn something, anything, about Tyler. Instead, I reluctantly forced myself to turn around and walk back toward the employee's exit.

"Hey, wait," Jan yelled at me, jogging down the hall. "Had to break down some equipment outside." She pulled off her Giants ball cap, pushed back her purplish hair, and put the cap back on.

"Very busy night," she added. "We had some technical problems that kept me running back and forth from the fifth inning to the end of the game."

She took a deep breath.

"You haven't heard from Tyler yet?"

"No," I said.

She glimpsed into the little radio booth at a red blinking light on the console, took her cap off again and fiddled with her hair.

"I don't know where he is. But for the last few weeks, there have been some strange things going down at the station. Can't talk now, but do you want to meet me at the Sports Pub in about thirty minutes?"

"Sure. OK. See you then."

The last thing I wanted to do was go to a bar. I wanted to go home and stretch out in a warm tub. My back ached from standing close to six hours and my hands and feet felt like blocks of ice. I wanted to walk away from what was left of the 25,000 fans who had attended the game, not rub elbows with them in the Sports Pub. It would be packed because the team won. I was sure all twenty-four of its televisions would blast different channels, different sports. I considered canceling, but my worry overwhelmed my sore, tired body.

CHAPTER 6

Laughing fans milled around the wide sidewalk outside the ballpark, even as the rest of the Bay slept. The fog had lifted slightly, but the air remained cool and damp. The crowd stood five-deep at the entrance to the Sports Pub. I elbowed through the mass into a loud, crowded, noisy bar. Every table, even the long, 'share with people you don't know' tables, were crammed with people. I inched my way through the crowd, bouncing off the fans who like to stand in groups, talk sports and drink beer.

I spotted one seat at the bar. I grabbed it, put my backpack in my lap, and glanced up at the kegs of beer stacked six high behind the bar. The guys next to me saw my jacket and beanie.

"Work for the Giants?"

I nodded.

"Great game."

"Yeah."

When they realized I had nothing more to say, they turned back to their friends.

"What can I get you?" the bartender asked, a forty-something guy with a big smile.

"Is it insulting to ask for something warm? Like hot tea?"

"Where were you working?"

"In the Garden. Did you see the fog? Moved across the field until it almost covered the lights in the outfield."

"Typical summer night," he said. "Not to worry. We have tea."

He stopped. "How about an Irish coffee?"

It sounded wonderful: warm coffee, a little whiskey, some sugar, cream.

"Better not. I don't drink anymore."

"Gotcha." He disappeared to get my tea.

The commotion of the happy, slightly drunk patrons surged upwards. Shoulders brushed mine. I moved closer to the bar and the crowd followed me, pinning me between two fans in Giants jackets and the highly-polished long bar. My throat grew dry and I couldn't swallow. The flight part of the fight-or-flight response settled in at the base of my neck.

"Too many people. Too loud. Got to get out of here," I said to no one in particular. I reached into my backpack to find my wallet so I could pay for the tea when someone tapped my shoulder. A voice close behind me said, "Over this way. They keep a room in the back for the broadcasters. We can talk there."

I turned to the voice as Jan grabbed my arm. Her smile dropped when she saw my face. "What's wrong?"

"Too much" was all I could manage.

She pulled me from the barstool and forced a path through the crowd. "Stand back," she yelled. "Lady about to be sick."

That did it. The crowd parted like the Red Sea. I let her guide me to a small but pleasant room off to the side of the kitchen.

"Works every time," Jan chuckled. "Now sit down, relax. I'll go get you a drink."

"I ordered tea."

"Be right back."

The panic gradually faded.

When she returned, a metal teapot in one hand and a mug in the other, she said, "The color has come back to your face. How do you end up with a job at the ballpark if you don't like big crowds and lots of noise?"

"I don't like heights, either," I said, ignoring her very reasonable question.

I sipped the warm liquid and let out a deep breath.

"So, what's going on at the station?" I asked.

Jan settled herself on a comfortable sofa across from me. She propped her black high-top sneakers on the scratched coffee table between us and sipped her beer.

"Well, a few weeks ago, a man showed up at the station asking for Tyler. He said he was a friend of his grandfather's and was trying to reach him. It was Tyler's day off, but I happened to walk by when he was talking to the receptionist. I offered to help him, said I would take a message and give it to Tyler, but we couldn't give out any information. He became more insistent that he had to reach Tyler's grandfather. Something seemed off. The man was in his late sixties, maybe seventies, well-dressed, but his face… his eyes were… I don't know… wild-looking. The receptionist was ready to call security, but I thought I might be able to help the guy without all that, so I tried something. Said 'Which grandfather is it? You know he has two living in the Bay Area?' The man stopped talking. But I kept going. 'Is it Sid in the East Bay or Benjamin in Sonoma?' So, the guy looks at me, takes a few steps back and says, "The man's name is Earl and I think he lives in Marin."

"I tell him that I just wanted to see if he was who he said he was. I promised that if he leaves me his name and number, I'll pass that info on to Tyler, who I'm sure will give his grandfather the message. So he gives me his information and leaves. Guy's name was Bernard."

"That is strange," I said. "What did Tyler say about this guy?"

"He thanked me, then got real quiet. I gave him the number and he said he would take care of it."

"Did he know the man?"

"No clue. Maybe. I couldn't be sure. Said he thought he was a neighbor of his from Oregon."

I stood up, ready to go home.

"Wait. There's more."

If I sat down again, I was so tired I would never get back up. So, I stayed standing.

"I saw the same guy outside the station a few times after that. And Tyler said that he felt like he was being followed, but he never saw anyone. I pushed him to tell the police, but I don't think he ever did. So, I told security to watch out for this old guy and gave them the best description I could. He never came back after that."

"Thanks. Maybe I'll talk to Earl and see if he knows who this man is. Both he and Ty lived in Oregon. He could be a neighbor. But why act so weird?"

Twenty minutes later, I climbed into my car, one of the few left in the deserted two-thousand space lot. I turned on the heat and grabbed a bottle of water from my backpack. Tyler was in trouble. You didn't need to be Sherlock Holmes to figure that out. Who was this man who kept visiting the station? Why was he looking for Tyler and Earl? I pulled out the tablet Lena had given me when I worked on my last case. Although I preferred to write things down on cards so I could move them around on a table, the tablet had its advantages. It could reference and cross-reference themes, names and locations faster than I could. I opened a new folder and named it Tyler. I used my first eCard to type down what little information I had about my missing friend and the odd stranger who'd been coming to his workplace. The one person who had more information wasn't a person. It was The Babe. I decided not to set up a card for him. Not yet, anyway.

After a glance at my phone—still no update from Jon—I pulled out of the dark parking lot into the even-darker San Francisco streets and turned on the radio. The baseball game usually replayed at midnight, but there had been a technical glitch, delaying the game for an hour. Instead, the station extended the aftergame call-in show. I'd know soon enough if Tyler had miraculously reappeared. The sports jock announcer often referred to him by his radio nickname "Einstein" because of his unlimited knowledge of sports statistics and unmanageable black hair. That didn't happen tonight. Tyler wasn't there.

When I pulled into Earl's long driveway, light from one window cast a weak shadow across the shadowy hedges. Stepping out of the car, I walked up the walkway and into a vacuum—little light, no sound. Inside, Dad dozed in front of the TV and Earl was absent, probably asleep upstairs. The Babe walked over to me, his nails clicking on the tile floor of the entrance as he did his hello dance, a speed walk in circles.

"Babe. Babe? Talk. Did you and Jon find anything?"

The dog ambled back over to my Dad and laid down.

I shook Dad's arm. He opened his eyes, "Hey, Trishie. Good game. The new centerfielder has promise."

"What happened, Dad?"

"Didn't you see him make that great catch? He bumped into the centerfield wall. You must have heard him."

"Not that. Jon and The Babe."

"Don't know what you're talking about."

"Didn't he … weren't you …?

"He was gone when I got here."

"Anything on Tyler?" I asked.

Dad shook his head. "Afraid not. To make matters worse, Earl's son and daughter-in-law fly in tomorrow. And they're staying here."

"Why not stay at their son's apartment?" I asked.

"Too small is what Earl mentioned."

"Maybe I should go to Lena's while they visit."

"I was thinking the same thing."

"No, Dad. We can't both go. You stay. They can have my room."

"Whatever you think best. Oh, your new credit card arrived today."

"Great."

Dad watched as I tore open the envelope, activated the card via my phone and clicked on my favorite online sock store.

"Going to bed. Sweet dreams, baby."

He ambled off to his bedroom next to the study with The Babe clicking after him.

I unzipped my jacket, stuffed my black knit beanie in a pocket and dropped onto the couch so hard, it lurched back a few inches. My eyes closed. *Have to get up. Don't want to fall asleep here.* But first, Lena needed a warning that I would be back in her house.

I pulled out my phone and sent her a brief text.

Former roommate needs place to stay.

She responded almost immediately.

Earl kick u out?

No. Has family coming. Why r u up?

Timmy's up. I'm up. Everyone's up.

Fun. See u tomorrow.

CHAPTER 7

I could hear Earl's son and daughter-in-law arguing about rental cars all the way up in my room. My clock read 10:30 a.m., a decent hour to get out of bed, especially if you went to sleep a mere eight hours earlier. I walked over to my deck and saw them standing in front of the house. Earl attempted to hug his son but was brushed off. He turned to his daughter-in-law and received air kisses on either side of his face. All the while, the couple never stopped bickering. I heard Earl say, "Let's go inside," and they did, leaving him to pick up their luggage and haul it up the front steps.

Dad hurried down the stairway to give him a hand. He grabbed two of the suitcases sitting on the brick walkway. He never had a chance to introduce himself to the couple. They walked right by him.

I threw on a pair of shorts and a faded Giants tee shirt. Then I pulled the sheets off the bed and replaced them and the towels in the bathroom. I grabbed some clothes, stuffed them in my backpack and headed for the staircase. All four people mingled below me at the bottom of the stairs. Earl was concerned. Dad was annoyed. The other two continued their bickering.

"Good morning," I remarked as I walked down the steps, smiled and stopped. The couple gawked at me with their mouths open.

"Dad, who is that? Is she your…?"

"No, no," said Earl.

"She belongs to me," said Dad.

"What?" said the son. He glanced from me to my father, then back to Earl.

"I'm Trisha," I said, standing on the bottom step. I held out my hand. They both gaped at it.

"That's my daughter," said Dad.

"Who are you?" they said almost in unison, seeing Dad for the first time.

"My friend from years back. He's staying with me for a while, and so is Trisha."

The couple exchanged glances.

"Robert, Trisha, I'd like you to meet my family. This is my son Gabriel, Gabe for short, and his wife, Elaine. They're Tyler's parents."

At the mention of their son, Elaine gasped and started to sob. Gabe put his arm around her and guided her into the living room.

"Well," I said. "I'm going over to Lena's."

"Earl, go with them," encouraged Dad, nodding his head in the direction of the living room. "I'll take their bags upstairs."

Earl turned and walked reluctantly into the living room.

"I can't get out of here fast enough," I said.

"Lucky you," said Dad.

CHAPTER 8

Dr. T was dozing on the couch, his black-rimmed glasses on the floor beside him, baby Timmy fast asleep on his stomach when I walked through the front door of Lena's small bungalow.

No doubt about it. They were father and son. Terrel's dad was black and owned a body shop on the Peninsula. His mother was a white middle school teacher. His dad loved Lena. Mom hadn't quite decided that my sister met her standards. Although her resistance started to thaw the more she played with her adorable grandson.

Timmy's caramel skin was like T's, only a shade lighter. But his hair had grown into a mop of strawberry blond corkscrew curls like my sister's. Timmy inhaled and turned his head on his dad's chest. He had been drooling and left a wet circle on Terrel's tee shirt.

Lena sat at a desk in her bedroom, which doubled as her office. She concentrated on a partially-designed website for goggles on her monitor.

"I picked up another national client. They manufacture leak-proof goggles, or so they say. I've never owned goggles that didn't leak."

Lena had the right touch for marketing the aquatic field, and she regularly fielded calls from prospective clients. She also dabbled in hacking when I needed her to find some information.

"That's a very domestic scene out there," I said as I walked into the messy room. Normally the mess involved clothes, mismatched shoes, and papers—boxes and boxes of papers—but now her typical clutter was mixed with diapers and onesies. Over in the corner on the floor lay a miniature Speedo for an infant.

"We'll put a portable crib in here with us and you're back in your old bedroom." She smiled.

"Lee, are the results final for the open water swim last weekend?"

"Not sure. Why?"

"The guy, Burk, who swam with me. He isn't listed."

"He could have been a jumper," my sister considered. "You know, didn't register, didn't pay the fee, but swam anyway. That happens sometimes."

"I hadn't thought of that. I wanted to thank him, but..." I shrugged my shoulders. "Have you ever seen him at these open water swims before?"

Lena thought for a moment.

"No. I haven't been swimming for the last few years, but I still recognize most of the swimmers who compete. Triathletes sometimes show up to swim. Maybe he's in that category."

"I thought you knew him." I stepped back in disbelief. "I was a wreck and you sent me off with someone you never met?"

"What's the big deal? This is a very trustworthy group. I never gave it a thought. Hey, has Tyler reappeared?"

"What?" I said, surveying the room. *How does the clinically-neat Dr. T handle this?*

"Earl's grandson, Tyler. That skinny guy with the electrifying black hair. Kinda looks like the male bride of Frankenstein," continued Lena, laughing.

"No."

"Where did he go?"

"That's the point. No one knows."

"But I bet you have some ideas?"

"Not this time."

Lena leaned over and switched off the computer. Her usually tanned skin had paled, and I noticed dark circles, like smudged dirt, under her eyes. Natural for someone who had a six-month-old baby.

"Fill me in."

"Well," I said, picking up one of Timmy's little undershirts that had some indescribable stain on it. I tossed the shirt over to her. She grabbed it with one hand and dropped it on the floor next to her desk.

"Lena, yuck."

"Are you going to tell me, or aren't you?"

I pulled out the tablet and showed her the puny amount of information I had gathered so far.

"This won't find anybody. Not even me and I'm sitting right in front of you."

"Listen, ok? Just listen. Someone is going through Tyler to find

Earl."

"Is Earl that hard to find?"

"I don't know."

"Have you talked to him about Tyler?"

"A bit. But I thought Tyler would turn up by now."

"You're not much of a detective, are you?"

She was right. For some reason, I hadn't gone into overdrive trying to find Ty. Of course, I hadn't been asked to. In fact, I'd been asked not to. That had never stopped me before. But with this, getting too curious or involved might jeopardize my somewhat precarious but luxurious living situation.

"Nobody is that keen on you snooping around, but we all admit—and I hate to say this—you do a good job. Does Tyler have a girlfriend?"

"I don't know."

"A boyfriend?"

"I don't know."

"Any friends?"

"Yes, he does have friends. I've seen one of them. He came to Earl's house."

"Looking for Ty?"

"No. Dropping some beer off for Earl a few weeks ago. Ty and his buddies make beer, something called Coyote Ridge. Tyler talked his grandfather into investing, I guess. According to Earl, the recipe sucks. He makes a face every time he takes a sip of their latest batch."

"Some investment." Lena stood and stretched. "Let's get you settled back into your bedroom." From the hallway, I heard Dr. T talking to Timmy in the living room.

"Guess who's here? Aunt Trisha. She's taking over your bedroom. That means you're bunking with Mom and Dad for a few days." Then he called out, "It's only a few days, right?"

"As soon as Tyler's parents leave, I'll be gone," I said.

"That's not the answer I wanted to hear," he admitted as I walked through to the kitchen.

Terrel settled Little T on the couch and joined me, pouring himself a glass of orange juice as he studied me carefully. "You here on official business?" he asked.

"What does that mean?"

"Lena mentioned that you want her help to find someone. I'm guessing that's the grandson?"

Terrel took a sip and aimed those intelligent dark eyes at me. I stayed silent.

"Do you want me to remind you of the restriction clauses when it comes to Lena helping you?"

"Can we talk about the Giants instead? This might be one of the good years."

Terrel's glare never wavered.

"You know there are rules that come with Lena when you drag her into your 'investigations.'"

"I can decide for myself what I want to do," came a voice from down the hall.

"Number one—her life is never put in danger."

"That works for me," called out Lena.

"And number one-and-a-half, neither is yours," said Terrel.

"I'm only worth a half?"

Laughter floated from Lee's bedroom. "Aw, you're worth three-quarters, at least."

"This isn't funny, Lena. I would never put you in danger."

"Number two—you will always keep the police abreast of any relevant information you find."

"How does that refer to Lena?"

"I'm all for that," said Lena.

"You know, you could be a little more supportive," I yelled in Lena's direction. "Dr. T., I know all this."

"But it needs to be stated so everything is crystal clear," said Dr. T. "Number three— Timmy is never involved ... never ... *n e v e r.*"

"Agreed," yelled Lena.

By now, my face had filled with heat.

"Okay, okay. No one will be put in danger. Ever ... *e v e r.* Your 'rules' are fine with me. No problem. But I think you're making this a bigger deal than it is. Tyler's only been out of touch five days. He's a young guy. I bet he's with friends or met a woman ..."

"You told me he didn't have a girlfriend," said Lena, still yelling from her room.

"Do you believe that?" asked Terrel.

"About the girlfriend?"

"No. That he'll show up."

I paused.

"That's why we have to have ground rules," he stated. "Over the past few years, Lena has been shot at."

"Me, too," I said.

"Drugged, experienced a severe allergic reaction. She went into anaphylactic shock, for God's sake."

"But—"

"There's more. Remember when some of your psycho friends dragged her off? Not once, but twice."

Sweat beaded on my forehead.

"I could have gone to jail for the things I did for you," called out Lena.

"There were a few missteps, I admit. They weren't all my fault."

"Trisha, I know where this is headed."

"I wish I did," I mumbled to myself.

"That's the problem. You don't," said Dr. T.

I couldn't fault his reasoning. Things often took a dip, sometimes a dangerous dip, before I could figure them out. Terrel provided the cool voice of logic and analysis. Great traits for an emergency room doctor but, as far as I was concerned, he lacked a little spontaneity on the home front. Taking chances weren't his thing.

Timmy began to whimper.

"Got work to do. Diaper change and then introduce Tim to the fine mechanics of my beautiful '73 Charger. It's time for him to check under the hood. Little dude, you stink."

I walked back into the bedroom that had been my home for two years before Timmy entered the world. Why Lena had kept the single bed in there, I didn't know, but she had. With the addition of a crib, changing table, and rocking chair, the compact space signaled that I would leave this room with bruises and bumps on my legs.

My phone buzzed. Jon. Finally. And it wasn't a text, but an actual phone call.

"There you are. I'd hoped to hear from you, maybe a little sooner," I said.

Jon paused.

"Trisha, remember I'm working. Can't always call when I want to."

"Of course. Sorry. How's work?"

I heard a sniff on the other end.

"Did you find anything?"

"Well..."

"Jon?"

"Nothing. Not a thing. We climbed down a trail, overgrown with brush. Babe was sniffing everywhere, but there was no sign."

"That's disappointing. Do you know where the trail leads?"

"Down to a small parking lot in Larkspur. It wouldn't be easy to get there since it was so overgrown, but I suppose it's possible."

"Did you try?"

"Yeah, we did. But some of the weeds were dense and the trail disappeared a few feet from where The Babe became the super-sniffer."

"Did you drive by the lot, by any chance?"

"Way ahead of you. It looks like it's been cordoned off for months. The lot and the bathrooms are closed for repairs. Nobody could park there, that's for sure. Maybe he left another way."

"He left? What are you saying? You think he disappeared on purpose?"

"I don't know, Trisha. If he took the trail, where did he go? Earl's house is at one end of the fire road that goes to Mill Valley. You told me his apartment is at the other. Did he fall into one of the canyons? Possible, but neither the police nor the rangers found him. There are only so many possibilities."

"Somebody took him," I said. "That's what I think."

"Possibly. Or maybe he took off, himself."

"Can we talk about this later?" I asked. My head hurt and this conversation wasn't helping any.

"Do I have a choice?" he asked. There was a smile in his voice.

"Not really … miss you," I said, just as he hung up.

I hadn't signed up to work the game that night, so I had plenty of time on my hands. I picked up the tablet and wandered out to Lena's small backyard with its beautiful view of Mt. Tamalpais. Deep afternoon shadows climbed up the steep hills and turned the Douglas oak and the California pine from dark green to a rich, brownish-black. Earl's home was closer to the base of Mt. Tam since he lived another canyon closer, but I liked this perspective best.

I sat on one of the lounge chairs and opened the tablet to view my notes about Tyler. Jan Johnson knew the most about Tyler's stalker. Maybe we could meet again, someplace quieter than the ballpark or a bar… Maybe the radio station, so I could talk to the security guard while I was there. I called the station and left a message on her voice mail.

If I'd had a copy of Tyler's house key, I would've just wandered over to check things out, myself. I'd grown comfortable with being in places I wasn't supposed to be. And I'd mastered how to tell little … tiny … white lies if someone found me. But I didn't have a key. I didn't even know where Tyler lived. Earl had been vague when I asked him. Just somewhere in Mill Valley on the other end of the La Cruz Canyon fire road. I hoped that Ty's parents would visit his apartment. I would put it on my to-do list anyway.

I hadn't given much thought yet to his beer venture. Maybe his business partners had a line on him. I did a search on Coyote Ridge. When a web address popped up, I blinked in surprise. *Wasn't this a hush-hush business until they worked out the recipe?* I clicked on the URL and again on a disclaimer that I was over twenty-one.

"Definitely that."

A stylish sketch of a ridge in San Rafael, popular with hikers and dog walkers, came into view on the homepage. Off to one side, a pack of coyotes peeked out from behind a grove of Eucalyptus trees.

"Nice design," I said aloud.

Lena walked up behind me. "I could do that," she said.

"You are so competitive," I said.

"I have to admit. That is nice. Someone spent some money. That's not the kind of artwork you'd find on the web for free. That isn't even paid stock. Someone drew this. Click on one of the tabs," Lena demanded.

I tapped the 'Beer' tab. Overlaid on the background of the ridge and the coyotes, some text announced, "We're not ready yet. Check back." I clicked the rest of the tabs, but they all said the same thing. Except for the "Contact" tab. There I found a phone number and an email address.

"That's my first step. I'm calling that number," I said.

Lena patted my shoulder. "Good luck with that. I have a date with a washing machine."

As she walked inside, I punched in the number and waited. The phone rang and as expected, it went to voicemail. I hadn't thought this through. *Would I get a call back faster if I said I was a friend of Tyler or Earl?* The beep sounded and I had to make a split-second decision.

"Hi, this is Arabella Stockman. An acquaintance told me about Coyote Ridge, that I might be interested in investing. Can you give me a call?"

I left my number and hung up.

My phone rang. It was Jon.

"Hey," I said.

"Have great news."

"You found Tyler?"

"Not everything is about Tyler, Trish. We've been invited to my sister's for dinner. She invited all the family. They can't wait to meet you."

There was a long silence.

"Trisha? You there?"

"Yeah. That sounds like ... sure ... would enjoy it. It's just finding time. It won't be easy."

"The Giants are on a ten-day road trip starting next week. I'm sure you can fit in one dinner," Jon said.

Another long silence.

It wasn't the first time Jon had asked me to meet his family.

"You have no excuse this time," said Jon.

"Honestly, I'm not ready to meet anybody."

"What's the problem? We've been seeing each other for nearly a year. I've met all your family, even family friends, even your family friend's dog. The Babe likes me, and I think everyone else does, too. Everyone but you."

"That's not true. I like you. So much. You know that. It's just... I can't..."

"Can't or don't want to?"

I couldn't answer him.

"Are you going to have dinner with me and my family, or not?"

"Jon."

"Are you?"

I gazed out the window. A deep blue sky sliced against Mt. Tam, now completely black.

"Okay. Of course. You're right. I'm sorry. Next week. Pick an evening. I'll go."

"Trisha, it's not supposed to be this hard, you know. I like you ... a lot. I want the people who mean the most to me to meet you."

"I know you do."

My phone's screen flashed. Maybe a call from Coyote Ridge.

"I need to get off the phone. Call coming in."

Before he could protest, I hung up and tried to answer the other call. "Hello?"

Lena stood by the screen door, shaking her finger at me.

"Rude. You are so rude. You hung up on Jon, the man who likes you. He's a good person. He treats you like a goddess, though for the life of me I don't know why. What is so wrong that you won't even meet his family?"

"Hello? Damn it." The call had gone to voicemail.

I glanced up at Lena glaring at me, her arms folded across her chest.

"I'm not ready. Not yet," I said.

Lena shook her head. "He won't stick around much longer if your attitude doesn't change."

"Lee, I realize you're worried about my love life, but I've got it handled. Really. Now, please go away." I turned around, then hit the voicemail button on my phone. The Coyote Ridge people had called back. They wanted to see me to discuss investment options. Immediately, if I was available. A perfect reason to leave my sister and my unfinished business with Jon.

CHAPTER 9

65 ... 70 ... 75 ... 80 mph. My ancient Honda wheezed and belched at the higher speeds but kept on going. I barreled down Highway 101, heading for the Golden Gate Bridge. I didn't care what the speed limit was. I wanted to rocket toward San Francisco as fast as I could. When I hit 85 miles per hour, my car started to shake, so I took my foot off the gas and slowed down.

For the first time in fifteen minutes, I glanced in the rearview mirror. I didn't see any flashing lights. So far, I'd been lucky, but it wouldn't last forever. The cars that I'd hurtled by were now far behind me; I moved over to a slower lane. Speeding always cured my stress.

My sister thought she had all the answers. She knew what guy I should see. When I should see him. How I should talk to him. Absentmindedly, I hit the accelerator again and almost rear-ended the late model Prius in front of me. I slowed down and glanced into the side mirror of the Prius. The driver, a woman with two kids in the back, was alarmed. Chagrined, I dropped back a considerable distance.

"Lena is going to get me killed," I ranted to my empty car. But deep down, I knew it wasn't her fault. I didn't like being pushed. She was pushing me. Jon was pushing me. I hit the accelerator again, snaked into the middle lane and flew past the Prius which was moving as far over as it could.

"I'll go when I'm ready and not before," I muttered to myself. Resolved, I settled down just in time to slam straight into a bank of fog near Sausalito. I couldn't see the Marin Headlands to my right or Richardson Bay and the waterfront marinas below to my left. Big drops of moisture splashed the windshield. I turned on the wipers. They smeared the grime around as they moved back and forth.

Traffic inched across the Golden Gate Bridge in the thick summer fog. Sometimes I could see the cars around me, but they soon disappeared into the grayness. Foghorns blared their deep two-toned alarms, the gloom so thick I could hold it in my hand.

My appointment to meet Jason Chang, one of Coyote Ridge's brewmasters, would take place in the outer Sunset District of San Francisco near the Pacific Ocean. He seemed more than happy to meet with me, a potential investor. As soon as I passed through the toll plaza and left the span, the fog lifted. I headed down 19th Ave and turned into Golden Gate Park, winding past lush, damp green trees and empty rolling meadows. I moved onto Sunset Boulevard, then turned right onto Noriega, skirting past small mom-and-pop stores and kitschy neighborhood restaurants, the tangy smell of the sea hanging in the air.

Jason Chang's house paralleled a narrow street, across from the ocean. I parked and walked up the pathway to a white stucco two-story home with a coral-colored entrance. I was reaching for the door when it hit me. I didn't know what I was going to say. Before I could even knock, Jason opened the door. He wore a gray rubber apron and rubber gloves.

"Hi, I'm Arabella. Call me Bella. I called earlier?"

"Yes, come in, come in. I'm happy you could come by so soon."

I followed him upstairs to the large living room with natural hickory hardwood floors, a comfortable couch and two extra-large chairs upholstered in blue, yellow and green stripes. Yet more proof money didn't equal taste. A large telescope peered out the front window.

"Not much to see today," I said, walking over and peering through the eyepiece. I could barely find the low greenery across the street. The ocean on the other side of the shrubs was nonexistent, a gray haze.

Jason scrutinized me carefully.

"How did you hear about Coyote Ridge?" he asked with a smile. A slight man of Asian descent, Jason had to be in his thirties, with dark receding hair. His lips were thin, and he wore black, square glasses. He chewed on the inside of his cheek as he pondered me.

"Friend of a friend. I recently came into some money and need an investment. Anyway, I knew he knew folks, so I cornered the guy. Asked a bunch of questions. And here I am."

I put my hands behind my back.

Was I talking too much? Did I make sense? Maybe I shouldn't have said I'm newly rich?

It was clear Jason didn't know what to make of me. He came across as more cautious than excited, even while meeting a potential "investor."

"The friend?"

"Friend of a friend," I corrected.

"Do you remember his name? I'd like to thank him for referring you to Coyote Ridge."

Should I tell him? Maybe not. Did it matter?

"Earl. I'm fairly sure his name is Earl," I said.

"I know an Earl," nodded Jason. "Let me show you what we're doing. Ever been to a basement brewery before?"

Could he be warming up to me? We walked back down the steps, went through a side door and turned into an ordinary garage that was now a brewing kitchen.

"Until we acquire some capital, this is where we make Coyote Ridge. We're working on the recipe. Earl ... probably the Earl that you know ... is helping us with that. Although we're trying to be scientific about the process, it's more like trial and error. Developing the recipe for a high-quality beer has been ... how do I say this ... challenging. That's why I'm not going to offer you a sip. Not yet. But we're getting closer."

"I'm impressed with your honesty," I said.

"I firmly believe in transparency with our investors," he said.

Stainless steel stoves, refrigeration, metal cabinets, hoses and large vats spread throughout the garage. It all looked official, but then, what did I know? I had never seen the inside of a small brewery before. He explained the process, step by step, but most of it was Greek to me.

"Understand?" he asked.

"Somewhat," I said, somewhat confused on the finer points of beer making. "Quite the process. You can't be the only one involved."

"No, I have two partners."

"And they are?" I asked.

"Friends."

He wasn't giving me much information.

"Travis something or other ... he's a partner, isn't he?" I continued to prod.

"Tyler. Not Travis. You know him?" Jason tilted his head and stared at me.

"Not really. But I remember Earl talking about a relative being involved. I thought his name was Travis, but now that you mention it, it was Tyler. And your other partner?"

He walked back over to the door that led out of the garage brewery.

"Burk, another friend of mine. From college. Let's go upstairs," he said.

"He has experience making beer?" I questioned.

Jason laughed. "No. Unfortunately, he doesn't. He's more of a computer guy."

Another Burk? Could it be the Burk I met? The swimmer? Mentioning that I knew him could come back to haunt me, especially if he set up a meeting with his partners and I was introduced as Arabella Stockman. But, not mentioning him had its problems, too.

I won't say anything. Not yet.

I smiled and followed him up the steps. Once settled in his living room, I changed the subject. "How does this work? Do you do the brewing?"

"We all do. I live here, so it's easier for me than the others. Bella, what are you looking to do here?"

If only I knew.

"A good investment," I said. "I have money to spend. I don't know much about beer, but if Earl recommends you … well, I trust him. And I like the name of your product."

Did he buy it?

"We have a portfolio and a business plan that you might like to see," he said.

Yes!

"Sure. That sounds like the right next step. Could I use your ladies' room?"

He pointed down the hall. Once inside the bathroom, I checked the medicine cabinet. Nothing. I flushed the toilet and turned on the faucet for a few seconds, then walked out. He stood by the front door with a folder in his hand.

"Here you go. This should answer your questions." He handed me the portfolio. Give me a call when you're ready and I can introduce you to my partners."

Not a chance.

"Well, it was nice to meet you. Thank you for showing me the setup. I'll read this over and get back to you," I said.

He smiled and we shook hands.

"Appreciate you stopping by. Say 'hi' to Earl for me."

Then he all but shut the door in my face. Shaken, I walked down the pathway to my car, got in, and locked the door, my heart pumping loudly in my ears. I did not intend to meet his partners, especially if Burk would be there. I thought about it for a moment. Was this the Burk I met at the swim? How much of a coincidence would that be? I drove down the street to Judah, next to the streetcar turnaround.

I wondered if Jason had bought my act. I'd tried to come off as someone who had money to spend but was naïve about investing. Given the fact it was a start-up—not to mention how bad their current batch had turned out—I thought he would've been falling all over himself to snare me. But he didn't seem that interested. In fact, it was almost like he couldn't get rid of me fast enough. I parked and went into a surfer hangout on the corner and bought a cup of coffee. By the time I returned to the car, my vital signs had returned to something close to normal. The fog had lifted slightly and danced over the fleshy ice plants that covered the center divide. I couldn't see the ocean, but it pounded and roared behind the grayness. I had turned my phone off while visiting Jason. When I switched it back on, it pinged incessantly. I pulled over to the curb before I reached the next stop sign. There were several texts ... every single one of them from Lena.

Really?

U R a jerk.

Call me now.

Don't be mad. Call me.

My earlier anger had drifted away like the fog. I'd have to connect with Lena eventually, but now was not the time. Before I started the car, I glanced to my right. Tyler stood on the corner. He rested against a beat-up mountain bike, a dark hoodie pulled tight around his face, his black hair sticking out around the edges. I opened the car door, but he motioned for me to stop.

"Stay there," he said.

I launched myself out of the front seat. "I've been hunting for you for almost a week. Everyone is worried. Earl is a mess, and your parents flew down."

I rushed toward him, stopping next to the bike.

"Keep your voice down," he cautioned.

"No, not until you tell me what's going on."

"I can't," he said, backing up.

I grabbed onto the handlebars to keep him from moving. The drippy fog clung to his dirty black hair.

"Tyler."

"You can't tell anyone you saw me."

"Why not?"

"I'm in trouble. Earl's in trouble. Because of me. I had to disappear.

And it needs to stay that way."

"Does this have anything to do with the beer guy or your stalker at the radio station?"

"Don't tell anyone you saw me or talked to me. Just stay out of it. And stay away from the house over the hill."

"What house? What are you talking about?"

He yanked the handlebars out of my hands and pedaled down a path through the ice plants to the sidewalk across the street. I dashed after him but in the time it took to suck down a breath, he'd disappeared, consumed by the fog. A horn beeped behind me. I was standing in the middle of the Great Highway, my hands on my hips.

"Lady, do you need help?" called out a burly contractor in a truck.

"No, sorry."

I jogged back across the median to my car, climbed in, started it up and turned on the windshield wipers. My heart thumped in my chest, again. Tyler was okay. I was so relieved. Relieved and troubled. Whatever the issue was, I had to find him and bring him back to Marin. For Earl.

I put the car in drive, moved toward Judah Street, then turned left until I was riding along the Great Highway. Ocean Beach and the Pacific Ocean were to my right, more ice plants to my left. I scanned each side of the road until I came to Sloat Avenue and the San Francisco Zoo. Cool fog silenced the neighborhood streets, and I thought about the thin hoodie Tyler wore. He must have been freezing.

Tyler could have stopped into any of the small restaurants and stores along Sloat or even ridden into the Zoo. I cruised up and down the street but soon gave up. A complete waste of time. I wasn't going to find him if he didn't want to be found. I headed toward 19th Avenue and the Golden Gate Bridge, switched on the heat and turned the windshield wipers up a notch while I went over the last few hours. Creepy Jason, the beer guy. Tyler, appearing like a ghost out of nowhere, warning me to stay away.

What could he have done that put him and Earl in harm's way? Maybe Tyler had lost it. Stay away from the house over the hill? He'd sounded like a character in a scary movie. *Give me a break.*

CHAPTER 10

Heavy traffic traveled north on 19th Avenue toward the Golden Gate Bridge, and I encountered red lights at each block. I switched on the radio.

"That's a line drive to center field... a shot no one was expecting," said the excited voice of the commentator. The Giants had traveled to Chicago and were playing the Cubs, leaving me with a free afternoon. Tyler clearly wasn't missing, but nobody knew that but me.

As soon as I heard the baseball game on the radio, my breathing slowed, my shoulders melted away from my ears. Maybe the constant patter of the two broadcasters relaxed me. *Better than meditation*, I thought as I crawled forward in the slow rush hour traffic. Tapping the steering wheel didn't speed anything up, but it didn't stop me from trying. I contemplated my options. I could either sit in traffic, see if Jon was around and head to his place, or call a friend I'd made in the San Francisco Police Department three years earlier.

I saw Inspector Carolina Burrell before she saw me. Inspector Burrell commanded attention when she walked into a room. She was a showstopper. A petite, small-boned woman, Burrell could be mistaken as delicate, even fragile, to those who didn't know her. Those who did understood she was tough, strong, smart and compassionate. Her stark white hair had grown, and she wore it piled high on her head with a few strands hanging loose next to her cheeks. I remember the first time I met her. The white hair had completely thrown me. In her late forties or early fifties ... not the elderly grandma I'd first imagined ... the woman had the deepest blue eyes I had ever seen. She destroyed bad guys with those eyes, just dismantled them piece by piece until nothing was left.

I watched as she stepped up to the counter and ordered coffee. Customers standing close by took a step back. Was it the badge or the persona? A light hanging above turned into her own personal spotlight. She stood there alone, talking and smiling to the counter person who appeared tongue-tied. I wondered if she had that effect on everyone.

She wore her police badge on a lanyard, hanging around her neck. On her left hip was a holster with a revolver resting inside. Handcuffs were attached to her belt. Inspector Burrell glanced over her shoulder and saw me. She waved.

"Trisha! Let me order something for you."

I didn't want to be a line jumper, but nobody objected.

"Decaf mocha."

Once we had our drinks and sat at a table away from the other customers, she said, "So, how have you been?"

"Still with the Narcotics division?" I asked,

"I am." She sat there quietly. Not speaking. Then she smiled. I felt terribly uncomfortable.

"Inspector Burrell?"

"Carolina. Please."

"Carolina, I know it's not your division, but you must know something about missing people, right?"

She nodded. "I might."

I explained the best I could about the quasi-disappeared Tyler. The more I talked, the dumber it sounded. Missing, not missing. What was I asking her?

"You meet the strangest folks," she said. "If I understand this correctly, a friend of your landlord—"

"His grandson."

"Okay. This grandson—"

"Tyler," I said.

"Okay. So this Tyler fakes his disappearance because he believes he's done something wrong. That because of what he thinks he did, he's in trouble, along with your landlord, his grandfather."

"Earl. Yes, that's it."

Inspector Burrell took out a small notebook and jotted down a few things.

"Let's start at the beginning. When was the last time you saw him?"

"Not more than an hour ago."

"Where was he?"

"Near his business partner's house across from the Great Highway."

"Did he see you?"

"Yes."

"Did you talk to him?"

"Yes."

"And?"

"He said something like, 'you never saw me.'"

"Why did he say that?"

"I don't know. My gut tells me that this isn't a minor situation. That whatever he did, it's going to come down on his grandfather."

"But you have no proof of that. Correct?"

"Correct. He's been reported missing, officially. And his parents flew in from Oregon and are staying with Earl, the grandfather."

"But he's not missing."

"Right. But they think he is."

"Is he being held against his will?"

"When I saw him, he was outside on his bike. So, I would have to say no."

Inspector Burrell put her pencil down and sat back in her chair.

"Let me explain briefly about missing people. Some of this will apply and some of it won't. Number one. You don't have to wait any certain amount of time to report someone missing. Whatever you heard in the past about waiting a day or two before reporting a missing person is not true. Number two … and we're not talking about minors here, but adults. The police will want to know if they left voluntarily or involuntarily or if the missing person was the victim of a crime or foul play. They'll check to see if he was in need of immediate medical attention or could be mentally or physically impaired."

"You sound like a police manual," I said.

"You need to know the basics. Being missing is not a crime. People disappear all the time and they usually show up after a few days, or even weeks later. Police resources are limited so when an adult walks away and disappears, more than likely, they're not going to do anything. People have the right to be left alone."

"But this is different. He said he was in trouble. He could fit into the crime category."

"What kind of trouble?"

"I don't know. He wouldn't say. Is there anything you can do?"

Inspector Burrell took a deep breath and said, "Well, this is out of my jurisdiction, but I can maybe… maybe… ask someone from the Taraval

Station to do a welfare check on the address."

"Thank you." I frowned.

"Not satisfied, are you?"

"I want to know what he's gotten himself into and why would it involve his grandfather. I'm worried about both of them," I said anxiously.

"Right now, there's no reason to suspect anything or anybody. The cops can't just jump in because someone said something that sounds odd to you. Bring me a reason to start an investigation."

"I thought I did."

"No, you didn't. Write down the address on the Great Highway; the police may be able to stop by. We'll go from there."

I picked up a napkin and wrote down Jason Chang's address. I heard chatter on Inspector Burrell's radio.

"Trisha, I have to go." She stood up. "There's one more thing. If the police find this Tyler person, they don't have to let friends and family know where he is. Not if he doesn't want them to."

"Well, that's not fair. We're worried."

"Be that as it may, people have a right to their privacy, whether you like it or not."

"But this isn't about privacy," I said.

Inspector Burrell stood up and turned her radio down a click.

"You know, in some missing person cases, the police often encourage the family or friends to seek outside help."

"You mean like an investigator?"

"Something like that. I have to go. I'll let you know what we find. It's been good to see you." She smiled. "And you haven't changed. Not one bit."

My face flushed. Inspector Burrell knew me to be … shall we say, creative in my endeavors to ferret out the truth. I didn't always have the complete facts, but my gut instincts usually rang true, and I didn't give up. I'd call myself persistent, but her word for me was annoying.

During my coffee break with Inspector Burrell, traffic had lightened up and now moved at a somewhat-normal speed toward the Golden Gate Bridge. I switched on my headlights, but only saw the stretch of freeway directly in front of me. Restless fog screened out my surroundings.

Inspector Burrell had all but said that since Tyler was an adult, he could drop off the face of the earth if he wanted to. I'd heard the same disappointing information when my husband walked out: if he didn't want to be found, there was nothing the Denver Police could do. Missing adults weren't a big priority. Although the police wouldn't put any effort into finding Tyler—or what he was so afraid of—they weren't opposed to someone else lending a hand. I planned on being that someone else.

I was nearly over the bridge when I remembered the baseball game. I switched on the radio to hear that our boys had won, and that the new center fielder, Sandy Miller, had some sort of a run-in with the mercurial right fielder, Edwardo Martinez... literally. From what the host said, they'd both made a play for the ball, collided, and ended up in a clump on the field. But then Miller stuck his arm straight up from the pile, the ball in his glove. I love that kind of drama at the ballpark.

Once I'd reached the Marin side of the span, a small patch of rich, dark-blue sky appeared as the fog floated away. I pressed down on the accelerator and headed for Lena's house.

50

CHAPTER 11

Lena was sitting on the couch watching the television when I walked in. She glanced over at me, then back to the screen.

"Are you mad?" she asked.

"Actually, I feel pretty good."

She clicked off the TV with the remote and patted the cushion on the couch next to her.

"Talk."

"Well, for starters, Tyler isn't missing, even though he wants people to think he is."

"What?"

"I saw him, just standing on the sidewalk. Told me to stop looking for him and to stay out of it. And something about a house over the hill. I have no idea what he's talking about. Anyway, he said he was in trouble, that he'd screwed up, and because of whatever he did, Earl was in trouble, too."

"What house?"

"Don't know. I never met any of Earl's neighbors."

"And what kind of trouble?"

"Don't know that either. But the police say I can find out."

"What officer of the law would ever say something like that?"

"Inspector Burrell from the SFPD. Remember her?"

"You know a lot of police officers. I get them confused."

"Funny. So, that's what I'm going to do. I'll figure this out and then Tyler can 'reappear' and Earl can relax."

"You want to go over that again for me? Maybe it's my mom brain, but when you stormed out of here, I don't know, four or five hours ago, you were incredibly mad. Now you're all smiles because a police officer

—"

"An inspector—"

"—An inspector has led you to believe you can solve this little problem on your own?"

"Most of that's right."

"Well, I know you. You're going to do what you want no matter what I say." She hesitated and then, "By the way, why don't you want to meet Jon's family?"

My pulse jumped about thirty points. I sat up straight on the couch. "We were talking about Tyler and Earl."

"Sorry. I thought we'd finished with that topic. It's only a question, Trisha. Don't go ballistic on me again," she appealed.

I stood up and started to walk around the living room, looking everywhere but at her.

"It's a simple question, Trisha."

"I don't have an answer."

I walked back over to the couch and picked up the photograph of me, Lena, our mom and dad at the Marin County Fair. Our family, before everything fell apart.

"You just don't get it," I said to my sister.

"Yes, I do. You've got all kinds of abandonment shit. I understand. First Dad, then your husband. I can see why you'd be gun shy. But Jon—Jon is great. And you're just pissing it all away because you're scared. Is that what you want? To be alone for the rest of your life?"

"Everybody leaves, ok? Jon will be next. It's only a matter of a time. I've thought about it over and over. No matter how hard I try, deep inside, I feel it's all my fault, that they left because of me. But I don't know what I did to make them leave. I don't know how to fix it. So, stop. Just stop."

"I'm here. I didn't leave."

"Oh, Lee, I know, and I'm grateful for that."

"And here comes the but."

Before I could continue, she walked out of the living room, down the hall to her bedroom. Her door closed.

Nothing is ever easy when it comes to Lena and me. Even with everything we'd been through together, it was like we spoke different languages sometimes. I clicked on my phone, checked my email. The final-final results from the open water swim had been sent. I was immediately drawn in, leaving Lena, Jon, and past life experiences behind me.

I'd come in thirty-fifth out of fifty women swimmers in my age group. Not bad for my first attempt while battling a serious case of open-water anxiety. I searched through the men's results. Burk wasn't listed. I checked the disqualified swimmers. Nothing there either. I combed through the overall set of results that combined both men and women of all age groups. No Burk. I tried to picture the last moments of the race, again. He'd followed me out of the water and ran through the finish line. Hadn't he? I couldn't remember. Had he been wearing a cap with his race number printed on it, his arms and legs marked with a thick black sharpie with those same numbers? Possibly. My fear had so completely overwhelmed me that I'd failed to register these suddenly-important details. I hit reply and composed a quick email to the event director, asking for any info about a swimmer named Burk, a tall guy in his late forties.

Now there were two quasi-missing men on my radar. Tyler and Burk. They were so different. Skinny, slight Tyler had frizzy black hair and a keen mind for sports statistics but wasn't athletic by any stretch of the imagination. Burk. Well, I didn't know much about him. Easy on the eyes, that was for sure. But also confident, a solid swimmer, and possibly a partner in Coyote Ridge. His anonymity irked me. I couldn't fit him into a neat little box, tied up with a bow, put in his proper place on the shelf of my mind. To be honest, I liked the way he had looked at me, how he'd talked to me in the water. I wouldn't have made it through the swim without him. But something seemed odd, and I didn't know what. Another gut feeling. In my mind, Lena's words ran through my mind, "You always find the weirdest guys to get involved with." I glanced at my sister's closed door and sighed.

I headed to Timmy's bedroom, scooted around the baby changing table and stood for a minute, staring out of the window into the darkness. *Why aren't things easier now?* I thought they would be. I had a nice, semi-permanent place to live, a solid part-time seasonal job, a relationship with my father and a boyfriend. At least, I hoped I had a boyfriend. Three years ago, I couldn't have dreamed of this existence. But living the dream hadn't filled the void, that developed when my husband left. It took working a case to get the blood flowing.

I'd turned into a danger junkie. Throw in some risk, uncertainty, verbal dynamite, a little physical danger, and I felt alive. No wonder everything else bored me. Normalcy could never compare to peril and crisis. In those moments, I could feel my mind growing sharper, adrenaline pulsing through my veins. I loved solving puzzles, often dangerous puzzles. Maybe that's why Burk piqued my interest. He was an unknown quantity, a hot enigma, a puzzle to solve. *Something is wrong with me.*

I sank down into the single bed, turned off the light and promptly fell asleep.

CHAPTER 12

I woke up to the sound of my phone chirping, Timmy wailing, and Lena trying to shush him. Poor baby. Poor Lena. Dr. T had four hours left at the hospital, lucky him. A message from the open water race director appeared on my phone. No one named Burk had participated in the swim, at least not legally. Then another alert from my bank popped up. My new credit card had been used, but not by me. Two charges were made in an East Bay big box store. Someone had purchased three laptops, noise-canceling headphones and a solar charger amounting to over $4,000. I guess all that shopping made the thief hungry, so he/she drove over to a Mexican fast-food restaurant and bought $60 worth of tacos and tortillas. I read the email in disbelief. *Not again.* I reread it, this time aloud.

"Lena," I yelled, jogging out to the living room. "My hacker is ... what's wrong with you?"

There was my sister, frantic. "I don't know what to do. I want to take a shower. I want to go to the bathroom, but I don't think I should put him down."

"Let me take him and you go do what you need to do."

"I don't know if that's—"

"Go." I reached for the crying baby and propped him up next to my shoulder.

"You have to be quiet so I can call the bank. There is someone out there who likes using my money. Well, the bank's money, but still."

Lena stood hesitantly in the hallway. "You were hacked?"

"Yes. A second time. Now, go. Take your shower."

With Timmy balanced on one arm, I contacted the fraud division of my bank and canceled the card, again. Another one would be sent to me, again. They were sorry for the inconvenience, again.

I voiced my frustration to Little T. The more I talked, the quieter he became.

"Let's go live off the grid, you, me, your mom and dad. Forget banking and credit cards. Forget guys who don't exist or go into hiding. You remember Tyler? That skinny guy you met at Earl's house? Well, that's what he did. He wants everyone to think he's missing. But he's not. He's done something stupid. Something that puts him and his grandpa in a lot of danger. What do you think it is?"

Timmy had stopped crying and was staring at me intently, giving me every indication he was listening. It was more than anyone else was offering.

"Ok, Detective Tim. Help me out. What do Tyler and Earl have in common?" Timmy turned his head and laid it down on my shoulder. "We know that they're related. Grandfather and grandson. They both like beer, but that's about it, as far as I can see. Are you hungry?"

I walked into the kitchen and opened the refrigerator. I noticed the bottle of beer I'd coveted the night before.

"You know Little T, I found Tyler near his beer-making buddy's house. What if his problem has something to do with Coyote Ridge?"

I shut the refrigerator and walked back toward the living room, only to stop half-way. "That's it. That's what Tyler and Earl have in common. Beer! Tyler makes it and his grandfather gives him and his partners money and brewing tips. Earl is supposed to be some sort of craft beer guru, remember?"

Lena called out from behind the closed door of the bathroom. "Who are you talking to?"

"Timmy." I glanced down at the baby in my arms. His cheek rested against my chest, his eyes closed.

Even he'd stopped listening. I didn't care. I went on prattling, anyway.

"So Coyote Ridge seems to be the connection. Are they stealing recipes? Couldn't be. Not Earl. He's too straitlaced for that. And if they were, you'd think the last batch would've tasted better."

Timmy gave a muffled snort in his sleep. I walked the baby back to his crib and laid him down. His eyes fluttered for a moment, but he remained in dreamland. I covered him with a light blanket, walked out to the living room and stretched out on the couch while I pondered my new discovery.

My phone buzzed with a text from Dad. The police had told Tyler's parents what Inspector Burrell had told me. Adults have the right to disappear. They didn't like that, so they packed up the car and headed to Carmel.

"I can go home!" I proclaimed to the empty room. Ten minutes later, a somewhat refreshed and clean Lena came walking down the hallway wrapped in towels.

"Where's Timmy?"

"Sleeping. You want something done, ask Aunt Trisha."

Before I could get the words out, Lena darted down the hallway to check on the sleeping baby. A second later, she walked back to the living room, her expression incredulous. "How did you do that?"

"He listened while I talked to the bank. Then we discussed Tyler and his grandfather and beer. We never got around to the beer making swimmer who doesn't exist, so I'll have to fill him in later. I'm going back to Earl's house. Tyler's parents have left, so I have my room back. I think Earl knows more than he's saying. About Tyler, about all of it."

Lena shook her head. "Here we go. Trisha's gone off the deep end, *again*! You need a better hobby."

When I left Lena's and drove up the hill to Earl's, I scoped out the houses I passed along the way. Nothing about them struck me as unusual. Maybe Tyler had been mistaken. The road was deserted except for two cyclists who rode by almost daily.

The Babe walked around in his customary circles as I came into the deserted house. I knew my father was with Earl, volunteering at China Camp State Park, part of a new daily schedule that kept him busy and happy.

The solitude of the house made me think about my own obligations. *I better take care of this now.* I pulled out my phone and called Jon. It went to voicemail. "I can't do the family dinner right. I'm sorry. Honestly, I am."

If I were brave, I would have said it to his face, but I wasn't, and I didn't want to. What I wanted was to find a bottle of Coyote Ridge. Four sat on the kitchen counter and two remained in the fridge, one of which had already been opened, its cap fitted back over the top. I picked it up, flipped off the cap and almost took a sip, but thought better of it. Instead, I sniffed the liquid in the bottle. It smelled like wet dog. *Well, that's enough to keep someone sober.*

Could this possibly be the beer that Earl had said needed 'slight tweaking'? If it were me, I'd throw it out and start from scratch. I pushed the cap back on and placed it back in the refrigerator.

Maybe Earl needed to be more hands-on and walk them through the beer making basics, step by step. How hard could it be? It's a recipe. Even I can follow a recipe. The Babe had trailed me into the kitchen and was stretched out by the table, body glued to the floor.

"What could make something smell so bad?" I mused out loud to the dog.

"They didn't clean the containers properly," said Earl, walking into the kitchen.

Surprised, I turned around. "You're back early. I didn't hear you drive up."

Covered in dirt and sawdust, Earl's body radiated heat.

"You're saying they didn't keep their bottles and mixing containers in the dishwasher long enough?"

"It's more complicated than that. This is a typical beginner's error," said Earl.

"Why don't you dump it out?" I asked.

"They need to taste it themselves, so they can see how bad it is," he said, moving me away from the fridge.

"Wouldn't they normally do that?"

"You'd think," said Earl. "But it doesn't look or taste like it."

"Did you try another bottle? Maybe it was just that one."

"Don't need to. According to Jason, all the beer came from one batch, and it was all stored together. They should all taste the same."

I took a closer look at my father's friend and noticed the dark circles that had settled under his eyes. "How are you doing?" I asked him. "You look exhausted. Have you heard anything from Tyler?"

"I'll be okay once I take a shower." I noticed he hadn't answered my question.

"Your son left?"

"Yep."

"Weren't they here to find Ty? Maybe visit his apartment?

"They did. They even convinced the police to go with them, but there was nothing out of the ordinary. The police told them to go on with their lives, that they'd be in touch if anything changed."

"If it were my sister, I'd never leave until I found her. Maybe he's closer than anyone thinks."

Earl tried to smile, but the corners of his mouth didn't cooperate.

"You have a good heart, Trisha, like your dad. But this is different.

Ty is different. His mom and dad are different."

"Can I ask you a few questions?"

"Does it have to be now? I'm tired. Been a tough day or two. I was planning on stretching out and taking a little nap after I cleaned up."

"Ok, just one then. Do you have any friends in the neighborhood?"

"Acquaintances mostly. No real 'friends.' To tell the truth, I never went out of my way to meet the neighbors. Why are you asking?"

"Just curious about the locals."

Earl shrugged and then turned to walk up the staircase.

"Do you and Ty work on other projects together besides beer?"

Earl stopped, shook his head. "No."

"Nothing at all?"

Earl turned and squinted at me like he was standing in bright sunlight.

"No, Trisha. Nothing at all. Why?"

"Just curious, I guess. Why don't you talk to his beer making buddies? They might know where he went," I said.

"Gonna clean up, lie down. Need to sleep."

He continued up the stairs, The Babe following. From the little I knew about my landlord, he had always been a person for detail … not the type to be blasé about a project, even if only mildly involved. He would never lend his name to an enterprise that didn't aim for perfection. Maybe Coyote Ridge didn't have to taste good. Maybe Coyote Ridge was a shell for something else. Something that only Earl and Tyler and their beer making buddies were aware of.

Before I headed up to see what Ty's parents had done to my room, I walked through the comfortable living room with its lived-in deep brown leather couches and chairs and out to the deck. Earl's drone rested on the patio's wicker sofa. He'd shown me how to use it once, when I first moved in. I often saw him flying it over the reservoir at the other end of La Cruz Canyon. Sometimes he followed the swimmers in the water. I had planned to ask him if he would like to be the air video expert for the next open water swim. If he videoed the whole swim and then hovered over the finish line as the swimmers came in, we could play it before the awards ceremony. It would be a first for Northern California.

I picked up the pint-sized flying robot and turned it around in my hand. Such a silly compact thing, with its tiny propellers, small black body and bug-eyed camera. I powered it on and saw the light blink.

"Let's go for a ride, shall we?" I sat the drone on the patio couch and pushed the control stick slowly forward. The little propellers whirled.

"And we are ready for takeoff." I pushed the throttle forward again, this time faster. Too fast. The drone went straight up.

"Shit!"

I pulled the throttle back to the starting position, trying to go slow, but it wasn't slow enough and the mini copter almost crash-landed right next to me. I turned everything off. I did a quick inspection of the propellers and the camera. Nothing damaged. Lucky its takeoff and landing platform were the soft cushions of the couch.

"That's enough for one day." I placed the controls where I found them, right next to the drone, and saw a folded piece of paper stuck in the corner of the cushion. On it were a few different sketches of these mini flyers. One was about the size of a large dragonfly. So tiny. In fact, he'd named it Dragon Fly200. Earl's neat linear handwriting had some notes on the minuscule bug. It would weigh no more than eighteen grams with its camera. By my calculations, that was around a third of a pound.

Under the Dragon Fly's weight were the words "Regular/thermal camera range of two+ miles, fly up to thirty minutes." At the bottom, he'd added, "Fits in the palm of your hand. Folds up to cell phone size."

Another sketch, this one called the "Batbot," had all its electronics under the main part of the body, making it look like, you guessed it, a bat. Next to the sketch were the words in precise penmanship: "Flight time under five minutes. Need different power source—high altitude lasers?"

Earl must be coming out of retirement if he'd started designing drones. But designing quadcopters that needed airborne laser beams to keep them energized? Sounded like science fiction or a military-grade invention. I pulled out my phone and took pictures of them, then refolded the piece of paper and stuck it back where I'd found it.

I wondered if my dad knew about Earl's designs. Best way to find out was just to ask him. I gave him a call.

"Hey, daughter of mine. What's going on? You at Lena's?"

"No, I'm back home. Lena's a little down in the dumps. Six months into parenthood, and I think she's realizing it's forever."

There was silence on the other end. Dad cleared his throat.

"Sorry, Dad. Didn't mean to offend."

"You didn't. I was the one who walked out. I have to live with that for the rest of my life. Is there something honestly wrong with Lena or is it just the new-mother blues?"

"She's fine. It's Earl that has me worried."

"The poor man. I've never seen him like this. He somehow thinks

Ty's disappearance is his fault. Not sure why. And his kids... what a piece of work they are."

"Dad, could I change the subject?"

"Shoot."

"What do you know about Earl's drone?"

"You mean Black Beauty? That thing he flies over the canyon?"

"Yeah. Black Beauty."

"Are you interested in getting one? I'm sure Earl can give you some suggestions, maybe a few lessons. You were never much of a driver, Trisha. You sure you want to start flying quadcopters?"

"No, nothing like that. I'm—"

"I tried it once, you know."

"Dad, listen—"

"Funny little things, hopping over the treetops."

"Dad," I said louder. "Listen. Did Earl design drones?"

"Well, let me think. He was some computer engineer genius, made all his money that way."

"Dad, I know this. But did he design drones? Is he designing drones now?"

"I don't know. We did have a discussion the other night about what the ideal drone would be like. The specs and all that."

"Why do you think he brought that up?"

"Oh, that's Earl, always looking to improve upon what is."

"Is there a reason, you think?"

"Nah. He likes to talk and think and invent things. That's who he is. Why all these questions?"

"Just curious, I guess. I found some sketches of what might be next-generation drones. Looked like Earl's handwriting," I explained, staring across La Cruz Canyon. Off in the distance on the fire road, the two cyclists who had ridden past me when I first arrived had stopped to chat. Or at least I thought it was them. Hard to tell so far away.

"Trish, are you thinking of buying a drone? I wouldn't if I were you. You'd fly it into the Canyon and never see it again. I remember when you learned to drive... that corner on Fifth and K... didn't you take out the stop sign?"

"Got something to do, Dad. Gotta go. Bye." I hung up. Sometimes talking to my father was like taking The Babe for a walk, Can't always keep him on track.

"What?" That's all I could say when I stepped into my bedroom. Ty's parents must have thought the hotel staff would be in to clean up after them. They had pulled the sheets off the bed and dropped them on the floor. Towels from my bathroom formed a damp trail to the sliding glass doors that opened onto the deck. The water dripped in the shower. Someone had managed to squeeze the toothpaste all over the sink and part of the mirror. Did they think I was the maid? If so, where was my tip? *Must have forgotten.*

My phone buzzed, signaling a text from Jon. *Not now,* I thought. *Can't deal with you and this mess.* Even I didn't know whether I meant the room or my relationship.

I'm not known for being neat, but I would never leave someone else's room in such disarray. I set the room back in order, vibrating with annoyance and getting angrier by the second. Jon's unread text wasn't helping my attitude, either.

I need to get out of here.

I changed into a pair of knee-length exercise pants Lena'd given me for my birthday and a gray crop top. Then I scrambled through the bottom of my closet to find the closest things I had to running shoes. I tied up the laces and picked up my phone. There were three texts from Jon and an alert from my bank.

"What now?" I said to the empty room. I opened my bank's website. Because of my inconvenience for the second time, they promised to next-day mail my new credit card. They reassured me again that I wouldn't be responsible for the charges. That was something, at least.

I stuck the phone in the waistband of my tights and trotted down the steps. The Babe wiggled around by the front door, watching me anxiously.

"Oh, all right. Come on." We jogged down the steps and took a side trail off the fire road, a path that led into the canyon and the reservoir at the far end. Tall redwoods crowded the path, framing the sky above me. The cool air and solitude helped minimize the concern over my violated room and breached credit card. The issue of Jon was not pacified so easily.

The wide dirt road was a perfect spot for a run … well, not exactly a run. Not even a jog, more like a fast walk. The redwoods dwarfed the small bushy Bay Laurel trees that grew alongside the trail. As the groves drifted into the deeper part of the canyon, mature madrones shedding deep red bark and exposing smooth yellow trunks replaced them. Their long twisting branches stretched out and shaded the trail, the temperature dropping at least fifteen degrees as we descended. The Babe obediently trotted next to me until something caught his nose and he scooted over to the edge of the trail and sniffed away. I kept going. In less than thirty seconds, he reappeared by my side, his tags clinking as he jogged along.

The trail straightened out as we reached the bottom of the canyon. After twenty minutes, I slowed down to a comfortable walk and then stopped. Sweat dripped down my forehead and I struggled to catch my breath.

"This is hard." The dog stopped and stood next to me, waiting for our next move. My anger had slipped away and with it, the urge to bolt. I looked down at The Babe. "We're almost there, bud. We can make it."

'There' referred to the reservoir. Even though it was now a considerable effort to move my legs, I started jogging again. Around the next bend, the water glistened through the trees and the shrubs. When the full reservoir came into view, I stopped and pulled out my cell phone to take a few pictures.

We started off along the shore for another ten minutes when The Babe suddenly made a hard right and ran into the tall grass by the water's edge.

"Stay with me. Come," and he did, sort of. But then he veered directly toward the water and jumped in, chasing a black and white waterbird with a needle-thin bill and hot pink legs.

"Babe, come. Now. Leave that … ah … thing alone."

"It's a stilt. A black-necked stilt, to be exact," said a voice behind me. I turned to find the shorter of the two cyclists I'd seen when I was on the phone with Dad. Next to him stood the other rider, a tall, ripped man with curly hair. His wraparound sunglasses hid his eyes, but he smiled broadly.

"I know you," I said to Mr. Smiley. "You swam with me at the open water swim. Burk, right?"

"That's right. Nice to see you again."

I faltered, searching for something to say. "You're not in the race results."

"You were looking?" he asked.

"Uh, just wanted to thank you," I stammered.

"You did."

I knew I should say something witty, something that would make him think I was funny or clever or both, but I couldn't let it go. "Why aren't you in the results?"

"A paperwork issue, that's all. I've been too busy to clear it up," he explained.

The Babe splashed through the water, headed for the trail and stood in the middle of the three of us, staring at me with expectant eyes. Then he shook, getting us all wet. Everyone stepped back.

"Sorry about that," I apologized.

"She's just being a dog," he said.

"She's a he," I said.

"Didn't you call him Babe?"

"Yeah, as in The Babe."

"Oh, that Babe. Babe Ruth. Gotcha," said Burk.

"I saw you taking pictures. Good place for a distance swim, don't you think?" his friend commented. "You know, if you swim and run, just add cycling and you could join us at some of the sprint triathlons."

"I'm a better swimmer than I'm a runner, and that's not saying much. And I haven't been on a bike since I was twelve."

"As they say, 'It all comes back to you,'" he pressed. "I should have known you'd name your dog after a baseball player," said Burk.

I took a step back. "The Babe isn't my dog and why do you think I'd name him after a baseball player?"

Burk took off his sunglasses. Startling blue eyes, bluer than robin's eggs, stared at me. I must have been completely freaked out to have missed them at the swim.

"Only a guess. You gotta be a baseball fan. I'm a season ticket holder and I've seen you at the Giants games half a dozen times. You usually scan tickets at the gates near Willie Mays Plaza, don't you?"

"You're right. I do." I was taken by surprise.

He stood there, that big grin still on his face.

A wave of uneasiness swept over me and a rosy flush crept up my neck to my face. I bent over to put The Babe on his leash.

"Sorry about the soggy dog," I managed to say, nodding to one man and then the other.

"See you at the next game," said Burk. He held my gaze for a minute. "What's your name again?"

"Trisha."

"That's right. Trisha, the anxious swimmer."

He held out his hand. "Burk Dennison. See you soon, Trisha. We ride by Earl's house all the time. We're neighbors. I'm around the corner, other side of the hill."

"Later," said the no-name cyclist. "Think about the triathlon. You'd have a lot of fun. We could train here in the reservoir for the swim."

With that, they rode off down the trail. I watched as they disappeared around a curve. My brain slipped into slow motion. He knew my landlord, but Earl hadn't mentioned a Burk when I asked him about his neighbors. Was his house on the "other side of the hill" the same one Tyler had mentioned? I had more questions about this guy than I'd had before this chance meeting. And why did I want answers so badly?

My pocket rang. It was Jon. I turned my phone off. I couldn't talk to him. Not now.

Later that evening, I sat on the deck off my bedroom, thinking about the probability of running into a total stranger two times in as many days. Burk didn't look like a stalker … not that I knew what stalkers looked like. And he was nice to look at. I wasn't completely opposed to running into him again.

"Trisha, is there something wrong with your phone?" Dad called up the stairs.

"No, it's just turned off."

"Well, your sister has been calling. The Giants are trying to reach you. Since you weren't answering, they tried Lee's home phone. They want you to work a special event tomorrow. You need to let them know as soon as possible."

"Okay, thanks. I will," I called down the steps.

The doorbell rang. The front door opened, and The Babe began to bark. It took less than thirty seconds before the tantalizing scent of warm pizza sauce, melted cheese and pepperoni floated into my room. My mouth watered.

"Come on down and have some pizza with Earl and me. We're tired of staring at each other… need a little female company."

"Let me call work first, Dad." I switched on the phone and called the Special Events office at the ballpark to let them know I would be there as requested. Jon had stopped texting me. I wasn't sure if that made me happy or sad.

CHAPTER 13

The event at the ballpark was billed as an annual sales celebration for a San Francisco tech firm. The company had booked the Club Level, or, more specifically, the entire second floor of Oracle Park. Guests wandered from one end of the Club to the other, eventually drifting to the ballpark seats to watch a video on the scoreboard about their company's accomplishments during the last year.

Inside, buffets with more food than anyone could eat spread throughout the Club. Young techies picked up their drink tickets and worked their way past the food and around the crowds to one of the jampacked bars.

"Are they even old enough to drink?" a co-worker asked me as he passed by.

"Some of them do look young," I agreed.

I watched the crowd, many of whom were thoroughly absorbed by the display cases of Giants memorabilia. This was one of my favorite spots in the ballpark. I especially liked the shelves of bobbleheads, bats and balls. At the far end, the three World Series trophies served as a backdrop for selfies. On this particular evening, I escorted the guests down one level, walked them by the Giants clubhouse and down another flight of stairs to the inside batting cage. There they could go one-on-one with the pitching machine.

Many of the guests delighted in the live music and crowded dance floor. Near the elevators, the heavy, pulsing, guitar-driven sound of the Led Zeppelin cover band pounded, punctuated by the undercurrent of laughter and conversation from around the corner. Everyone was enjoying themselves.

Two of my co-workers were in the midst of a heated discussion. I walked over and heard the tail end of the conversation. "John Bonham... known for his speed and power... always in the groove."

The other man said, "I'll take Ginger Baker any day."

"Are these guys the two outfielders the Giants are interested in?" I asked. They gaped at me as if I had grown horns.

"No," said the second man, "They're drummers. Rock drummers." He pointed down the hall toward the band.

A voice came from behind me, "John Bonham played with Led Zeppelin until the night he drank so much he vomited, choked, and died in his sleep. He was one of the best."

I turned around. There stood the blue-eyed cyclist, Burk Dennison. *What's he doing here?* I took a step back and stuck my hands in the pockets of my khaki work pants.

"Ginger Baker, on the other hand," Burk continued, "was probably the first superstar drummer. We're talking mid-sixties. They're both in the Rock and Roll Hall of Fame."

My co-workers nodded. "The man knows his drummers." They slapped him on the shoulder and walked toward the band.

"Hello," I said. My stomach lurched. "You're everywhere, aren't you? Do you work for this company?"

"No, but I'm a guest of a guy in the C-Suite."

"Come on, be honest. You're stalking me, aren't you?"

Burk looked surprised. And a little amused.

"You have to admit, it's starting to get a little weird. What is this, accidental meeting three or four?"

"Trisha," said my supervisor as he walked by, "I need you to run the elevator until the event is over."

"Sure thing." I turned to walk away. Burk grabbed my elbow and gently pulled me back.

"I have to tell you something. I recognized you at the swim. I ride in that neighborhood a lot. And I've seen you. You know, I happen to believe in serendipity. So, maybe ... just maybe ... we're supposed to spend some time together."

He stepped closer, pulled out his phone, and tapped contacts. Then he typed in, *Trisha, the swimmer,* saying it out loud with each keystroke. When he said my name, the throbbing of the band, the laughing partygoers and the ballpark vibe, evaporated.

Don't do it. Don't. Don't. Don't. Burk exuded perfection, on the outside ... warm, caring, and genuinely interested in me. But life taught me that perfect didn't exist. My cynical side concluded he was most likely dicey on the inside. Unfortunately, I had a weakness for dicey.

"Last name?"

"Not important."

A loud cheer went up from the crowd as the band finished a set. I blinked and took a deep breath, then dictated my number.

"My turn," I said. I took the cell out of my pants pocket and clicked through to find my contacts.

"Trisha," my supervisor said, as he came up beside me. "Need you now. For a few minutes."

His voice startled me, and I dropped my phone. Burk grabbed it before it hit the ground.

"Go. I'll add my number," said Burk as he waved me away.

I hesitated and reached out for the cell.

"Come on, Trisha," said my supervisor.

"Don't worry," said Burk. "I'll be right here. Not going anywhere."

"Now, please," said the supervisor.

I turned and followed him through the crowd. He posted me at the top of the escalator on the other side of the Club.

"One of the employees had to leave suddenly. Someone is being redeployed and should be here in a few minutes," my supervisor said.

"Sure thing," I said, wondering if I would ever see my cell phone again.

Five minutes later, my replacement arrived, and I scooted toward the display cases. Burk held out my phone.

"Here you go," he said. "Now, back to our conversation. I'm thinking we should have dinner."

"Maybe. Working here keeps me busy."

"Trisha," the supervisor called out as he walked back in my direction. "Don't forget the elevator."

"On my way," I called. The chemistry building between Burk and me, fueled by adrenaline and a certain amount of fear, disappeared.

"Good running into you," said Burk to me as he waved at my supervisor. "Long lost friend. Haven't seen her in years." He walked toward the band and the third-base side of the Club level.

My co-worker and sounding board, Charlee Ann, stood next to the elevator and shook her head as I approached.

"Who's that?"

"Nobody. Just a friend."

"Girl, tell that to someone else. Does Jon know about him?"

"There's nothing to know. Just someone I met who keeps showing up unexpectedly."

She cocked her head. "Uh-huh. You're headed for trouble, sister."

"Go back to work," I said with a chuckle.

That night at the ballpark turned out to be a party no one wanted to leave. I didn't blame them. It was a great event. Eventually, they all cleared out and I was free. I took the stairs down to the women's changing room. I fumbled with my jacket as I pulled it from my locker and dropped my work badge when I went to tag out. Then I tripped over the curb as I walked into the parking lot, heading for my battered Honda. Was I just exhausted or was I rattled from my encounter with Burk? Perhaps a combination of both, if I was honest.

It being midweek after 11 pm, traffic had disappeared. Shimmering lights on the Golden Gate Bridge gleamed against the amber towers. The routine summertime fog had moved further west into the Pacific, uncovering the mysteriously beautiful span that linked the city and Marin County. The rush from running into Burk again had melted away. I usually associate that sort of strong physical reaction, that spine-tingle, with my detective work. I hadn't expected it from a man I barely knew. He was eye candy, and I had just experienced a sugar rush. That was all. Wasn't it? I hit the accelerator, launching my car off the bridge and into Marin.

Once I passed through the Robin Williams tunnel, the highway grew dark … only a few cars, no streetlights. Burk running into me had to be deliberate. Had to be. Even with his bullshit explanation about knowing Earl and his reason for being at the ballpark, these meetings couldn't be accidents. Not both of them, anyway. My mind revolved on its hamster wheel again.

Pulling off Highway 101, I decided to take the back route to Earl's house. The road started at the bottom of La Cruz Canyon, not far from the side exit to the reservoir, and wound its way up past evergreens and new-growth redwoods on one side. High decorative gates protected the houses tucked behind them, only a few scattered streetlamps brightening the narrow two-lane road. Out of the darkness, I saw a car rushing up the hill behind me, its lights glaring in my rearview mirror. At the next bend in the road, a small pull-off appeared, so I moved over, letting the small car zoom pass.

I rolled the windows down, then switched off the lights and the engine. A faint ticking came from under the hood then faded away. At first, total darkness, but then shapes appeared. I heard the howl of a coyote from deep inside the canyon, then a deep bellow joined in. Barking, growling and high-pitched yips layered over the howl. I used to believe the symphony came from a pack of some sort, seven or eight animals at least. But Earl had explained that coyotes can make several different sounds at one time. What sounded like many might only be two or three. A defense mechanism to trick bigger, meaner predators into thinking a pack of coyotes lay in wait. Pretty smart when you thought about it.

Most of the homes around me were dark, but I'm sure their occupants heard the increasingly-loud howls. As suddenly as it started, it stopped again. Total and utter silence. I had the bright idea that maybe I could see them. I grabbed the binoculars I kept in the glove compartment and crossed the road to the top of a trailhead between some houses. A few streets below, a solitary streetlight illuminated the entrance gate to the reservoir. It cast long narrow shadows that stretched almost to the coal-black water.

I scanned the trees and caught the glitter of eyes staring back. Then another pair. *Were these the noisemakers?* We stood staring at each other; their legs as rooted as mine. The spell broke when I heard a door open and close and saw a flash of light for a second or two, no more. I turned and saw the bottom level of a house. Curtains blocked out most of the light, but a faint yellow glowed around their edges. Someone must have walked in. Outside, four or five bikes leaned against a wall. The door opened again, another brief flash of light and sound.

"Later," I heard a man say. He quietly closed the door, picked up a bike and headed toward the road on a sidewalk hugging the house. A shorter man with an almost unnoticeable limp walked by him, nodded and slipped into the home. Another two minutes went by, and the cyclist zipped past my car on the side of the road, lights on his helmet and front and back fender. I watched as he stopped under the one streetlight to adjust his pedals and I got a good look at him. It was the same guy who had been riding with Burk in the Canyon. These coincidences were starting to creep me out.

I took a few steps on the grassy trail that led down the hill and into the canyon. The animals I'd been watching had long disappeared into the darkness of the tall trees and shrubs. As I turned around, something hovering near the trees caught my eye. Terrified it was a bat, I almost screamed, but caught myself. Whatever it was, it was mechanical, not biological. It moved, silently, toward the house until it was hovering almost directly opposite the door.

I had seen Earl practice this maneuver many times with his drone, making it hang in the air near the tree line so that it became all but invisible. The drone moved up to the other side of the house that was closest to me, then sailed around a detached garage I hadn't noticed.

The door opened again, and another voice said, "No worries."

A man walked around to the garage and pulled up the door. The drone moved above him, capturing his movements. Banks of computer servers lined the garage. He vanished into the humming garage. While he was there, the lights blinked. A few minutes later, he walked out, pulled down the door, and moved quietly to the house and slipped in. "Fixed," is what I thought he said to those inside.

I watched, fascinated, as the black drone lifted, flew parallel to the trees and then melted into the night.

I walked quietly up the trail to the car and got in. The house over the hill. Could this be the house Tyler had warned me about? Given what I'd seen, it was more than likely. The drone. Burk's biking buddy. The fact that it was this late on a weekday and there were people still awake in Marin. Could it be a computer start-up? I heard that people often worked all night. But here? Deep in a canyon where the Wi-Fi is sketchy, at best? I was about to start my car when a small beat-up Ford passed me and stopped at the front gate of the house. The driver punched in some numbers on the keypad and when the gate opened, drove in. The sliding fence closed silently behind him.

For after midnight, this place was buzzing.

Dad and Earl sat watching television when I walked in, both holding a Coyote Ridge beer bottle.

"Earl, did you happen to be flying your drone about fifteen minutes ago? Over on the other side of the hill?" I asked.

Dad laughed and turned to Earl. "Didn't I say not to spy on our neighbors?"

"Just trying out my new night vision apparatus," said Earl. "How'd you know about that?"

"Long story. Do you or maybe Tyler know who lives there? What they do?"

"No, can't say I do. This house had its lights on, some outside activity. Perfect for testing my equipment."

I didn't believe him, but I wasn't going to confront him in front of

Dad. "Does that awful beer taste any better?"

Dad took a sip and cringed. "Still skunky."

"Then why are you drinking it?"

I bent down and picked up the cap that Dad had knocked on the floor and stuck it in my pocket. It didn't matter how old they were. Men were just big messy boys.

"I'm going to bed. So tired."

My feet dragged as I climbed up the staircase. Inside my room, I collapsed on the bed.

"Ow." I reached around to my back pocket and pulled out Dad's bottle cap. Someone had spent a lot of money on the design for the label as well as the cap. The graphics included an outline of two coyotes from the neck up and the initials CR in black.

Classy. I picked up the remote and turned to a rerun of a sitcom I'd watched a million times before. Usually, watching television calmed me down from the excitement of working a game. I slipped off my work clothes and dropped them on the floor next to my bed. As I sank into the silly story, I turned the cap over and over in my hand. I was thinking about the lecture Earl gave me about beer and beer bottles.

"Only use brown bottles. If they're clear or green without coating on them, the UV rays go right through the bottle and into the beer, changing the taste. No one would want to drink it, that's for sure."

He hadn't mentioned caps. I stroked the little tin cover in my hand. Tyler and his friends had obviously put a lot of thought into this little thing, but they'd forgotten to manage the taste of the beer. To me, they had the whole thing backward. First, create a good product. Then worry about the marketing. I turned the cap over. The underside had a thin layer of plastic tightly fitted against the top. I couldn't remember the inside of caps looking like that, but then, I'd never spent much time looking. When beer drinking consumed my life, all I cared about was getting the cap off.

I kept rubbing my finger on the inside of the cap while I watched TV and listened to the canned laughter. My eyes grew heavy and began to close. I snuggled deeper into my pillow.

Beer was flat. Cap was flat. Beer was flat. Cap was flat. My sleep mantra stopped suddenly. The beer cap wasn't flat. I saw a slight indentation under the plastic film. When I closed my eyes, I touched an inconspicuous bulge. Maybe just a bubble of air. I tried pressing down on the pocket of air, but it didn't give. I picked at the film of plastic, but the edges held tight against the cap.

What a crazy waste of my time. I tossed the beer cap on my nightstand and turned off the light. But I couldn't sleep. I kept wondering about Tyler and what sort of trouble he was in. I didn't have any idea. My mind spun faster and faster. And going nowhere. I sat up, shaking my head; I would never fall asleep tonight. Trying to think about something else … anything else … I grabbed the bottle cap and tossed it up in the air and caught it with the other hand. I did that a few times successfully and then tried to do it with my eyes closed. The bottle cap missed my outstretched hand and landed with a kerplunk in a glass of water on the night table.

Oh well. Not ready for prime time. I wiggled my fingers into the glass and pulled out the cap. The bubble of air had a more solid squareness to it. What could be concealed under there? Finding a pair of tweezers, I pulled at the edges until one side came loose. I yanked it and ripped off the plastic. That something flew onto the floor.

It was a ridiculously small microchip. I laid it on the smooth light-colored bedspread and took a picture. Then I turned it over and took another photo. It had to fit into something. But what? A computer? A reader of some sort?

I texted the photos to Lena.

R U up? What's this?

T is up. So I'm up. A microchip. Smaller than most.

Why would someone put a microchip under a beer cap?

Dunno. U R the detective.

What does this do?

Dunno. Bring it by tomorrow. I know someone who can help.

I wrapped the minuscule chip in a tissue and put it carefully into an empty paper clip box. I did the same with the cap and the plastic film.

"Trisha," called out Earl from downstairs. "Did you pick up a beer cap? The one from the Coyote Ridge bottle?"

"Yeah. I'll toss it down to you."

I reached for the bottle cap, walked out on the landing and said, "Catch."

"Trish," said Earl, sounding puzzled. "Are you sure this is it?"

"It's the only beer cap I picked up."

Instead of moving back into my room, I stayed on the landing to listen to the conversation between Earl and my father. All I heard was "beer … top … missing." For a few minutes, I heard the rustling of plastic bags and Dad then said, "I'm not digging around any more garbage for a ridiculous beer cap." I couldn't catch the muffled response.

"Have you lost your mind?" Dad replied. Then he walked down the hall to his bedroom.

Earl stayed there for at least thirty minutes shuffling through the mess, examining and shaking each piece of refuse. Was he hunting for the chip? I arguably should return it to him, but not yet. I wanted to know what it did.

CHAPTER 14

The next day, I picked up Lena and Little T early since the Giants were back in town and I was scheduled to work the night game.

Once she fastened the car seat and the baby securely, she climbed in next to me. I handed her the paper clip box with the tiny microchip. Lena didn't know I found it under the beer cap.

"It's a chip."

"I never would have guessed," I said, rolling my eyes. "I think it belongs to Earl."

"So, give it back to him."

"If I do that now, he'll know I found it and took it. And I'd like to know what's on it."

"That's the real reason. You're so nosey. Why do you even care?"

"I'm not sure. I'll give it back … sooner or later."

"Right," said Lena, giving me the side-eye. She rubbed the tiny object between her fingers. "I've never seen one so small. I don't know what it's used for, but Crypto will."

"Crypto? His name is Crypto?"

"Crypto*king*. That's his hacking name. I don't know his real name. Just to warn you. He's extremely suspicious of anyone not in his inner circle."

"Why is that?"

"Nature of the beast, I think. Hackers are wary of the outside world. Somewhat paranoid. It takes a while to gain their trust."

"But he trusts you?"

"Yep. We met in a private chat room for hackers. He's helped me out in the past, and you're the only person I have ever asked him to meet. That's why we're doing it in person. So he can check you out."

"Got it," I said.

She turned to check on Timmy and said, "Let's go. Larkspur Street. Across town in the Canal."

I backed out of her driveway and then the questions started.

"Have you heard from Jon?"

I didn't answer.

"Why am I not surprised."

I stared straight ahead as we made our way by the public library, one of San Rafael's vintage public buildings. We passed City Hall and a large parking lot that housed several police cars and the CSI trailer.

Lena opened her mouth to say something else, then hesitated. She changed topics. "Where'd you find this chip again?"

"Under a bottle cap. I think it was put there on purpose. And there's something strange going on with Earl. He was flying a drone around a neighbor's house last night, after midnight. He made it sound like no big deal, but that house had people coming and going and they have a garage packed with servers. Something is off about the whole thing."

"Wait. Let me get this straight. According to you—"

"And Tyler."

"And Tyler, that house is weird at best, bad news at worst."

"So it would seem."

We drove down East Francisco Boulevard and turned left.

"Park here. His office is just through that doorway." She pointed to a small entrance most people would never see.

"Are you sure?"

"Yep. There's a parking place. Take it. Now."

I did a quick U-turn and pulled into the spot.

She climbed out and wriggled Timmy, now asleep, into a front pack. I followed her to a small narrow doorway with the number 470 written above it in faded black paint. Peeling gray paint covered the door. Lena pressed the button next to the speakerphone. I heard a click.

"Yeah?" came a male voice with a faint southern accent. He turned the one-syllable word into two distinct sounds.

"It's Lena."

"I know," he said.

The door unlocked from the inside and popped open. I expected to see a narrow hallway, but instead, there was a wide anteroom with a fat-tire bike leaning against the wall. Faded concert posters of notable punk rock groups, including The Ramones, The Clash, and the Dead Kennedys graced the dirty green walls. Down the hall, an extra-large closet opened off to the side, two servers resting on floor-to-ceiling racks. One had blinking green lights; the other solid yellow. Both were connected with miles of blue, yellow, and white cables. A massive air-conditioning unit pumped out cool air into the small narrow room.

Lena led me into the main office. A tattered leather couch with a rip on one of the arms and a wide flat-screen TV on the wall told me all I needed to know about this guy's decorating style, or rather, lack of it. Discarded monitors, keyboards, laptops, even printers, took over most of the floor space. In the middle of the equipment trash heap sat a large desk drowning under piles of paper and candy wrappers. CryptoKing sat with his back toward us, staring at the three monitors in front of him. Whoever this guy was, he wasn't a neat freak. "How did you know it was me?" Lena said.

"Cameras." He spoke hesitantly and quietly, drawing out each word. He pointed to a small monitor that displayed the video feed captured by the security camera perched above the door frame. He turned around.

"Little Tim is growing," he commented to Lena. They chit-chatted while I stood there awkwardly.

Crypto wasn't exactly what I expected for a computer guru. He had heavily-hooded, bloodshot eyes, long dark hair that covered his ears, and a sense of sadness about him. He looked like a human basset hound.

"I'm Trisha," I said, sticking out my hand. He glanced at me. Then at my hand. Then back at the monitors. I was obviously in the "not-to-be-trusted" category Lena had mentioned.

"I know."

"You do?"

"Your sister told me the two of you would be stopping by."

A long pause followed every word and made me wonder if he'd forgotten what he planned to say. Compared to Crypto, I babbled at a rapid-fire pace; Lena buzzed at warp speed.

"Why did you come over?" he asked.

I pulled out the paper clip box and unwrapped the tissue. He picked up the little chip and turned it over in his hands. Then he moved over to his messy desk, pushed some papers aside and turned on a jeweler's magnifying lamp. The bright piercing light illuminated the small microchip. He held it with a set of tweezers and turned it over.

"You found this where?" The southern accent was becoming thicker.

"On the bottom of a beer bottle cap. Under a thin sheet of white, very sticky plastic. I didn't see it. I felt it. What is it?"

"It's a memory card. I've heard about these micro-minis. Never saw one, though."

"Like the memory card in my phone and camera?" I asked.

"Yes," said Lena, as if she was addressing a preschooler. "Similar to the one in your phone or camera. Only much smaller and thinner."

"I want to know what's on it. Can you do that?"

"It'll take a bit. I'll have to transfer the data—if I can get to it, that is."

He dug around the pile of electronic gear on his floor, shook his head, then walked at a glacial pace over to a shelf and retrieved something the size of a small cell phone. He turned it over in his hands, running his fingers over the openings.

"This might work. Can't say until I try."

I don't think Crypto knew what the word 'hustle' meant. He'd take a few steps, stop, poke at the thing in his hand and then start to walk again. If he didn't pick up the pace, I'd be late for work. He made it back to his souped-up computer and sat down. He pulled a headlamp on to his forehead, switched on the light and attached the new piece of equipment to the PC. With extreme care, he pushed the little card into the smallest slot, then typed in some code. The screen read "Access Blocked." He typed in more code. The same message popped up.

"Well, I'll be," he said, pushing his chair back from the desk. He closed his eyes for what seemed like three minutes. I mouthed to Lena, "Is he on drugs?" She ignored me.

"Someone is being very careful with whatever is on this memory card. Let me try another way." He typed again and "Access Blocked" appeared again. But instead of deleting it, he kept typing. With the hit of the last keystroke, a video popped up on all three of his computer monitors.

"Got it," he said and pushed his chair back again, resting his hands on his stomach.

"This was taken during the day," I concluded, peering over his shoulder.

"No, it wasn't. See ... There's a timestamp. 11:28 p.m. Someone was using a thermal imaging scope. It picks up the smallest of differences in heat. Hunters use things like this if they're doing their thing at night. Huntin' for hogs, maybe."

"That's La Cruz Canyon. I don't think there are any hogs living there. Coyotes for sure, but no hogs. This must be from—"

"A quadcopter," said Crypto. "Given the angle."

"Just what I was going to say."

I watched a black and white video with touches of faded color. The copter followed the edge of the canyon, then swept toward the homes nestled into the hill. It hovered near one house and captured people, mostly men, coming and going. It zoomed in on two, in particular. I saw profiles, but even as advanced as the camera was, I couldn't identify any features. At one point, the door opened and someone walked out, went to the garage. The drone had followed. Inside were banks of servers. That left no doubt. This was the same house I'd seen the night before.

The house over the hill.

"I know where that is," I said pointing at the screen. "I saw that place last night and I saw the drone watching it. It had to be close to midnight."

When the man shut the garage door and went back inside the house, the quadcopter must have flitted around to the road in front. It captured someone cycling up the driveway, moving through the gate and disappearing into the darkness. Then the video ended.

"This has to be footage from Earl's drone. He even admitted he was filming last night," I said. "But why hide this chip under a beer cap?"

"No, not last night. A few nights ago. See?" Crypto pointed to the time and date stamp again. "Maybe this Earl guy is keeping watch on someone or somethin'," said Crypto.

"Any guess as to what they're doing in that house?" asked Lena.

"With all that weight in the garage, it might be a startup," Crypto figured.

"If this was shot from Earl's drone, why his interest in this house?" asked Lena.

"Is this Earl into computers?" asked Crypto.

"Yeah," I responded.

"Once a computer guy, always a computer guy. Maybe he's watching for developments in the field," Crypto said.

"Then he should go and knock on their door and ask. This drone crap is stupid," said Lena.

"I agree. This goes way beyond natural curiosity," I chimed in.

"This Earl you're talking about? It's not Earl Cunningham, is it?" asked Crypto.

I nodded. "He's my landlord."

"He's a legend in the industry. He was there when everything started," said Crypto, staring at me in awe. He gave me a silly grin and started to nod his head.

What a fanboy. But if it got me into the "trust-by-association" category, I was all for it.

CHAPTER 15

The baseball game dragged on, each inning taking longer than the one before. Luckily, Jan, the sports guru from KSPT, broke the monotony when she tracked me down in the Garden. She gave me an odd look and motioned for me to follow her.

"Gonna take my break now," I announced to my co-workers. I followed her out and we headed for the small studio down a hall crowded with fans in line for beer and food. A few stopped and waved.

"Hey, Jan, have time for an autograph?"

"Sorry, no. Gotta be on air in thirty. Next time, ok?"

She pulled me into a small room adjacent to the studio. Stacked against the wall were cardboard cartons filled with bottled water. The cardboard gave off a musty smell.

"What's this all about?" I asked.

"I have to be quick. I'm on soon. More strangeness at the studio. Tyler came by the station. Said the head honchos gave him leave because of family illness. His grandfather, I think."

"Earl's not sick."

"Well, that's what he told them, and they bought it. Anyway, that's not the important part. The older man who wanted to find his grandfather was back. Almost distraught. Security called the police and they hustled him out of the station," said Jan.

"Did he say what he wanted?"

"Same as before. He was hard to understand. I'm not sure if he'd reached Earl and Earl wouldn't talk to him, or if he was still trying to reach him. He was rambling about surveillance, but he made no sense. Anyway, he created a major scene. Sorry, but I gotta go. I'm doing production on the rest of the game. But you stay here."

"What? Why?"

She didn't answer, but quickly walked out, leaving me standing there. Five long minutes crept by before the door opened again. It was Tyler.

"What the hell is going on?" I yelled.

"I'm not sure I should tell you, but you're all I have," hesitated Tyler.

"I'm standing in a fucking closet. You better tell me."

He had purple circles under his eyes, and someone had pulled the plug on his electric hair, now matted and greasy. The hoodie, still pulled tight over his head, smelled like he'd slept in it. Repeatedly.

"When was the last time you took a shower?" I asked.

Tyler groaned and pulled a small energy drink from his pocket.

"I didn't want anyone to get in trouble, certainly not Grandpa Pearl."

"What are you talking about?"

"You know that guy who keeps stopping by the radio station? He asked my grandfather to do a little spy work for him. It was supposed to be fun."

"That's an oxymoron if I ever heard one."

"No, really. It wasn't supposed to get serious like this."

"Who's he spying on? And why?"

Tyler avoided the question.

"It's gotten out of hand. And now I've complicated the entire situation, and I'm worried it could get Grandpa hurt."

"Does he know that?"

"Not exactly."

"It's a simple question, Ty. Does Earl know what you've gotten him into?"

"No. Well, yes."

"Am I right in thinking our neighbors on the other side of the hill, Earl's drone, your awful Coyote Ridge beer and that mini-chip are involved?"

Tyler looked surprised. "How did you know about the chip?"

"I found one. But go on. This little spy game of yours became dangerous ... because?" I asked.

"So, his quadcopter did some snooping from the air, all nice and anonymous. Nobody had to meet anybody. I know I could have just arranged to have the chip picked up and delivered, but Grandpa thought that wasn't very creative. He wanted a challenge. We thought it would be clever to hide it so it could be transferred back and forth, no one the wiser."

"Back and forth to who?"

Tyler shrugged his shoulders, but kept his mouth closed.

"Seriously? Fine. So you settled on bottle caps."

"We did experiments with different places on the bottle. We tried putting the card under the label, but it just got wet. Killed all the code on the chip. You know how Earl likes solving problems. He was determined to figure out a way to transport the chip and keep it dry. So he came up with the bottle cap idea. Smart, huh?"

I moved over to a stack of cardboard cartons and sat down. I had a feeling this would take a while. Tyler continued standing in front of me, shifting his weight from one foot to another.

"You know Earl has aged a gazillion years from worry, don't you? Worrying about you. Can't you even tell him that you're safe?"

"I know, and I'm sorry. But I don't want him to know where I am. That way—"

"He can't tell anyone if he's asked," I said.

"Right."

"Why all the subterfuge?"

"It's the people who want the chip."

"Okay."

"I've decided not to give it to them."

"You what?"

"They lied to us. The surveillance wasn't what it was supposed to be."

"Earl has been watching a house in the neighborhood at night with his drone and recording it. Right?" I asked.

Tyler nodded.

"But what he thought he was watching turned out to be something else?"

Tyler nodded again. "What's going on in that house isn't what we were... uh... led to believe. It's much bigger, and more dangerous. Let's say a business, we'll call it Shadowcorp, wants to know what their competitors are doing. There are ways to find out."

"And you and Earl and the fellow visiting the station were part of the ways?"

"We thought we were just doing a little surveillance. See who was coming and going. Peek in the windows. Report back to the company. All done from the comfort of Earl's house."

"So, these people at the house are 'Shadowcorp's' competition?"

"That's what we thought. At first. But not too long ago, Jason Chang

—"

"The beer guy."

Tyler gave me a weird look, then shook his head. "Yes. The beer guy. He's also an employee of Shadowcorp."

"Let me guess. He's the one you're sending the chip to. And he sends it to Shadowcorp's headquarters," I said.

Tyler hesitantly nodded. "He let it slip that we weren't spying on a competing company, but a number of high-level employees from their own company."

"They're spying on their own employees?"

"They thought the Marin group had gone rogue. And they were right."

I started to ask him a question, but he stopped me.

"Look. We think we've figured out what's going on, but we need confirmation. Earl and I can't get in there, so I'm wondering ... hoping ... that you could come up with a way to get inside."

"You gotta be kidding, Tyler. What happened to 'stay out of it, Trisha'? Besides, I don't break into houses ... anymore."

"I'm not asking you to do anything illegal, but if you happen to find yourself in the house ..."

I stood up. "You made it very clear that I wasn't to go near that house. You just said that it could be dangerous. Now you're asking me to figure out how to get inside? To put myself at risk? What's in this house that's so important?"

"Numbers."

"That's a little vague. What kind of numbers?"

"Probably a list of about twelve numbers and symbols. My guess is that they're hidden downstairs somewhere, but likely not in the main room. Do you know what ransomware is?"

"Someone shuts down a computer with it and wants money or something from the owner to open it back up. Kind of like blackmail."

"Close enough. I think that's what we're dealing with. Trisha ... I don't know who else to ask. We—Grandpa and I—we need to find those papers. I'll be in touch. Oh, and don't tell Grandpa that you saw me or talk this over with your dad, please. He's not good at keeping quiet."

With that, he opened the door of the small room and disappeared into the crowd.

It took forever before security shooed the last enthusiastic fan out of the ballpark and I couldn't wait to leave for home. I kept replaying my conversation with Tyler. He and his grandfather were working for people who thought nothing of spying on their employees. Why? What were they doing? What did Tyler mean by 'gone rogue'? This was obviously more complicated than I'd first thought. But one thing was for sure. Tyler wasn't missing. Never had been.

I took the back way home again, winding up the dark two-lane curving road. I switched on my bright lights and the edges of the narrow roadway fell into the quiet shadows. This time, no one tailed me up the hill. I slowed down and glided into the pull-off where I'd stopped the first time. I turned off the car and listened. The soothing hoot of an owl filled the night air from somewhere deep in the canyon. I kept my steps light as I walked across the road and down the hard, rocky path. The trail crept up a slight incline and I had a perfect view of the back of the deserted house.

No lights glimmered behind the blackout curtains. But even from where I stood, I heard the steady hum from the closed garage. I walked a little further and noticed the bikes were gone. The owl hooted again, much closer this time. I turned on my phone's flashlight and the glare caught the eyes of two deer standing behind a grove of redwoods about twenty feet away. They scuttled deeper into the darkness as I inched closer to the house.

Nothing to see. Not even Earl's quadcopter. I turned to head back to the path when I heard the rumble of a car coming up the hill. I shifted behind a tree and waited quietly. The car pulled up to the gate. After a few seconds, the motors whirred and the entryway slid open. The car pulled into the long driveway and the gates closed behind it.

A car door opened, then slammed shut and footsteps moved toward a side entrance. I shifted a few feet back into the canyon, off to the side where I could get a better view of the front of the house over the low fence.

A man stood at the door, scanning the dark. He must have heard me move through the underbrush. After a tense moment, he pulled out a key, unlatched the door, reached in and turned on an outside light. He turned and glanced around again. This time, I dropped to my knees, hiding behind the thick bushes and shrubs. He took a step in my direction, then paused. I stopped breathing. I thought my heart would hop out of my chest as I waited for him to spot me.

Eventually, he shrugged and walked back to the house and went inside. The light switched off and I heard the door lock. The edges of the curtains glowed with the faint light from inside. But even that disappeared, leading me to believe he'd moved into the front part of the house as another dim light came on inside. No noise escaped from the dwelling; the crowd that had been there the night before had gone.

I walked as silently as I could back up the path, then across the road to my car. I didn't turn on my headlights until I was already several feet down the winding, pitch-black road. When I could no longer see the house or its driveway in my rearview mirror, I stopped the car and took a deep breath. I had recognized the man who had scanned the woods so diligently. It was Burk, the tall, hunky athlete with the blue eyes and the smile, who made a habit of running into me.

CHAPTER 16

I didn't sleep well. Seeing Burk had unnerved me, and my meeting with Tyler kept me tossing and turning all night. I woke up feeling hungover. I grabbed a robe and wandered onto the deck absentmindedly staring at the midsection of the redwoods and evergreens in the canyon across the road. The sky was a light blue and the sun bored into the side of Mt. Tam, casting razor-sharp shadows from the tall trees.

I needed to wrap my head around everything that I had learned, and to do that, I had to talk it out with someone. I wondered if Jon could spare a few minutes for coffee. That way I could apologize in person for canceling the family dinner.

There was a knock on my bedroom door.

"Trishy, you up?"

"Yeah, Dad. Come on in."

"What are you wearing?" I said, trying not to smile.

"Well, this belongs to Earl. Said I could try it and if I liked it, I could have it. He has another one."

Dad had stuffed himself into a wetsuit, the kind that surfers wear. Black, slick neoprene. Long sleeves, long legs. Black booties covered his feet and he wore heavy gloves.

"Did you swallow a beach ball?" I asked.

"That's not nice, Trish," answered Dad, patting his round stomach as he admired himself in my full-length mirror. "I'm going to lose weight, firm up like you did."

"Don't tell me you're going to learn to surf?"

"Yep. Might be the on-your-stomach kind or the stand-up kind … not sure yet. I can do the stand-up paddle off China Camp. Maybe we could do it together? Get your sister involved. Make it a family thing."

My phone pinged. Jon. "I have to answer this, Dad."
"Of course."
He shuffled out of my room, glancing at himself again in the mirror. "Looking good, if I do say so myself."
"Yes, stunning," I called after him.

Jon agreed to meet me early in the afternoon at a small coffee shop not far from where he worked. Frankly, this surprised me, since it was obvious that I'd been avoiding him.

Jonathan Angel had put up with my persistent sleuthing for almost two years. We met when I worked at Fort Mason, a converted Army pier that jutted into San Francisco Bay. A security guard for the National Park Service, he glided along the dull white corridors, nodding and sometimes saluting as he passed my office. Things had changed when, one foggy morning, he'd stopped in and brought me a mocha.

Brown hair combed straight back, clear-eyed and a smile ready to explode at a moment's notice. He was bigger, broader than most men I knew. The wooden chairs would creak when he sat in my office at Fort Mason. He didn't mind my constant, one-sided 'What do you think about this theory?' conversations. In spite of all my misgivings, we became closer than friends. Lovers. But now, according to Lena, as he itched for more commitment from me, I was pulling away. That's not how I saw it, but my sister has been known to be right, on occasion.

The café sat on the grounds of Crissy Fields, a completely renovated airstrip with marshes, running paths, and picturesque retired Army buildings. It offered a unique view of San Francisco Bay and the Golden Gate Bridge, where the summertime fog smothered the tops of the North and South Tower. I walked in and took a table by the window.

A fireplace kept the shop cozy and warm. I ordered a hot chocolate in tune with the overall vibe. I didn't see Jon walk in, but I recognized his voice as he ordered coffee. I watched him nervously as he thanked the barista and came over to sit across from me.

"I thought you fell into La Cruz Canyon or lost your phone. Or your voice," he said. His easy smile was missing.

"I know I owe you an apology. I'm sorry. I can't visit your family right now. I just can't."

"You've said that already."

"Please don't be mad. I just need a little more time."

Jon reached out to take my hand. I'd missed his warm and

comforting touch.

"I get it. You're scared."

"I don't want to talk about it. I can't."

"Trisha. This is the time to talk about it. I'm here. Now."

I managed to ignore the earnestness in his voice.

"There is something I do want to talk about."

"What?"

"The missing-not missing Tyler."

Jon dropped my hand and his disappeared beneath the table.

"You're saying this conversation has nothing to do with you and me?"

"Not totally."

The silence lengthened as the waiter brought over his coffee and my hot chocolate.

"I should have figured."

"You're good at working these things out. There is so much I don't understand. I ran into Tyler at—"

"You know what, Trisha? I'm not interested. I'm tired of being a sounding board, something to bounce your wild ideas off."

"You're more than that. Much more."

"Not to you. When you want to talk about something that matters, like us, let me know."

He stood up and walked toward the front door of the cafe, leaving behind an untouched cup of coffee. *He didn't just walk out, did he? Wasn't he going to help me?* He always helped me. I squeezed my eyes shut for a second and then slowly opened them. Through the window, I watched his white truck as it drove away toward Marina Boulevard.

I pulled out my phone and punched in a number. Lena picked up.

"Lee?"

"Not a good time, Trisha. Timmy's burning up, his face is bright red ... leaving now for the doctor's. Talk later." She hung up. The comfortable warmth in the café intensified almost immediately. I started to sweat. I didn't know what to do. I picked up the cup of hot chocolate and took a sip. It tasted like chalk and I almost gagged. The room, now oppressively hot, began to spin. I was suffocating, about to faint. I sat the cup down harder than expected, the muddy liquid spilling onto the table and floor. A waiter rushed over to clean it up.

"Very sorry. Clumsy." I could barely get the words out.

"Are you all right?"

He handed me a napkin and I wiped down my forehead, my face, my neck. "I have to go."

Outside, the dull fog was grayer, denser than it had been fifteen minutes earlier. The air damper, the wind colder. My hand shook as I tried to unlock the car. I gritted my teeth in frustration when I dropped the keys. After what seemed like forever, I climbed inside, tears rolling down my cheeks. I couldn't breathe. It had been a while since I'd had a panic attack, but I recognized this one as an old friend.

Make that enemy.

I picked up my phone, hoping for a text from Jon. I focused on its tiny screen for what felt like forever, willing it to ring or buzz or flash. Then I waited some more, staring at the massive base of the Golden Gate's South Tower. The fog sank lower and would soon smother the restless tide below. I could relate.

It's strange what you think of at times like these. I heard my father's voice telling a story I had heard many times. "You know, in 1987, May, I think it was, the bridge had its fiftieth birthday. It was closed to cars. Only foot traffic was allowed, and your mother and I took a walk down the middle of the bridge, along with one million other people. Caused the bridge to flatten out. There are photos, you know."

The seagulls soared on the air currents flowing down Chrissie Field and landed on the damp grass. I'd let myself have a moment. Now, it was over, and I had things to do.

When I turned onto our hilly street, Dad was standing next to a driveway about three houses down from Earl's. He was chatting with a guy in a sporty, gray BMW. Dad threw back his head and laughed. I was glad he was back in my life … so far. Right now, however, I didn't want to talk to him or anyone else.

Dad waved as I drove toward him. Then the man in the sports car stepped out, causing me to stop just shy of the driveway. It was Burk. Of course it was. Who else would it be? The hair stood up on the back of my neck.

Burk smiled when he saw me. "Hey, neighbor," he said.

"I have to park," I called out.

Willing myself to stay cool, I pulled around his car, drove up the stone driveway, parked and got out.

"Dad, can I get your help for a minute?" The smile on his face disappeared when he reached me.

"Something wrong, cupcake?"

"What's he doing here?" I hissed.

"He stopped and introduced himself when he saw me outside. Said he knew Earl and you. We were discussing cars. I like that little thing he's driving, don't you? Did you know that he had the same kind of truck I did about ten years ago? What a—"

"Coincidence?"

"Exactly."

"He's the master of that. Dad, there is something strange about him. Make him go away. Now."

I headed up the front steps.

"He's a neighbor. Just being friendly, that's all. Good to know your neighbors," Dad called after me.

"Then enjoy your neighborly conversation. I'm going inside."

And I did.

I watched through the open door as Dad said a few more things to Burk before he waved and drove away. Then, I stomped my way on to the deck off the living room. Dad joined me.

"Why were you getting so gosh darn mad about that man? I thought you were going to chew up nails and spit out a barbed wire fence."

"Jon broke up with me," I confessed.

"Oh, Trishie, I'm sorry. Do you want to talk about it?"

I didn't say anything. I couldn't even look at him.

"Why? Was it because you wouldn't go to dinner with his family?"

"I don't know. Maybe."

"Small potatoes, Trish. People don't break up over that. Something else happened, didn't it?"

"I was a terrible girlfriend."

"Now, Trish."

"I was. He deserved better."

"I'm sorry about Jon," Dad said.

The grimness of failure and shame flooded through me. I knew that feeling—intimately—and didn't like it one bit. I put up both hands in defense, backed away and ran up the steps to my bedroom, slamming the door behind me. I know that Jon had been there for me, time after time. But now, I really needed him. Why didn't he understand?

Someday, I'll have more than a bedroom to stomp in, I thought to myself as I thumped around the space. It didn't help. I was still miserable. I walked out to my deck and peered down at the canyon, turning from the deepest of greens to dusky ebony in the afternoon shadows. I wanted to dive into that darkness and hide from my dismal life.

I was sound asleep, glued to the mattress, when my cell phone rang. I reached an arm out to the bedside table without picking up my head or opening my eyes, groping for the persistent chime.

"'lo." I managed to say, my eyes shut.

"Hey, Trisha, did I wake you?"

"It's the middle of the night, so, yeah. Who is this?"

"It's me, Terrel. And it's 6:00 am. Why are you sleeping?"

I opened one eye and saw the pale early morning sun stretched across my bedroom.

"Oh, I don't know. Since the Giants are out of town, I thought I'd take the opportunity to sleep past dawn. Why are you calling so early, anyway? Is Little T okay? Did his fever get worse?"

By now, I had hoisted myself to a sitting position and pushed the hair out of my eyes.

"He's fine. His fever is gone, but Lena—"

"Dr. T, what happened?" I asked, imagining the worst.

"Nothing serious. My sweetie is just feeling a little under the weather. I wondered if you could come over and spend some time with her. Maybe keep an eye on Little T so she can rest?"

"Is Lena sick? Did she get what Timmy had?"

"No, I don't think so. She's been up for the last two nights with Tim. She needs some sleep, that's all. You'll come over?"

"Of course. Give me an hour."

"Great. I have to be at the hospital for rounds." There was a considerable pause, and then "There's one more thing."

"What's that?"

"I hate myself for saying this. Can't even believe I'm thinking it." Another long pause. "You know that missing guy—"

"Yeah?"

"Well, you know I haven't been too keen on Lena's involvement in your quasi-detective work in the past."

"Yeah, so you've said before. And it's more than quasi, and you know it. I've solved two murders."

"Right. You're right. Um … well, Lena needs a diversion. Timmy is taking up so much of her time and she's tired. I'm concerned she will get sick if she doesn't take care of herself. She even put some of her design clients on hold for a few months. Between you and me, I think her mind is turning to mush. She needs something to think about, other than—well, you know."

I smiled.

"And I'm said 'diversion,' is that it?"

"You're my best option, believe it or not."

Where have I heard that before? Had he been talking to Tyler?

"Just make sure it's not dangerous."

"Does this mean you think I've done some actual good with my quasi-detective work?"

"I hate to admit it, but yeah. I have to go, or I'll be late."

"So, you think I'm pretty good at what I do?"

"Need to go."

"Close to great?"

"Girl, you can be obnoxious sometimes." Dr. T hung up.

"Bye-bye, T."

"Dad? Earl?" I yelled from the second floor. No one answered, but The Babe came over to the bottom of the steps and wagged his fat little stump of a tail.

"Where'd everyone go?" The Babe continued wagging.

"Why don't you come with me? You can distract Timmy for a while."

The dog tilted his head.

"Walk? Want to go for a walk?"

I'd said the magic word. He ran to the door, ran back to the steps and then ran into the living room to get his stuffed raccoon. Then he darted around in circles with his toy in his mouth. "You taking that with you? Fine with me."

I pulled his leash down from the hook on the wall by the front door. A basket of mail rested on a side table. My newest credit card had arrived. I wondered how long this one would stay completely mine. I stuck it in my backpack.

"Let's go," I said to the pleased dog. He trotted by my side as I walked to the car. I hadn't done a very good job parking when I came in yesterday. My car was at an extreme angle and taking up two spaces. I'd have to apologize to Dad and Earl.

I was at the bottom of the driveway, ready to turn into the road, when Burk rode up on his bike and stopped in front of the car. I froze.

"This is a coincidence," he said.

I nodded. "Yet another. I have to go."

"We're going out for dinner soon, right?"

I smiled and drove off, leaving him standing there, watching me. Before I could hit the gas, it dawned on me. He was the key to that house. I threw the car in reverse and backed up until the car reached him.

"Sorry, didn't mean to be rude. My sister isn't feeling well. Going over to help out."

"With the kid?"

His response jarred me. "How do you know she has a child?"

"I met all three of you at the swim, remember? So, is dinner a plan, then?"

"Yeah, it's a plan. Give me a call." I smiled a smile I didn't feel. I wondered if the corners of my mouth even turned up. Then I gave a lackluster wave and drove off.

CHAPTER 17

"I'm telling you … the guy wants something," I declared to Lena as we sat at her kitchen table. The Babe was lying on the floor in the living room, keeping an eye on Timmy, who sat in his play center. The Babe took his babysitting duties very seriously. The gentle dog would put his face right in front of the baby's and start licking him. Timmy would giggle. The more Timmy laughed, the more the dog licked. They both were in heaven.

"What guy are you talking about?" asked Lena. Dr. T had been right. Lena was losing it. What a mess! Her corkscrew curls were pulled straight back into a very unbecoming mini ponytail. She wore one of Terrel's faded blue scrub tops, milk stains and I'm not sure what else ground into the cotton. She had on a pair of cut-off jean shorts that had seen better days and had completed the ensemble with flip-flops held together with duct tape.

"You know, cut-offs went out of style when you were in high school."

Lena ignored me. "What guy?"

I toyed with lying, but I decided on the truth.

"The swimmer who helped me a few weeks ago. Burk. Do you remember him? He's been turning up everywhere. He doesn't live far from Earl."

Lena smirked at me. "Are you crushing on him or something?"

"I wouldn't call it that."

"Lusting after him?"

"Well, I was. But now I'm creeped out."

"Are you over Jon?"

"No. But he's over me. He broke up with me in a coffee shop at

Crissy Field."

"He broke up with you?" She stared at me a second, contemplating. "You know this is your fault. You just can't commit."

My eyes filled with silent tears. "I haven't cried in years. Now someone mentions Jon's name and I fall apart."

I grabbed a napkin from the kitchen table and held it over my face for a few seconds. The look on my sister's face told me she wasn't all that sympathetic.

"It's not that easy, Lena. Everyone in the world has told me how wonderful he is. 'He treats you like a goddess, Trisha. You found a keeper, Trisha.' Blah, blah, blah."

Timmy fussed from the other room. Lena stood up and peeked around the corner. Then she said,

"We … all of us … want to see you happy. Maybe we went a little overboard about Jon. Not that he doesn't deserve it, but I could see how you'd feel pressured. You like this other guy?"

"A few days ago, he was all I could think about. But it's getting strange. The more I see of him, the more freaked out I am."

I tossed the napkin into the trash and followed Lena into the living room where she picked up Little T, sat down on the couch and started nursing him.

"Meaning?"

"It's like he knows where I'm going to be and then shows up."

"He's stalking you?" Lena asked, her voice doubtful.

"Could be. It's not so crazy." At Lena's incredulous expression, I continued. "You know that house? The one on the video?"

Lena nodded.

"He went there last night. Late."

"And how do you know that? Sounds like you're stalking him. Maybe he lives there. Maybe that's why you keep running into him. You use that road going and coming from work. You walk—"

"Run," I corrected.

"Run? Seriously. You?"

"Yes, me. I have started to run. Well, jog."

"Okay. You jog down by the reservoir with The Babe. It doesn't sound that odd that you'd run into him."

"He knew about you and little Tim."

"Of course, he did. He met all three of us at the swim, remember? Maybe not. You were in the middle of a full-fledged meltdown."

"Ok, fine. Anyway, my hookup expectations kinda disappeared. It just creeps me out, turning up everywhere I go. But, if I play along with him, he might invite me into that house."

Lena stared at me like I'd grown another head. "If he's such a weirdo, why would you want to go anywhere with him, much less his house?"

I told her about my most recent conversation with Tyler.

"He and Earl were doing some surveillance on that house. 'Playing at being spies,' is the way he put it. He wants me to get in there and see if I can find some numbers. I said no."

"What kind of numbers?"

"I don't know. Something to do with ransomware."

"Wait a minute. Tyler is involved with a ransomware scheme?"

"Something like that."

"This could be serious, Trisha. Way beyond your scope. You'll need a crash course on what ransomware can do, at the very least. It does more than capture someone's credit card. Do a search; 'ransomware, Atlanta, Georgia,' or maybe 'ransomware Baltimore, Md.' Ransomware shut these cities down. With a few keystrokes, they'd locked the files for everything from payroll to personal information on cops and city officials. Do a little research," she insisted. "You'll see. I'm going to take a nap."

Lena stood up, laid a now-sleeping Little T on his blanket on the floor, and walked toward her bedroom. Then she stopped and turned. "And Tyler wants you to what? Climb into a window to find these 'numbers?' You're not going to, are you?"

"Well, I won't break in. But if Burk invites me in…"

Lena shook her head then disappeared behind her bedroom door. Timmy lay cuddled up next to The Babe. Both snored delicately. I pulled out my tablet from my backpack and typed in ransomware. In less than a second, I had close to twenty-five million results.

"I wonder if there is a 'Ransomware for Dummies?'" I mumbled to the snoring pair.

I scanned the pages of results and settled on an online encyclopedia that explained in the simplest terms, what I needed to know. Ransomware was an especially malignant form of malware that infected a computer or a network and locked it down, often encrypting all the files. Money proved to be the magic key to unlock the frozen files. Private money. Money that changed hands on the dark web, using bitcoin.

I kept scanning. A well-known cybersecurity firm reported that the use of ransomware had jumped 118% since the previous year and had cost victims billions of dollars. The malware crept into a computer when a naïve user like me clicked on a link or an email that they shouldn't have. I immediately thought of the new credit card in my wallet. Someone had hacked into my information. I had accidentally invited him or her in by clicking on something that infected my computer.

Most ransomware attacks came from outside of the United States, places like Russia, India and the Middle East. But this was close to home. Somehow, Burk, Tyler, and Earl had a finger in this pie. I was determined to figure out how and why.

I needed to update the eCards on my tablet. I brought up Tyler's card and filled in the information from my conversations with him, the first near Ocean Beach and the second at the ballpark. I added bullet points for "ransomware" and "numbers." Then there was Earl's crazy friend who might be less crazy than I first thought. Although I hadn't met him, he deserved his own card. This man knew Earl, had offered him a job spying on someone (or something), and now wanted to warn him about … what? The spying? Something else? All that went on the card.

I had an almost-empty eCard for Jan.

Works at the sports radio station. Connects with Tyler. Has purple hair.

Not much there. Jason Chang, the bad beer maker, involved with the mini-chip and its source, the fictitious Shadowcorp, needed a card, too.

Burk Dennison deserved more than a card. He deserved his own page. He acted as if he was interested in me. He knew where I went and who I met. He knew where I worked. Stalker? Counterspy? Future boyfriend?

His friend, the other cyclist, needed a card, too. But I didn't know much about him, except that he and Burk were buddies and worked in the same house.

The house. Although I usually kept the cards for people, the house warranted a card. Traffic came in and out late at night. Burk lived there. Earl spied on it with his drone. Tyler believed that something illegal was going on inside. Crypto had questions about the servers and networking technology in the garage.

Maybe a card for Shadowcorp. I wished I knew the real name.

I didn't want to, but I had to type out an eCard for Earl. Such disloyalty toward a man who had been nothing but generous to me. In spite of my hesitance, I knew it was important. Everything revolved around him. A retired computer genius. "A legend," Crypto had gushed.

Tyler, the sports nerd, knew as much as I did when it came to the underpinnings of a computer. But he'd discovered he'd gotten his grandfather in a cybersecurity scheme that could get them both hurt, and Tyler wanted to keep him safe. Did Earl need protection? Did Tyler? They'd been pseudo-spies for at least six months, and everything was fine. Then something changed. What was it?

I started another category: Contacts. In this file, I added a page for the basset-hound computer guru, Crypto, who'd helped me access the footage on the mini memory card. He might be a good source of background information.

Burk called just as I hit the power button to turn off the tablet.

"Hey," I said, trying to feel enthusiastic.

"How's the sister and the baby? What's his name?"

"I thought I told you." I never did, but I wondered what he would say.

"No, never did."

That made me feel better, but Timmy would remain nameless.

"What are you up to today?" I asked, ignoring his question.

"I'd like to see you."

"Well, you do see me … a lot. You keep running into me. I'm starting to wonder if that's all by design."

That stopped Burk. Then he laughed. It sounded a little forced.

"I'm between homes right now, so I'm staying with a friend who lives close by. You know how life can get. I'm trying to figure out what I want to be when I grow up."

"Yeah, I've been there. In fact, I think I'm still there. What do you do, normally?"

"Ride bikes."

"For a living?"

He laughed again, this time a little more genuinely. "No, just for fun. Wanna grab a cup of coffee … maybe a sandwich?"

"Okay. Sure." I noticed he hadn't answered my question. One more thing for the Burk card.

"That's what I wanted to hear. How about you shoot me a text when you get back from San Rafael and we'll go from there."

"I'll do that."

We both hung up and I sat there staring at the phone. *Had I mentioned that my sister lived in San Rafael?* I couldn't remember, but I didn't think so. A shiver passed through me and my heart thudded. About an hour later, Lena strolled back into the living room. She looked almost human. The short nap had helped.

"You an expert on ransomware yet?" she asked.

"What did you say?" I asked, still thinking about my phone call.

"Ransomware? Remember?" She carefully picked up the napping baby and returned him to his crib.

"I'm going to meet Burk for coffee."

Lena pushed her curly hair back from her face. "That was the idea, right?"

I nodded.

"Well, why do you look so ... I don't know ... puzzled?"

"You can track phones, right?"

"With my eyes shut. Why?"

"Can you set it up so you can track my phone when I'm with Burk?"

"Trisha, if you're that worried about this guy, don't go."

"I'm going. But if I drop off the face of the earth, I want you to be able to find me."

"I don't like this."

"He's connected with that house, Earl and Tyler, and Tyler's friend and his skunky beer. If he has anything to do with ransomware, I need to find that out, too."

"Skunky what?"

"Means the beer tastes bad."

"You're making me nervous. Don't go back to his house alone. Promise me that."

"We're just going for coffee."

"Most people don't ask their sister to track their phones while they're on a date. This doesn't feel like a good idea. Why don't you start with something less ambitious?"

"Like what?"

"Try talking to Earl."

I paused.

"I have something better in mind."

CHAPTER 18

A few hours later, The Babe and I returned to Earl's house. No cars were in the driveway so both he and Dad had left, most likely for China Camp.

"Earl? Dad? Anybody here?" I waited. No response. "Good."

Just to make sure I wouldn't be surprised, I locked the front door and climbed the staircase to the second floor to Earl's bedroom, located at the far end of the hall.

Earl was a neatnik. His room—or what should be called his suite of rooms—personified Ben Franklin's quote: "A place for everything and everything in its place." The expansive bedroom, painted a pale green, had a deck off to one side, with a view of La Cruz Canyon, like mine. A gentlemanly coverlet in shades of brown and tan engulfed the king-sized bed. The bed was precisely made. I bet it had knife-sharp hospital corners. I wondered for a moment if Earl had ever served. Antique pine bedside tables with delicate, blown glass lamps on top, graced either side of the bed. Nothing rested on the amber-colored tables except for his phone's docking station. No dimes or nickels, no pile of paperbacks, no crossword puzzles. Not even an empty wine glass.

Two pine chests of drawers stood against the other wall, photos of his son and daughter-in-law, Tyler's high school graduation picture and a large portrait of a pretty woman scattered across the top. Given the young woman's stiff "beehive" hairdo, it must have been taken in the sixties. Earl's wife, maybe? I didn't know her name and Earl never mentioned her.

The comfortable room was clean and organized, just how I would suspect a wealthy-yet-unpretentious computer scientist would keep it. It was also a little boring for my tastes. Too much brown. The only sign of personality surfaced with the photographs. Off to one side was a large modern bathroom that had a control panel by the entry door. Earl could order up a warm shower while in bed, have the cool tile floor heated to perfection before his toes hit the ground, and his towels warmed on electronic towel racks while he showered.

A walk-in closet held more suits, shirts, and shoes than I've ever seen outside of the men's department at our local department store. Strange, because I never saw Earl dressed in anything but casual clothes and faded tees.

Earl's study had two entrances: one from the bedroom and the other from the hall. It overwhelmingly outsized the bedroom. You could tell it was the more important room; it had a more lived-in feel. Against one wall were floor-to-ceiling bookcases with half a dozen diplomas and certificates on one shelf. A framed crayon drawing of a boy walking with a man near the ocean, done by his son or maybe Tyler, sat front and center on another shelf. Next to the drawing, a black and white photo displayed a shirtless twenty-something Earl in skintight jeans, his long hair pulled back in a ponytail, dancing to music that had ended years ago.

"My goodness, Earl. Look … at … you." The photo had been taken outside, and Earl swayed in front of a packed group of young people at a concert. The boy next to him wore striped pants and a tie-dye shirt; the girls dancing behind tossed their shoulder-length straight hair. They dressed in long flowing skirts and wide floppy sun hats. In one corner of the frame, I found the girl with the beehive from the bedroom photo. Only now, her light hair hung loose around her shoulders, her arms high over her head, her eyes closed. Braless, her breasts pushed against the thin gauzy top. Like everyone else in the photo, she beamed.

I picked up the frame, undid the clasps on the back and pulled off the cover. On the back of the photo, it said, 'Woodstock, August '69, Catskills.'

Earl had been at the infamous concert. I wondered if he and his wife had met at Woodstock. What a story that would be. I replaced the back and set it down on the shelf. I pushed down an urge to hunt for more photos. I needed to keep my focus and continue the search. The only problem was that I didn't know what I was searching for.

The rugged black cases that held his quadcopters were on the next shelf. I knew he had two of them, but I counted three large cases and four, exceedingly small cases, about the size of cell phones. I opened the large cases and found drones, controls and drone parts. No extra sheet of paper, no notes, no extra video cards. I did the same with the small cases. The first mini drone was about as big as a dragonfly. It looked like the one I'd seen in the sketch. The next two were even smaller, half the size of the dragonfly. Once they were airborne, they'd be all but invisible.

The perfect spying machines.

I walked around behind his desk and sat down in the swivel chair. The sketches of the drones I had seen the other day lay strewn across the desktop, plus a few more. I opened the middle drawer. Nothing but the usual drawer junk that even a man as organized as Earl kept. The top side drawer housed operating manuals for some kind of server. I pulled opened the next drawer and found a small plastic container of the mini memory cards, like the one I'd found in the beer cap. A hole punch took up the third drawer. So far, my little expedition had been a colossal waste of time, except for the discovery of the Woodstock photo and the mini memory cards.

I got up, walked toward the wall of books and let my hand drift across the bindings of the books, skimming the titles. Nothing out of the ordinary there. They were mostly technical tomes I had never heard of and would never make any sense to me, even if I decided to read one. I turned, ready to leave, when I noticed a computer textbook, slightly out of line with the others. The author's name was Cunningham. Earl Cunningham.

I pulled the book off the shelf and flipped back the cover, skimming over the introductory page and the table of contents. What didn't he do in this field? I turned the page and found a cut-out square that held a waterproof black pouch, the type that divers often carried, and a short barrel revolver. The handgun covered the smooth pouch that had an air-tight sliding seal. I put the fake book down on the desk, took out the gun, and set it gingerly on the desk. Then I lifted the pouch and slid open the seal. Tucked inside were a big blue marble, a man's wedding ring and a paper with a list of nine complicated letter-and-number sequences that stretched to fifteen digits long. They all started with the same prefix—U8Q—and ended in sequence, like A1, B2, C3 and so on.

I carried the paper over to the desk, pulled out my phone and took a picture. Just then, I heard a car crunching across the stones in the driveway.

"Hey, Trisha," Earl called out. "You need to come out here and repark. I can't get in."

Oh no, I did it again. I put the paper back in the black bag with the blue marble and the ring, then placed it in the book. I added the revolver.

Then I flipped the fake book closed and hurriedly pushed it back in the bookcase, making sure the binding stood even with the other books. I darted out the door, ran down the hall into my bedroom and peered over the deck.

"Sorry, Earl," I called down. "I'll be right there."

I apologized profusely to Earl. "It won't happen again."

He smiled and patted me on the back. "Don't worry about it. But in the future, please be more considerate about me and your dad. We're getting older, you know. Eyesight's not as good as it used to be. Don't want to ding your car."

I followed Earl into the kitchen. "How was China Camp?"

"It's the busy season. The parking lot is crowded. Beach is crowded and so is the snack bar. I'm tired," he said, sitting down heavily on a solid wooden chair.

"Let me get you something to drink. You want a beer?"

"Sounds good. But not Coyote Ridge."

"Don't blame you." I flipped off the cap on a tall-necked brown bottle I found in the side door of the fridge, handed it to Earl and sat down.

"Heard anything from Tyler?" I asked.

He shook his head. He seemed strangely unconcerned.

"I'll leave you alone." I started to walk out, then changed my mind and turned. "Actually. . . I have a question for you. About the house on the other side of the hill. You've been watching it with your drone, right? Any particular reason?"

Earl regarded the beer bottle for a long time.

"There was a lot of activity. Good place to practice. That's all."

"They have a garage full of servers. Did you know that?"

"I'm tired, Trish. Need to take a shower." The tone of his voice made it clear he wouldn't be answering any more questions.

"Sure. Okay."

I walked up the steps to my room and glanced down the hallway to Earl's study. Next time he went out, I would pay his suite another visit.

"Earl?" I yelled from the door of my room. No answer. I walked to the staircase. "Earl?"

"Yes, Trisha?" he said, walking up the steps with The Babe by his side, his voice suddenly very tired.

"Do you know where Dad is?"

"At China Camp, I suppose. He and a few volunteers were working on the pier when I left."

"Think I'll take a drive out and visit him."

As I walked down the hall to my room, my phone pinged. A text from Burk.

Back from SR yet?

Does he know I'm home or is he fishing? I didn't respond.

CHAPTER 19

I hadn't been out to China Camp since the summer before, when Shari Granter's body washed up on the shore. Sheri and Lena grew up together and spent afternoons in pools all around the county. Her death, quickly deemed a murder, shocked everyone. I'd spent a lot of hours driving back and forth on the winding road to the popular state park on the edge of San Pablo Bay trying to figure out who had done it and why.

This time, driving there didn't have the same fierce sense of purpose. I wanted to talk to my dad about the missing-not-missing Tyler, even though I'd promised I wouldn't. But to be truthful, I just wanted to see him.

Both Lena and I were shocked when he slipped back into our lives last summer. After he left, so many years ago, not everything I did to care for Lena had been legal. I'd managed somehow, but it changed me, and it definitely changed my sister. She was only ten. Once she realized he had no intention of returning, her heart closed.

The thing was, he did return when he learned about Lena's pregnancy. Apparently, he'd kept track of us during his lost years. He'd been around for about a year now, and never stopped working his hardest to make it up to both of us. Lena continued to be snippy with him. But for me, there were times, like the present one, when I needed someone to bounce ideas off, especially with Jon no longer around. In all honesty, I needed a parent to talk to. I needed my dad.

The road to China Camp skirted a forest-like drop off to the Bay on one side, and steep wooded hills on the other with snatches of water through the trees. I parked in the upper lot and walked down the hill to China Camp Village. The former shrimping village closed at sunset, but that was a good three or four hours away. Being midweek, only a few people remained at the beach or walking through the museum dedicated to the Chinese settlement.

I saw Dad at the end of the fishing pier with a few other men. They were deep in conversation. He turned for a second and I waved, both arms over my head.

"Hey, Dad." He waved back, said a few words to the men around him and walked back toward me.

"Trisha, this is a surprise. What are you doing here?" He wiped his hands on a green bandana he had in his jeans pocket.

"Do you have a few minutes? I need to run some things by you."

"For you sweetheart, I have all the time in the world. Let's get something to drink and we can sit at one of the picnic tables."

He pushed open the screen door of the small snack bar that belonged in the 1950s while I walked over to the nearby cluster of tables. The sun dropped behind the China Camp Hills, and a long cool patch of shade moved across the parking lot toward the beach. I found a table that gave us as much sun as possible and sat down.

Dad came out with a can of root beer for himself, a diet iced tea for me and a bag of chips. We sat for a few minutes munching away. I recognized the vroom of a powerboat skirting across the Bay. But our silence went on ... and on. Dad turned toward me.

"You want to tell me what you'd like to talk about? Or should I guess?"

"I'm not supposed to be talking to you. Tyler thinks you're a blabbermouth. But there are some things that confuse me and I need your opinion."

"Tyler? I thought Tyler was missing," Dad said, sounding surprised and relieved at the same time.

"He's not. Not really."

"Trish, either he's missing, or he isn't," he said sternly. "I can't believe that he didn't contact Earl. To tell him he's alive, for Pete's sake."

"That's what I thought. I've seen him a few times."

"What! And you didn't say anything? I get it if you didn't want to talk to me, but not to tell Earl? What were you thinking?"

"I'm sorry," I said. "Tyler didn't want me to tell anyone. But ... "

"Go on."

"He and Earl have been 'spying'"— I made air quotation marks with my fingers— "on a house over the hill, closer to the reservoir. And they've been passing information back and forth in the Coyote Ridge beer bottle caps. Some guy that Earl knows, the one that got him to take this spying job, now feels he's in big trouble. And Ty thinks that ransomware is involved somehow. Anyway, Tyler wants me to find out what is going on."

"How are you supposed to do that?" he asked.

"He asked me to find some kind of proof—a paper with some numbers on it. He thinks it's inside the house over the hill, and he wants me to try to get it."

"Sounds dangerous to me. Don't do it."

I groaned.

"Why does Tyler think I'm a blabbermouth?"

"Dad, that's beside the point."

"Well, I'd like to know."

"Dad, be serious for a second. What's your take on this? It might help me figure it out."

"If I heard this story from anyone else, I'd think they only had one oar in the water."

He stood up from the picnic table and walked toward the beach. Uncertain of what to do, I stayed where I was. I wanted to tell him about the fake book in Earl's study but was having second thoughts. He turned around, walked back and sat down on the table again, took a sip of his root beer and then tossed the can in the recycle bin a few feet away. He wore the same faded yellow tee shirt that he'd had on last year, the first time I saw him again. He ran his fingers through what remained of his hair.

"I knew something was up. But Earl isn't the type of guy who talks about his life."

"Is it just me, or does it seem like he doesn't seem to care that Tyler is missing anymore?"

"I've gotten that feeling too."

"I think he knows he's not missing."

"You might be right, Trish."

"He hasn't said anything to you?"

Dad shook his head. "Not me. We're guys, Trisha. We talk about the Giants, his new drone, how awful Coyote Ridge tastes, our volunteer work. We pretty much stay away from personal things."

His glance drifted to the pier. "We have a few hours of daylight left. Might be able to finish up the repairs."

He stood up and leaned over to kiss me on the forehead. "Don't know why Tyler thinks I'd spill the beans. Never would. Never," he declared. "Need to have a talk with him next time I see him."

"No, Dad, please don't. I'm not supposed to be sharing this with you."

He walked toward the pier mumbling to himself. "I can keep a secret with the best of `em."

On my drive back to Earl's house, I got a call from Dr. T.

"Lena tells me you have a new boyfriend."

"Hello to you, too."

"Hello. Well, do you?"

"I love you T. You're my favorite almost brother. But this isn't any of your business."

"She says that this new guy sounds like a creepadouche—her word, not mine—and that you asked her to track your phone when you meet him."

"That's right. And?"

"Trisha, there are too many sickos out there. I know. They show up at the ER all the time. I think—how do I put this—"

"I shouldn't go out with him?"

"Yeah, that would cover it."

"T, you're not my father."

"Well, I bet he'd agree with me. Did you tell him?"

"No. I don't have to tell him about everything that I do … or everyone I meet for coffee. Lena's behind your call, isn't she?"

"Think I'll run this by him."

"You will not. This is none of your business. I am an adult. This conversation is, as you like to say, 'o-ver.'"

"Don't hang up. We don't want you to end up in a garbage dump, that's all."

I knew he cared about me, like a brother would. But it didn't stop the warmth from creeping up my neck and into my cheeks as I listened to his preaching. My breathing accelerated. Not realizing it, I pressed down on the gas pedal and raced around the curves of Point San Pedro Road.

"T," I said, louder than I expected. "I appreciate your concern. But I can handle this."

I hung up. I pulled my foot off the accelerator and slowed the car to a reasonable speed. I wondered if Lena and Dr. T were right.

CHAPTER 20

I didn't connect with Burk when I went home. Even if I had wanted to (and I was ambivalent about 'what I wanted'), I didn't have the chance. Earl was having a very animated conversation with the nutso man who had been trying to track him down through Tyler and the radio station.

"Bernard, slow down," I hear Earl saying over and over as I sprinted up the steps and slipped through the wide-open front door. Bernard careened from the deck to the living room and into the kitchen, then through the dining room, his arms flailing.

"They're going to kill me. They're going to kill you. What don't you understand?" His words mashed together at a rapid-fire pace. It took me a moment to untangle his gobbledygook.

"Please sit down," said Earl following him. "Please."

"Earl, what's going on?"

"Old friend … visiting … a bit upset." He tried to grab Bernard as he flew by us.

"A bit?"

I had an idea. I walked into the living room and stood in front of the couch. Bernard galloped my way, but he glanced back at Earl.

"We have to do something. Danger … we're in …"

He turned around and paused for a micro-second when he saw me. That's when I lunged for him, grabbed him around the waist and pushed him onto the couch, my feet and legs flying behind me. I pulled his hands up over his head, barely keeping them together.

"Earl, help me hold him down."

"You tackled him," he said in disbelief. "You tackled him," he repeated.

"Help me. Grab his arm."

"No, Earl, help me," begged Bernard from the couch where I knelt his chest. He tried to sit up, then stopped and gaped at me. "Please, get off me."

"Will you be good now?" His ribs sagged beneath my knees. He nodded and I pushed myself up and off him to a standing position.

"Sit up," I ordered him, and he did. "Would you like a glass of water?"

He nodded.

"Okay, I'll get you something. But don't you dare get off the couch, understand?" He nodded again. Earl came over and sat next to him.

Instead of walking into the kitchen, I jogged up the staircase and made a beeline for my room. I had to calm down. I sat on the bed and fell backward onto the comforter. *What did I just do?* My arms trembled. I scanned the ceiling and took one deep breath after another. "Breathe in … breathe out … breathe in … breathe out." My body relaxed.

"Frida, what's in the fridge to drink?"

"Nothing," said the robotic voice from the refrigerator.

"You're no help."

Then I stood up and walked into the bathroom. My cheeks flushed a vibrant pink. I turned on the tap and let the cool water run through my fingers, then splashed my face, once, twice and then again. As my face faded to its natural hue. I ran a comb through my hair and headed back downstairs.

Earl was deep in conversation with Bernard when I came back with the water. They stopped talking when they saw me.

"My apologies," said Bernard. "I never should have acted like that … let myself get out of control. I'm terribly sorry."

Bernard and Earl sitting side by side were a portrait in contrasts. Earl was the poster-boy for California cool with his gray ponytail and state flag tee shirt embellished with a faded brown grizzly bear. Bernard, on the other hand, was buttoned-down and pin-striped to the extreme. Even his buzzed salt-and-pepper hair was obsessively neat.

Earl reached for the water and gave the glass to Bernard.

"Thank you, Trisha. But we need to speak privately for a moment or two."

"Nice try, but I'm not going anywhere." I sat down.

Both men stopped talking.

"Okay, let me put it this way. You—and Tyler—are spying on the house over the hill, using your quadcopter to film it, and then passing the media thingy off to someone via a Coyote Ridge bottle cap."

Earl stared at me open-mouthed. "So far, you're on target," he said.

"What I want to know is why? Why are you doing this? And why has it suddenly become so dangerous?"

Bernard put the glass down and cleared his throat. "I'm to blame for that," he said.

"You're not," said Earl. "I willingly jumped on board when you discussed this with me."

"Will somebody tell me what is going on?"

Earl spoke first. "We're spying on spies."

Then Bernard shared a tale that started decades ago in the Pacific Northwest where he lived.

"I've known Tyler since he was a little kid. A sports statistics wizard, even as a child. Well, years back, Earl was drawn to the Bay Area because of all the bright computer minds who had ended up here."

"Bernard, is all this important? I just want to know why Tyler won't come home and what it has to do with that house."

"Trisha, don't be rude."

"Sorry. Tyler wants me to help, but he won't tell me anything."

"Then he's doing what I asked him to do," said Earl.

"I knew it! You've talked to him," I said.

"Let's discuss that later, okay? Bernard, finish your story."

"Yes, of course, Bernard. Please go on." I deadpanned, barely containing the sarcasm.

Bernard's demeanor had dramatically changed since I'd entered the house. Quiet, calm—almost meditatively—he told his story, A retired, comfortable but bored computer security analyst who had jumped at the chance to get into a little computer espionage.

"You know," explained Bernard, "find out what the competition is working on and who they're working with."

"But you're retired. What competition are you talking about?" I pestered. So far, he hadn't mentioned that the competition was Shadowcorp's own employees. I wonder if he knew.

"Trisha," said Earl, glaring at me. "Stop interrupting."

"OK. Sorry. Go on."

"To answer your question, Trisha," Bernard said, "Other computer security companies. Anyway, Tyler contacted me. A friend of his ... he never mentioned who ... asked if he knew someone who was available to do a little reconnaissance work for them. They didn't want much … not really. Just keep an eye out, when I could, on who was going in and out of a house a few blocks from my neighborhood. I was free most days, needed a challenge … so I thought, 'Why not?'"

"Tyler was down here in the Bay Area during most of this. He had never done anything like this before, but the extra paycheck was too good to pass up. He was trying to get on his feet, you see. He had just moved out of Earl's house and money was tight. The company who had hired us flew him up to Oregon to be the go-between. They gave him a drone for me, paid for a few lessons on how to operate the gadget and I was in business. Unfortunately, not much happened at the house. I'm not sure what they expected to find, but this was a typical suburban home. A family with two teenagers and a white cat lived there. I'd film early in the morning until an hour after the family left the house, and then again in the late evening. Occasionally, I'd film during the day, but there wasn't any real reason to. I'd give the SD card to an Uber driver who doubled as a delivery person and he'd give me a clean card."

"Did Tyler ever say who hired you?"

"No, and he said not to ask. So I didn't."

"Maybe it doesn't exist." *I bet it's Shadowcorp.*

"Trisha," Earl said sternly.

"Why were they spying?" I asked.

"They told Tyler they wanted to know what their competition was up to. I took it at face value."

"Doesn't seem too smart. Working for people you don't know."

"Trisha. Let the man speak," said Earl.

I rolled my eyes, but clamped my lips shut and nodded at Bernard to go on.

"I was getting paid … good money, too … but after a month or two, the bloom was off the rose, so to speak. I told Tyler I was bored, wanted to quit. He relayed that information, and they asked if I knew anyone else that might be interested in this type of work … maybe someone in San Francisco. I told Tyler this sort of thing might interest his grandfather. I knew that Earl was getting frustrated down here. Needed something to take up some time. Tyler agreed, but he didn't want Earl to know he was involved. So, I played along. Agreed to tell Earl the idea—and the connection—was mine. By the time we talked, Tyler learned that the company wanted him … you …" he pointed to Earl, "to do surveillance on a house in this neighborhood."

"The house over the hill, close to the reservoir?" I asked.

"That's the one. Earl accepted the job and all that was left was to figure out a way to pass the data. It seemed harmless," Bernard said.

I sat back in the chair.

"You want my take? The house you were watching in Oregon was a dud, a decoy. They wanted to get to Earl and this house over the hill. That was always the goal."

"Earl, do you think that's true?" Bernard asked.

"It's a roundabout way to get the information they wanted," said Earl. He closed his eyes and readjusted his ponytail. "But it makes sense. Things have accelerated tremendously over the past few weeks."

"There's something I don't understand, though. You obviously know where Earl lives," I said. "Why all the effort to hunt him down at the radio station?"

"There's something I haven't spoken about to anyone, not even Tyler. Not long after I bowed out, my landline wasn't working properly, so I had the cable guy run some tests. He found a bug. My phone was tapped. When he went down under the garage, where the coaxial cable meets the cable box, he found another bug right there, plain as could be. Someone had access to my phone, my computer and internet, and my TV. He pulled them out and said he would report them to his supervisors. I also filed a report with the local police department. I'm not sure they believed me, but I gave them the contact information for the cable company anyway."

"So now you were under surveillance. I can see why you'd start to panic."

"There's more. The next day I was visited by two men who said they were from the FBI. They told me I was involved with a computer espionage ring that had spread from the Pacific Northwest down to California. They said that this spy ring was dangerous—wouldn't hesitate to kill me or my family."

"Why didn't you tell me?" Earl was close to shouting.

"I didn't know who to believe. What was true, what wasn't. And I was scared. I left home that night. I was too afraid to take my own car, so I got a rental and bought a couple of burner phones. I've been in the Bay Area for a few weeks now, trying to get ahold of Earl to warn him and Tyler. I couldn't just come here. I was too worried I was being tailed."

I couldn't believe what I'd heard. "I wonder if they were the real deal. Did these men give you a card?"

Bernard hunted in his wallet and pulled out an official-looking business card with the FBI seal embossed on one side. The name of an agent, Theodore Pinehold, and his phone number were printed on the other.

"Let me try the number," said Earl.

"No, don't," I said. "We can't use any phone that's in the house or our cell phones. I know someone who might be able to help."

I kept staring at the card, hoping it would tell me something, but it didn't. I knew, just knew, it was fake. I needed to check it out.

"How did my grandson get involved with all of this?" Earl mumbled to himself. "All he cares about is sports. He's not an agent, a counteragent, a spy. I didn't think he even knew this much about computers."

"Did he ever say anything about ransomware?" I asked.

Earl shut me down. "Never."

That's when Dad walked in.

"Hello. I'm Robert, Earl's roommate," he said, extending a hand to Bernard. "Trisha, are you going somewhere?"

"I'll be back soon." I was already at the front door, pulling on a sweatshirt.

I placed the card in my pocket, picked up my backpack. "Okay if I take The Babe with me?"

Earl nodded.

"I'm going to see what I can find out about this card," I said. "Earl, catch Dad up, okay?"

CHAPTER 21

Finding a place to park on Larkspur Street wasn't as easy this time. Instead, I pulled into the large, crowded parking lot by the local bowling alley. The Babe and I walked a few blocks past Mexican restaurants, multiple car repair shops, and a few closet-sized cafes, their menus written in Spanish, hanging in the windows. A steady stream of traffic whipped by.

I rang the bell for Crypto's apartment.

"Yeah?"

"This is Trisha Carson. I was here—"

I heard the door unlock. I walked in with the large pup by my side, his nails clicking on the tile floor, his nose in full gear, sniffing every corner of the new surroundings.

"You know, I never was formally introduced to you," I said to the sad-eyed man sitting on his rolling desk chair, the three monitors lit up like Christmas trees. His long hair was now pulled up into a messy man bun.

"Call me Uly."

"Is that Russian?"

"Nope. What can I do for you?"

"I want to make a call, but I don't want the number to be traceable."

"Get a burner phone." He turned back to his keyboard and started typing.

"That's it? Get a burner phone?"

"Yep." His fingers clicked and tapped, and lines of code started running across the three screens. I stood there, feeling stupid.

"Okay." I turned to leave.

Uly turned to me. "You sure that's all?"

"Well, now that you ask." I gave him the Cliff Notes version of what I learned from Bernard. Uly didn't say anything. Instead, he stood up, stretched and walked over to a filing cabinet. He pulled open a drawer packed with brand new phones.

"Try this." He pulled a phone out of its plastic wrapping and handed it to me. As soon as I took it, he grabbed it back.

"Just a minute." He pulled the back off the phone and walked over to a flat table, then turned on the jeweler's desk lamp. He flipped back the top of a narrow flat box with about twenty small compartments and pulled out a pair of ultraslim tweezers. With the tweezers, he picked up a tiny black dot out of another compartment and placed it in the phone. I tried to peer over his shoulder, but he hunched over the phone, blocking my view. He slipped the back on and handed it to me.

"Here."

"What was that?" I asked.

"It'll tell me where their phone is when they pick up."

"What if no one picks up?"

"Guess you're screwed. Go ahead. Dial."

I did. I watched The Babe trot around the room, sniffing at all the corners, while I punched in the numbers. Finally a man answered.

"Seven. Four. Nine," said a hurried male voice.

"Seven. Four. What? Is Theodore Pinehold there?"

"No, he's not."

"Excuse me, but where have I called?"

He hung up.

"I don't think that's the FBI." I gave Uly back the phone. "He answered with a number. 749. Does that mean anything to you?"

"Some security companies give their agents numbers. Might be something like that. Did you say the FBI?"

Uly went over to his computer and connected the smartphone to a USB port, hit a couple of keys and numbers and letters appeared on the screen. At the bottom of the list were the words "San Francisco."

"The phone is in the city."

"Can you be more specific? Like maybe an address?"

"Might be downtown. Can't tell yet."

"Can you find out who answered?"

"Unless you have a voiceprint I can compare it to, not likely."

"OK. Thanks. I have to go. Here's my cell number. If you find the street address, can you call or text me?"

Uly nodded and turned back toward his keyboard.

"One more thing."

He remained motionless but eventually turned around. "What?"

"I'm going to meet someone from that house ... the one that was being videoed. You know, from the quadcopter? Say I wanted to video the inside of the house. Hypothetically, of course. Is that possible?"

"Yes. It's possible." He turned around and stared at the monitor, but his fingers didn't move on the keyboard. After a moment, he glanced back at me. "I'm guessing you want some help with that?" he asked.

"Yes. Please."

With a loud sigh, he rolled back his work chair, his saggy, basset hound-eyes lost in thought. Then, he stood up, stretched and shuffled over to a metal cupboard on the other side of the room. He pulled open the doors, rummaged around and walked back with something in either hand.

"This is a wire. Tape the speaker on your upper chest where it can't be seen. Near your bra is usually good." He blushed at the word bra. It was almost endearing. "Word of caution. Use tape that you can pull off easily. Otherwise, it could hurt."

He held up a tiny digital recorder. "This records what you're taping."

"How am I supposed to turn that on and off without someone seeing me?"

"It's voice-activated. That means—"

"I know what that means. Thank you for this. It's nice, but I want more than audio. I need video."

Another deeper sigh. He held up a black diver's watch with various dials under the glass.

"This watch is a mini-video cam. Just press the button on the right side to activate it. Aim the watch face at whatever you want to shoot. You can use it at night. It's sharp enough to recognize things in the distance, even faces. It has eight gigs of built-in memory, so that gives you about an hour of video without the use of a memory card. Very nifty gadget. And it's waterproof."

"If I want to view what I've recorded?"

"Use the cord I'm gonna give you. Attach it to the watch and your computer. Then download the files. Easy."

"I suppose it records audio as well."

"Sure."

"Then why did you give me the wire?"

He looked like he had to struggle to keep from calling me an idiot.

"Think about it, Trisha. If all you need is a voice, use the wire. It's the simplest of these devices. If visuals are more important, use the watch."

"I'll do both."

"Whatever," he said as he turned back to this computer.

"'Bye and thanks. Come on, Babe." I stuffed my two new favorite toys in my backpack, and we let ourselves.

"Think about it, Trisha." I mimicked Uly's light drawl. "What e-vah."

CHAPTER 22

The next morning, my smart refrigerator, Frida, woke me playing melodic Hawaiian music. She signaled the coffee maker to brew me a cup.

"Frida, what's on my schedule for today?"

"You are scheduled to work tomorrow at 5:00 pm."

"Anything else?"

"You have a text message," said the robotic female voice.

"Can you read it to me?"

"Weren't you going to call me, emoji telephone, question mark, Burk," said Frida, emphasizing each word precisely. "Would you like to respond?"

"No. Thank you. That's all Frida."

"You are welcome."

'That's all' was the command to turn Frida off. I felt a little awkward talking to an appliance that controlled my room and everything in it. I enjoyed the convenience of having an invisible assistant, of course, but Frida … well, she was involved in too much of my life, and remembered all of it. Better than I did.

I picked up my cup of coffee and wandered out to the deck. Fog encased the pine trees and redwoods at the bottom of the canyon, then dissolved into swirling mist toward the top. Hovering, not more than ten feet in front of me, was Earl's Black Beauty. I waved. "Hey, Earl, how's your psycho friend?"

The Babe started to bark in the background so I couldn't catch all of Earl's comments, but it sounded something like "Not as crazy as—"

The drone disappeared.

I walked back in, picked up my backpack and pulled out my new spy toys. I put the watch on my wrist and slapped the wire underneath my PJ top in the middle of my chest and tucked the mini recorder into my pocket. Then I walked into the bathroom and discretely pressed the side button to activate the smallest video camera I had ever used. I pointed it toward the mirror, ran my other hand through my hair and tossed my head back.

"Mr. DeMille, is it all right if I say a few words? This is my life. It always will be. The camera—"

"Hey Trisha, you want a donut?" Dad called from downstairs. I blinked once, twice and settled back into my Norma Desmond impersonation from the 1950's film, *Sunset Boulevard.*

"All right Mr. DeMille, I'm ready for my—"

"Donuts, Trish?" yelled Dad.

"—closeup. Yeah, Dad. Save me a chocolate one."

I pulled on a sweatshirt and bounded down the steps. Earl and Dad were parked in the dining room, munching on the sweet treats.

"Try one of these," said Dad. "You'll love it."

The donut he offered was covered in chocolate with slices of raspberries spread across the top.

"Dessert for breakfast. Tempting." I said. "I'll have half. I'm watching what I eat."

"Well, you can watch it while you eat it," snorted Dad.

"Ha, ha. Dad jokes. You're supposed to be my support system. Not my enablers."

"Like the snake in the garden of Eden, holding the apple or in this case, the donut, out to Eve," said Earl.

"Think I'll have cereal," I said as I rummaged around the cupboards. "What happened to Bernard?"

"It took him a while to completely decompress, but he did. Then he left."

"Where is he staying?"

"He wouldn't say. Thought it was too dangerous for me to know. Did you call the FBI?" asked Earl.

"I did, and let's just say, those guys who came to visit Bernard were not agents."

Both men said 'hmm' at the same time.

"Well, who were they then?" asked Earl.

"Dunno. Earl, does the number seven, four, nine mean anything to you?"

Earl shook his head.

"Whoever answered the phone listed on the card is in downtown San Francisco."

"And how do you know that?" asked Earl.

"I have my sources. I'm trying to find the exact location, but it might take some time." I'd planned on telling them about my new spy gear but thought better of it.

After my donut/cereal break, I climbed back up to my room and onto the deck. I dropped into one of the lounge chairs, took off the wire and laid it on the side table. I undid the strap for the watch and turned it over in my hands.

So clunky and unattractive. Maybe I could go into business making spy thingies the right size and design for women. I played with the watch and the mini tape recorder until they felt familiar in my hand. Then I remembered—I'd never checked back in with Burk. I found my phone, gave him a call, and left a message.

"Sorry about yesterday. There was some stuff going on at my house. No time to do anything else. Do you have any free time today? I'm going to go for a swim down at the reservoir this afternoon around two. Wanna join me?"

I hoped the message sounded enticing and apologetic enough. If Burk failed to appear, it would be the first time I'd gone into the water without a swimming companion glued to my side. I wondered if I could do it. I pictured the reservoir: brownish-green water sweeping across the canyon floor until it reached a blockade of new-growth redwoods. In my mind, the shadowy water grew deeper and cooler. *Maybe I'll just stay on the beach.*

A message popped up on my phone, the bank wanting confirmation I had received the replacement credit card. It gave me a link to click on. I started to, then thought better of it and called my bank to make sure they were the ones emailing me. They were. After a brief conversation, they recommended that I change my username and password on all my accounts. I had a few minutes, so I came up with new usernames and passwords for my bank, two email accounts, cable, and health insurance.

CHAPTER 23

The afternoon sun blazed white hot. Beachgoers who didn't have a day job—or who had called in sick—packed the local reservoir. I spread my towel by the lifeguard's tall, white chair. Lena taught me this trick. "If you're by yourself, or your whole group decides to swim at the same time, always chat up the guards. Good chance they'll notice if some random person decides to steal your stuff," she told me once on a trip to the beach.

Out in the water, safety lane lines dotted with small oval blue and white floats separated the roomy rectangular swimming area from the rest of the reservoir. At the furthest edge, a wide lane was cordoned off for lap swimmers. One length measured about fifty yards, twice the length of a regular swimming pool. In the past, I'd swum out there comfortably when my sister stayed closed and if I tucked myself next to the lane lines. But not today. My heart rate vaulted up a full ten points and my whole body stiffened when I glanced at the water. I turned around and concentrated on the white wooden rung of the lifeguard chair, trying to steady my breathing.

"Safe. Safe," I spoke quietly. "I'm safe." My shoulders slipped down from my ears. I twisted my neck around in circles, one way, then the other.

I glanced up at the guard sitting with a red lifeguard tube on her lap.

"Okay if I put my towel here?" She nodded but kept her eyes on a group of laughing children pushing each other underwater in the shallows.

"You have a crowd today for midweek."

"I don't know where all these people come from," she replied, her eyes never leaving the water.

I fastened the video watch to my wrist. Maybe I could practice if I was calm enough to get in the water. "Anything I should know about the reservoir today?"

"It's warming up … maybe sixty-eight or sixty-nine degrees. There's no current, no angry sea monsters. Watch out for the rocks under the surface when you first get in."

"Thanks."

"No, thank you. You're the first person this summer to ask about water hazards. I wish more people did that."

Sand, a lot of sand, had been trucked in to make this beach. It was the coarse kind, not the fine powdery stuff found on tropical beaches of Florida or Hawaii. Today, it seared my feet as I tiptoed down to the water's edge. I slipped on two caps for extra warmth, fitted my goggles to my face and forced myself to walk into the water up to my knees. *Breathe in. Breathe out. Control the breath; don't let it control you.* I dipped both hands in and splashed water on my face and the back of my neck. *Chilly, chilly, chilly.* I walked in farther until the water circled my waist, then I held my breath and sank under the surface. I pushed off the bottom and stood straight up. I glanced over my shoulder. Nobody on the beach paid any attention to me. I took another deep breath, bobbed up and down a few times, and walked out a few feet more. I stared back at the beach, at the lifeguard in her chair. If I could see the guard, she could see me. Then, I ducked under the water and stayed there. I opened my eyes. My hands and arms were veiled in soft brown silt. Then I stood straight up. Goosebumps covered my legs.

Take a stroke. Just one stroke. Instead of diving in the water and starting to swim, I carefully stretched out on my back and floated. I imagined the lumpy white cloud above was a camel. It changed shape into a mountain. Water gurgled around the edge of my cap. I raised one arm over my head and took a stroke. Then another. I rotated on to my stomach. Light filtered through the dark, greenish water. It had a fuzzy quality to it, hazy, not shimmering and sparkly, like a chlorinated swimming pool.

The goosebumps disappeared as I got into a rhythm. I enjoyed watching the trees climbing to the top of La Cruz Canyon when I turned my head to breathe. This fisheye view gave me a new perspective of the land. I started to daydream, and unexpectedly, ran smack into another swimmer. Our arms locked at the elbows and we both stopped with a jerk, water splashing around us. Our arms disentangled and I pulled my face out of the water to find a man more bewildered and alarmed than I was.

"I'm so sorry," I said. "I wasn't paying attention." My legs were kicking in circles beneath me to keep my head out of the water. "Are you okay?" I asked.

On the edge of panic, he swallowed and spit out a mouthful of reservoir water.

"Yeah," he managed to say.

The swimmer was in his forties and wore tinted goggles, now half-full of water. He had on a sleeveless wetsuit. He would never sink with that on, but even so, he was rattled.

"Sure you're okay?" I asked.

"I'm going in."

"Do you want me to swim with—" but before I could finish, he took off, headed for shore with spray flying around him like glittering beads.

The cordoned-off area for lap swimmers took shape an arm's length away. The water pulled at my shoulders. The white lifeguard chair on the shore had shrunk to the size of a toy. *How did I swim so far away from the beach?* Alone, I treaded water, trying to stay calm. I glanced down; there was nothing below my waist, not even my legs. Only the greenish-brown water. Something nibbled on my toes ... or did it? My heart rate jumped up again and goosebumps, this time from fear, spread across my arms. I pulled my legs up to my chest, away from whatever was in the water with me. I tried to slow my breathing again with my 'breathe in, breathe out' mantra. Instead, I managed to suck down a mouthful of water. I longed to be on my towel, safe on land. I began to sprint after the man in the wetsuit, sighting on the lifeguard chair in the distance.

My arms churned through the water until I had to stop and catch my breath. Starting slower this time, I began again. The steady movement of arm over arm settled my breathing. Eventually, the water grew shallow enough to stand, and I stretched my legs beneath me until my feet sank into the muddy bottom. I could tell the lifeguard didn't consider me in danger. The sun grew warmer, so did the water, and the children playing at the shoreline welcomed me back to shore. Or so I thought. They never noticed me. I pushed my legs through the thigh-high water toward shore, only stopping when it was around my knees.

Burk was standing by the lifeguard chair. I had forgotten all about him. But he hadn't forgotten me. I waved in his direction and he waved back. As I transitioned from water to beach, I pulled off my goggles and caps and tugged at the bottom of my swimsuit.

"Hey," Burk called out as I jogged across the hot beach.

The lifeguard leaned over when I was closer. "What were you and that other swimmer doing out there? Dancing?"

"Ah … no. We hooked elbows and I think it spooked him, so he came in."

"I saw that," the guard said. "You weren't far behind. All that empty water and you two collide."

I nodded.

"You okay?"

"Yeah. Just a little winded, that's all."

"You have a nice stroke," she commented as her radio crackled, and she turned away to answer it.

"Nice stroke," said Burk, nodding and repeating the guard.

"She probably didn't see me gasping for air. For a minute, I thought I was being chased by some sort of shark."

"I don't think we get those here," said Burk.

I sat down on the towel, pulled another one from my bag and started to dry my shoulders, then my hair.

"I'm surprised you went out by yourself. You must be feeling better about the whole open water situation?" he said, sitting down beside me.

"I forced myself to go in. With a lifeguard watching, I felt safe." My hands hidden in the terry cloth, I clicked on my watch. Now I had to figure out what to do with my left arm so I could film him, not the kids building a sandcastle a few feet away.

I reached my left arm across the front of my body, rested my hand on my right shoulder, and pointed the watch directly at Burk.

"How about you change, and we go get something to drink?" He stared at me then reached over and kissed me on the cheek.

I pulled back and my arm dropped.

"Sorry, but you're so appealing."

"Something cold to drink sounds fine. Need to keep it non-alcoholic," I told him, trying to recover from the unexpected kiss. "I'll be right back." I climbed to my feet, picked up the swim bag Lena had lent me and walked to the changing rooms. I clicked off the watch.

When I was dressed and walking back on the beach, I saw Burk standing in the parking lot next to his bike.

"Where should I meet you?" I asked.

"Is your car here?"

"Yes."

"I'll ride up the hill and leave my bike at the house. Here's the address. You can pick me up there. Do you mind driving?"

"No. Not at all."

This is good. One step closer to getting inside.

I reached the house before Burk, so I glided into the pull-off that I had stopped at a few nights ago opposite the dwelling. I climbed out of my car and stood by the large electric gate until he arrived. That long, steep, windy hill had no effect on him. No huffing, puffing, not one bead of sweat. I switched on my camera watch again. I stood close to him as he reached over to the entrance gate and I aimed the watch face at the control box.

"I'll be right out," he said after he punched in the gate code and it slid open.

I walked next to him as he peddled in.

"You can wait here if you'd like." He pointed to a comfortable chaise lounge on the deep green front lawn.

"You mind if I come in? Need to use your ladies' room."

For a second, Burk hesitated. He glanced at the door, then back at me.

"It's kind of an emergency," I said, dancing from one foot to the other, like a four-year-old. "Please."

"Sure. Of course."

He moved ahead of me and opened the large front door painted a rich salmon color. Inside, a couch, a few folding chairs, and a large TV mounted on the wall occupied the living room. The spacious dining room had floor-to-ceiling windows with a spectacular view of the canyon, but nothing else. As I turned around, I caught a glimpse of the kitchen. It had nothing on the counters but a takeout bag.

"This place is empty. Do you really live here?"

"The restroom is down that hall."

Four doors, all closed, lined the hallway. Burk took the steps in the kitchen that led downstairs. When he was safely out of sight, I opened the first door to a spacious bedroom with a walk-in closet. Completely empty. No furniture at all, but blackout curtains covered the windows. Door two led me to the same results: empty room, blackout curtains, no furniture. Door three led to a different scene. I aimed my watch cam at the shelving that lined three walls of the room. Each shelf held various electronic products: cords, batteries, monitors, PCs, a few laptops. All were carefully labeled with a product name and date.

A row of computer books and magazines accumulated dust on the wide window ledge. I aimed the watch and scanned the small library. I picked up one binder after the other that were filled with pages of schematics that meant nothing to me. Then I walked out, switched off the mini cam, closed the door behind me and scooted into the bathroom. It was obviously a guy's bathroom, grimy with dried soap splatters everywhere. Nothing of importance hidden in the medicine cabinet; just a mostly empty bottle of acetaminophen and a small screwdriver. I flushed the toilet, pretended to wash my hands and walked out.

"You might want to put some towels in the bathroom," I suggested, shaking my hands. I walked into the kitchen and found some napkins next to the paper bag which I used to dry my hands. Burk leaned against the refrigerator. He had changed from his black bike shorts and multicolored skintight jersey to a pair of jeans, a deep green polo shirt, and flip-flops.

"Sorry about that. We're not equipped for company. But how about some freshly squeezed orange juice? My roommate makes it every morning."

"Sounds delicious, right now. So thirsty. Probably from swimming."

Burk handed me a red Solo cup full of OJ, like we were at a frat party. Boys.

"Thank you." I walked over and took it from him. He grinned at me.

"What?" was all I could manage between gulps.

He shrugged. "Nothing. You look pretty at the moment, especially with that damp beachy hair."

"Did you say bitchy hair?"

"Beachy. You know, like you just came out of the water at a beach. Isn't that what you girls call it?" He walked over to the front door and opened it. He was fidgeting.

Smiling, I wandered around the kitchen to find a trash can for the plastic cup. A stiff, brown grocery bag did double duty as the waste bin. I took aim at the bag, tossed the cup and missed. When I walked a little closer, stooping to pick up the cup and drop it in, I noticed something shiny at the bottom. A beer cap from Coyote Ridge. I took the napkins I used to dry my hands, leaned over and picked it up. Burk called to me as he walked out the front door.

"Just leave the cup on the counter. I'll take care of it later."

"Need to clean up. That's what my mother taught me. 'You make a mess. You clean it up.'" I pretended to fuss around the counter and the makeshift trash can, searching for other bottle caps. Nothing. I stuck the one I'd found in my pocket.

"Ok, ready to go." As I walked over to him, I tapped my chin, then pointed at him.

"Some kind of cream. On your chin," I said. "Right there." I stood close to him now. With my other hand, I wiped it away. He rubbed his chin and smiled. He leaned toward me, but I walked past him, outside to my car. He followed me, rubbing the dirt off my back window with his hand while he waited for me to unlock the car. He didn't try to hide his expression.

"Only thing I can afford right now," I explained as I opened my door, climbed in and reached across to open his.

"Roll-down windows. I didn't think they existed anymore," he said as he brushed the sand from the passenger side seat. He took the towel draped over the seatback, folded it, and put it in the back. I never thought about the appearance of my car, but seeing it now, through his eyes, made me cringe. It was out-of-date, no style or pizzazz, filthy; a car he would never be seen in, if he had a choice. For the first time in a while, I was reminded that I didn't quite measure up to the standards of Marin County. I turned the key, checked the rearview mirror and pulled out.

"Well," he said, "At least it runs."

"Hey, don't patronize my car." With that, I pushed down on the accelerator and sent gravel flying out behind me. The car surged ahead, hugging the corners of the narrow road as it tore down the windy hill.

About ten minutes later, I pointed to an ice cream shop with tables outside. He shook his head. "Down the street. Pull in here."

He pointed to the parking lot of a local bar, a nice local bar, but still.

"I don't drink anymore. I thought I told you that. I was thinking of a smoothie or a glass of lemonade. Besides, I'm not feeling too well. I'm getting a headache and feeling a little dizzy."

"You need something to drink and eat. This is the spot. Great burgers."

"I'm not sure this is a good idea." The back of my neck started to burn.

"Come on. You've been swimming. You need sustenance."

I did get headaches and lightheaded when I hadn't eaten for a while. But this was different. I wanted water, gallons of water. And my neck burned as hot as the sun.

I climbed out of the car, feeling woozy. Burk was watching me intently. It made me nervous.

"I need healthy food … and water, a lot of water. Maybe I should just go home. Sorry, but I don't think I should go in there. I don't feel good."

I leaned against the car, let my head hang forward and closed my eyes. I knew that feeling creeping up the back of my neck. I was going to pass out if I didn't sit down.

"Of course, Trisha. I didn't mean to push you. The guys in the house come here all the time. The food is great. I bet the chef would whip you up a smoothie or a salad or something. Just give it a try. It's an okay place."

Why was he pressuring me? The sun weighed down my shoulders and my knees began to buckle.

"Not for me." I opened the car door and almost fell in. I fished out a water bottle from under the seat and took a long drink. It did nothing. Burk walked over to the car and rested both arms on the roof.

"You don't look well. You shouldn't drive. Come on, you're only a few feet from an ice-cold drink. I know it'll help."

"Can you get a ride home?" I asked.

"Sure, but … let me drive you," he said.

What's happening to me? My body felt as though it was disintegrating. I never felt so weird before. I didn't care if Burk was the key to the house on the hill and some enormous computer plot. It wasn't worth it. I had to get away.

"I'm leaving."

With that, I inched away from the curb and drove down the two-lane street, trying desperately to stay awake. My eyes closed and my head dipped down to my chest. I managed to glance up. The car in front of me morphed into two cars. I saw two traffic lights hanging above me. Both were green. Or was it one? I couldn't be sure. So tired. Two of everything. Needed to close my eyes. An entrance to a parking lot for a grocery store appeared. The concrete roadway grew bigger then smaller. I drove over the curb into the lot, toward a parking space under a tree and passed out.

"Ma'am wake up. You can't sleep here."

I heard the voice, but it was so far away. I opened one eye. A policeman and his partner waited off to the side of the car.

"Ma'am, you have to move your car. You can't sleep here."

"You have a twin," I said.

"Ma'am, please get out of the car."

"I don't think I can."

"Get out of the car, now."

I put my hand on the door handle, pushed it down and the door opened. I swung my feet around and touched the pavement. I peered up at the policeman ... ah, police*men*. How sweet. So young. They had brown hair like mine. I smiled at both, stood up and collapsed into darkness.

CHAPTER 24

I woke up in Mercy Marin Hospital almost six hours later. My stomach was churning and my body trembled. Lena stood at the window, talking quietly on her phone. Dad sat at the foot of my bed, staring at me.

"She's awake. Lee, your sister's awake."

"Don't talk so loud, Dad. It hurts my head." I closed my eyes again. "Oh," I moaned and vomited into the plastic bucket sitting on the bedside table.

"Trisha, it's me, Lena." She handed me a napkin to wipe my mouth.

"I know who you are," I mumbled, eyes closed. It was an effort to open them, but I managed it. Both Dad and Lena stood next to the bed, so close, they were almost in there with me.

"Where am I?"

I studied my surroundings. Wires and tubes extended from multiple parts of my body. "Am I in a hospital? What happened? Did I pass out while I was swimming?"

I tried to sit up. "Oh no," and I threw up again. And again.

"Was I in the water?" I mumbled.

"No," said Lena. "You were in Tarantino's parking lot."

"What was I doing there?"

"That's what I was going to ask you."

I laid back down. I couldn't recall what happened. Then, an image emerged from my spinning mind.

"I was so tired. I couldn't keep my eyes open. I remember seeing two of everything and wanted to get off the street. I saw twin policemen and now I'm here."

"Trishy, is that all you can remember?" asked Dad.

"Have a sip of water, sis," Lena urged, holding a cup in her hand.

"No, the thought of it makes my stomach—" and I hurled again.

"An ice chip?" begged Lena. I turned away from her.

The faces of my family were portraits of concern.

"I don't remember much else."

"And that's normal, considering what you ingested," agreed Dr. T as he walked into the hospital room with another doctor.

"What?" asked Lena and my father together.

"I'm Dr. Patel," announced the woman. She had large dark eyes behind bright, pink-framed glasses. "We found Rohypnol in your system."

"From the reservoir?" I asked.

Dad and Lena glanced at each other. "No," they both said.

"Do you remember taking anything? Anything at all?" asked Dr. Patel.

"No."

"Did you have anything to drink?"

"I had a glass of orange juice and some water. I'm confused. I did go swimming, right?"

"This has nothing to do with swimming or the water in the reservoir."

"Rohypnol, often called Ruffies, is a date rape drug," informed Dr. Patel. "It acts like a tranquilizer and is easily ten times stronger than Valium."

Everyone stared at me.

"Was I raped? I don't remember having sex. Did I have sex?" I asked Dr. Patel.

"No, you weren't. Thank goodness. From what the police told us, they found you passed out in your car at—

"Tarantino's," I said.

"You remember that?" the doctor asked me.

"No. But, my sister just told me."

"Terrell, do you agree?"

"Yes, I saw the results of your blood tests. You were definitely drugged," said Dr. T.

"I want to go home. I have to pick up my car." I tried to swing my legs over the side of the hospital bed and immediately began to throw up. I took a breath and looked at my distressed family. My body trembled.

"I can't stop throwing up," I managed to say between episodes.

"This isn't an uncommon reaction to the drug," said Dr. Patel. "We'll give you something to settle your stomach and we've already started pumping fluids into your body. You are severely dehydrated."

"I have to pick up my car," I said as my head fell back on the pillow.

"We have it," said Dr. T. "It's parked in front of Earl's house, like always."

"Depending how your recovery goes, you might be here for a day or two. By then, the drug should be out of your system, and you should be able to remember more. The police want to talk to you when you feel up to it."

"More police," I said as my eyes closed. Before I drifted off, I tried to search through the fog that blanketed my mind for what happened. I remembered swimming, getting out of the water, walking to my towel … and Burk. I said his name aloud.

"What? Irk? Jerk? What are you saying, Trisha?" asked Dad. "Lena, get off your phone. Trish said something. It might have been 'hurt.' Do you hurt, Trishy?"

"No, Dad. Burk. She said 'Burk.' I bet he was the guy who did this to her."

I spent the next two nights in the hospital, drifting in and out of sleep.

"Ooo, I feel terrible. My head hurts," I said to the room when I woke up. Dad snored lightly, curled up in the empty hospital bed next to mine.

A nurse walked through the door. "Good to see you up. Want some breakfast?"

"No food. Please don't mention food." But for the first time in three days, my stomach stayed calm.

She glanced at the monitors and changed a clear saline bag that had dripped its last drops.

"Hey, Dad, wake up."

I picked up an extra pillow from my bed and feebly threw it at him.

"What? What?" Dad scanned the room wildly. His gaze settled on me. "Trisha! How are you feeling?"

"I have a headache and I feel weak."

"You sound much better. Do you remember what happened?"

"It's starting to come back, bit by bit. I want to go home."

"They do hospital rounds at 8:30. Maybe your doctor can release you then," said Dad.

It took a few more hours, but I was back at Earl's house before noon. Had I been gone for only three days? It seemed like a month. For the first time, this place felt like home. I settled down as soon as I walked in the door, overjoyed to be there. Earl and Dad treated me very gently. No probing questions, no demands for answers. They plied me with, chicken soup and saltines and a mountain of pillows. I drifted into an erratic dream filled with policemen, orange groves and anonymous swimmers. When I woke, there was a small glass of apple juice sitting on the table. I stared at the amber liquid and my heart started to pound. My hands trembled when I picked it up. Drops of juice flew everywhere. I couldn't drink it. I couldn't drink anything I didn't pour for myself. I placed the glass carefully on the floor so it was out of sight.

My phone buzzed with a text from Lena.

Don't tell anybody anything yet. I want to hear.

I scrolled down my messages. Nothing except some frantic texts from Lena a few days ago when she tried to locate me. I wandered unsteadily out to the deck, studying the trees in front of me. I had thought I was seriously dehydrated—it never occurred to me I'd been drugged. I'm not a stranger to fainting, so I recognized the signs. But this had been different. Drinking plenty of water and sitting down always helped in the past, but it had done nothing to improve my condition. But Rohypnol?

In the pile of release papers was a card from Detective Mark Hamilton, Central Marin Police Department. I had met him the year before when I was trying to find out who'd killed Lena's friend. I called and he promised to stop by within the hour.

Twenty minutes later, Lena walked in with baby Tim in a stroller, Detective Hamilton right behind her.

"Well, you're on the road to recovery," my sister said, lifting Little T up and gently putting him on the floor. The Babe came over and started cleaning Tim's face. They both crawled off to another part of the living room. When everyone was settled, I launched into my story. Meeting Burk at the beach. Driving to his house. Going inside to use the restroom. Drinking the orange juice he gave me and driving us both to his local bar.

"And then?" asked Detective Hamilton.

I told him what happened. Everything I could remember until I passed out.

"So, Burk drugged you. It must have been the orange juice," said Lena. "Why did you accept a drink from someone you barely know?"

"Who puts drugs in orange juice?" I asked.

"Why did you ever agree to see him? I thought he creeped you out."

"He's a sicko," said Dad, who paced back and forth as I talked. "I want him arrested!"

The officer glanced at my father, then back at me. "Can you think of any reason he'd do this?" he asked. I didn't want to tell him why I'd gone to Burk's house in the first place, or what had led me there.

I shrugged. "I barely know him."

"Anything else you remember?"

I bit my bottom lip, closed my eyes, then opened them.

"No. Sorry."

"I say we find this Burk and get some answers," demanded Lena. She was also pacing around the room, ready for action.

"Lee, how did you know where I was?"

"Remember when you asked me to track your phone? Well, I never turned the app off. I found you in Tarantino's parking lot. You never go there, ever. You always say it's too expensive. After two hours went by and your car hadn't moved, I knew something was wrong, so I drove over. That's when I saw the police and the ambulance."

"Your sister contacted everyone," said Dad.

"The police didn't say very much, only that you were being taken to the hospital. I wasn't very nice to them," Lena said.

Office Hamilton stood up. I gave him all the information I knew about Burk: a description, his phone number, his address. He said he would drop by his house and the bar on the way to the station, then left. Earl and Dad, reassured that I was fine, left for China Camp. It was just me, Lena, The Babe, and Timmy.

"That man was going to rape you."

"I'm not so sure about that. If that was his plan, why take me out of the house? Kidnap me, maybe."

"You've got to be kidding. Is there a reason to kidnap you?"

I reached into my pocket and pulled out the Coyote Ridge beer bottle top and put it on the couch beside me.

"What does this have to do with anything?"

I picked up the bottle top and tossed it at her. "Check this out."

Lena gave it a quick once-over. "Ok."

"This is from a beer bottle like the ones that are in Earl's refrigerator. The caps carry micro mini memory cards back and forth. You know all this."

"Yeah. But why would Burk have one? I don't know, Trisha. It's called the date rape drug for a reason. Although I don't know why he thought he needed it … just a few days ago you were ready to lay it all out on the line for him."

"Was not."

"Were, too."

"A momentary lapse of judgment. But I changed my mind."

"You change your mind so much; I never know what you're thinking."

"That's not true. Give me the cap back. I want to see something."

Lena tossed over the cap and I checked the inside.

"There's nothing here."

For a second, I closed my eyes, trying to remember what Ty had said about the bottle caps. He'd never mentioned who the caps, meaning the mini chips, were meant for. Just that some anonymous computer company wanted information. Jason Chang, the beer maker, had mentioned that a Burk was a partner in the business. It was presumably this Burk, so finding a bottle cap in his trash would make sense. But it all seemed a little strange in a way I couldn't quite put my finger on.

"Lena, listen to this." I told her the theory percolating in my mind.

"So, you're saying that the cap went from Earl's to the beer making house off Ocean Beach, then ended up at Burk's house?"

"I think so. If he had a chance to view the video, he would know that his house was under surveillance. If he traced the chip back to Earl, that might be why he wanted to kidnap me. Maybe he—they?—wanted to trade me for information."

"The cold war comes to Marin," mocked Lena, scooping up Timmy who had fallen asleep next to The Babe. "Keep thinking. You'll figure it out. I've got to go. Maybe you shouldn't go to work tonight. Stay home. Take it easy."

"That's the plan. I don't think I could handle standing for six hours."

Lena draped the sleeping baby over one shoulder and the diaper bag over the other.

"Thanks for finding me. I have a feeling I would be in jail or worse if I hadn't blacked out and you hadn't found me."

"I could tell something was wrong. You never liked that store. You don't even like to park in their lot. How come?"

I didn't want to go into the story now. It brought back an unfortunate incident that happened nearly twenty-five years earlier. It still bothered me.

"Seriously, sis. Why don't you like Tarantino's?"

"If I tell you, promise not to tell Dad?"

Lena put the diaper bag down on the floor, shifted Timmy to the other shoulder. "Talk."

"It was my favorite store at one time. When I was eighteen, nineteen,

I could shoplift to my heart's desire there. No one bothered to notice. It was just you and me then, and we needed the food. I hadn't figured out the financial aid system in the county. Anyway, one day they caught me with a pint of ice cream, a package of hot dogs and a head of lettuce. They said they wouldn't call the police if I never stepped foot in the store again. So I haven't."

"I didn't know that."

"Well, now you do."

"You were getting food for us."

"Yeah. This store had the best produce. You know, the freshest."

"I get it. Thanks for doing that," said Lena.

"I remember the ice cream flavor. My favorite—chocolate with little marshmallows and a ribbon of chocolate syrup."

"I don't know what to say. You risked going to jail to keep us fed. I never knew," said Lena, staring at me.

"We had to eat," I rationalized. "And if I had to … ah … liberate a little produce, I wanted it to be the best I could find."

Lena walked over to me, bent down and kissed me on the cheek.

"Thank you for taking care of me."

CHAPTER 25

A few days later I headed back to the ballpark. Across from Oracle Park, the wind rolled down the Second and Third Street hills, the damp gray fog tumbling after it. The blasts of air picked up newspapers and street trash and forced them into little cyclones outside the ballpark.

"Heavenly Jesus, it is chilly out here. Reminds me of Candlestick," said Charlee Ann as we walked through the employee entrance toward the time clocks. "You weren't working with the Giants when they played there, but it would get so cold and windy, we'd have hot dog wrappers flying all over the place."

"You have fog in your hair," I said as I examined her short, tight brownish-red curls. Drops of moisture clung to each strand, like a glittering hair net. She patted her hair.

"Girl, you're a poet."

I had brought a scarf with black and orange stripes, heavy ski gloves and warm black ski tights to wear under my khakis, but I had a feeling it wouldn't be enough. Contrary to what the rest of the country thought, California, especially Northern California, lacked sunshine and warmth, especially in the summer.

We went our separate ways after checking in; Charlee Ann walked into the crowded breakroom to put her lunch in the refrigerator and I turned into the locker room. I had a killer headache. *Probably should have stayed home.* I sat down on the wooden bench and put my face in my hands.

"Did you hear that Martinez broke his little toe? Out for six weeks, at least," said an employee one row of lockers behind me.

"Freak accident, is what they're saying."

"The guy's a hothead. Bet he kicked something after the game,"

GLENDA CARROLL

laughed another woman.

"No, I heard he tripped and slammed his foot into a curb. Bet the manager's not happy with that," said the employee.

Charlee Ann walked into the locker room and sat down beside me. I didn't move. "You okay?" she asked. "Not sick, are you?"

"No, it's just that—"

"You're investigating again, aren't you? I know that gleam in your eye. It's like you can't tell the time of day. Lost in your thoughts."

I tried to smile.

"I thought you gave that up." She reached over to straighten my collar.

"Something happened to me. Someone put something in my drink. Drugged me. My head still hurts. And sometimes I can't breathe."

"Say what? You tellin' the truth?"

"Unfortunately, yes."

"You just find the bad ones, is what I know. What happened to that nice guy you were seeing? Jon, right?"

"We had a falling out." I bit my lip to keep from crying.

"Bet he never slipped anything in your drink now, did he? I got to get to my station, but you take care. Don't be drinking anything but what you get for yourself."

"Yes, mother," I said, drawing out the word. Chuckling, I shut the locker with a clang and closed the lock. "You don't have to worry. I'm sticking to water fountains."

Our pitching ace stood tall on the mound, mowing down the batters. The flags over Triples Alley stretched out like they were dipped in starch. The wind blew hard, straight from the batter's box to the outfield. The fog thickened as it spread across the field and players appeared and disappeared like ghosts. When the ball dropped out of the mist, outfielders often found themselves in the wrong place with no chance of catching it. Other times, pushed by the wind, the ball exploded off the bat, landing in the bleachers for a home run.

"Tonight, this game depends on the elements," said a fan standing next to me, squinting to see where the ball landed. "It has nothing to do with talent or smarts."

"You're right," I agreed as he walked past me down to his seat, a few rows from the field. The innings passed quickly. Batters up. Batters down. It was already the middle of the seventh and the Giants trailed the visiting team by a run. As the ballpark organist began to play *Take Me Out to the Ball Game*, every baseball fan stood, singing and swaying from side to side.

An older man wearing a leather Giants jacket with patches from all the team's world series and pennant wins stood off to the side of my aisle. He leaned over the last row to talk with his friends.

"You know, the Giants inspired this song."

"When they were in New York?" asked the woman wrapped up in a black Giants sweatshirt and an orange and black blanket.

"Jim, I've heard you tell this story a hundred times," said the man.

"Well, I haven't," said the woman.

"The guy who wrote it was a songwriter in 1908. Never been to a ball game in his life. Name was Jack Norwood. So, he's riding this subway in New York, sees a billboard that says, 'Baseball Today—Polo Grounds.' He gets this inspiration for the song about going to a baseball game. And do you know who was playing at the Polo Grounds? The New York Giants."

By that time, everyone within listening distance was enthralled with the old storyteller and fascinated with the tale of the song.

"Great story," I marveled.

"All true. Check it out. You'll see for yourself."

The bottom of the seventh inning started and the old timer disappeared into the moving crowd behind me. An inning later, the visiting team's mid-reliever dropped a ball right in the zone and the batter hit it into McCovey Cove. That was it. Two runs scored. The game concluded with a win in the Giants column. Fans streamed up the steps on their way to the ballpark exit giving me high fives as they passed.

It took another twenty minutes to completely empty the ballpark. Only employees remained and we were about to start the sweep. Each of us took a row and walked the curve of the stands, from one end of the ballpark to the other searching for items people had left behind. In the past, I've found sunglasses, umbrellas, jackets, even cell phones. They all ended up at Lost and Found.

"Everyone ready?" asked my supervisor standing in the aisle, four rows closer to the field. With that, we moved forward, stepping around leftover garlic fries, peanut shells, and hot dog wrappers, the usual mess found at any ballpark following a game. The ballpark cleaning crew would move in once we were done to power wash the stands. Halfway through, the first set of lights high above the field switched off.

Out of habit, I glanced at my phone and clicked on my email. No emails popped up. Instead, across the screen diagonally, the words 'unknown user' popped up.

"Of course, you know the user. It's me," I corrected the cell.

"Who are you talking to?" asked a stocky co-worker one row over.

I shook my head and continued walking, scanning the cupholders, the seats and the concrete floor. We stopped at the end of our rows. I volunteered to take what had been found—a Giant's ballcap, a grocery tote bag in orange and black, and a green thermos—down to the Promenade level to Lost and Found.

"It's all yours," said the supervisor. "Thanks, everyone. See you next time."

After I dropped off the forgotten items, I walked over to the seats and glanced from one end of the cavernous ballpark to the other. The massive scoreboard, now dark, stared down at the empty baseball diamond. Circling the bleachers, diving seagulls bombarded the stands, escaping with tidbits of leftover fries and hotdogs. Below. the grounds crew hosed down the field while security stood in the exits and maintenance workers emptied the endless number of recycling bins. I glanced at my phone. My email said, "Unknown User." I clicked on Settings and then clicked on "Sign Out." The page went blank. I remembered Lena once saying that a forced restart would take care of some glitches in a phone's underpinnings. I pressed and quickly released the volume up button. Then did the same with the volume down button. I held down the side button and my breath at the same time. The phone logo appeared and my phone hitchhiker was gone. *What a tech genius.*

I headed for the elevator to go down to the locker room. Employees deep in discussion about the game hung around the time clock. I had carpooled into the park with some co-workers and they waited for me.

"Trisha, let's go."

"Almost ready. Need to stop at my locker and check out."

Fifteen minutes later, I sat in the back seat of the car, my hand in my pocket clutching my cell phone. I pulled it out, turned it back on and clicked on my email. My email messages had returned.

"Did you ever have your phone say, "Unknown user" when you checked your email and then your messages were gone?" I asked my three colleagues.

There was a chorus of no's and a few snide remarks about what a techno birdbrain I was.

"You should change your password," said one of my co-workers.

"I tried a forced restart and it worked."

"A forced what?" said the woman sitting next to me.

"Never mind. Things like this happen with technology," I said smugly.

"Only to you," giggled the carpool driver.

CHAPTER 26

"Trisha, wake up. The police are here to see you," yelled Dad from outside.

Great. Now the whole neighborhood knows.

I stumbled out of bed, walked onto the deck and saw Dad talkin'' with Detective Hamilton, the officer who'd questioned me before. Their conversation grew more animated; I heard Dad say, "not safe." If he was talking about me, I had to agree with him. I was not safe. Not anymore.

"Be right there." I waved at my father and the officer. They barely noticed me. I threw on a pair of black tights, a wrinkled Giants tee shirt, slipped into some flip-flops and went downstairs.

"Ms. Carson, there seems to be a mix-up," said Det. Hamilton. "The address you gave me for this man named Burk isn't valid. He doesn't live there. In fact, when I stopped by, I found a woman and a little boy, a toddler. She mentioned that she and her husband had been there for almost two years."

"That can't be. I was in that house two days ago. There was no family there. At all. The place was bare except for a few folding chairs and a flat-screen TV." The detective looked at me skeptically. "I'll show you. I have proof."

Detective Hamilton and Dad followed me up the stairs, into my bedroom and waited patiently as I connected Uly's video watch to my computer. I clicked on the icon and the interior of Burk's house, the almost empty interior, appeared on the screen.

"See. No family. No kids. No toys."

"And you shot this?"

"Yes," I responded.

"When?"

"Right before I was drugged."

"You want to tell me why you were filming this guy's house?"

When I just stared back at him in silence, he sighed and shook his head.

"Ok, tell me the address again. Maybe I wrote it down wrong." The officer took out a small notebook and pen and waited expectantly.

"I have a better idea," I said.

I sat in the backseat of the patrol car as we drove over the winding hill to the large house behind the sliding gate. The officer pulled up and pressed the button by the speaker and a female voice answered, "May I help you?"

"This is Officer Mark Hamilton from the Central Marin Police Department. I'd like to speak with—" he paused for a moment, checked his small notebook and continued, "Mrs. Norcastle."

"Mrs. Norcastle is out for the rest of the day. I'll tell her that you were here."

"Ma'am, please open the gate." It clicked open and the officer walked briskly up to the front door, me following behind like his shadow. A tiny round woman, not more than five feet tall, her dark hair pulled straight back in a severe ponytail, opened the door.

"Can I help you? I'm the housekeeper."

He handed her a card. "Please ask Mrs. Norcastle to call me when she gets back."

The little woman nodded. "I will." She peered down at the card but made no move to go back inside the house.

Det. Hamilton turned back toward the gate and started walking, leaving me standing there. I stretched to one side, trying to peek over the housekeeper's head into the house. The officer glanced back and gestured at his patrol car. Reluctantly, I followed him. We stopped next to the passenger side door.

"That doesn't make sense," I said. "Did you see her and the little boy?"

"Yes, I did. In fact, she invited me in. The house was furnished, toys everywhere. What I would expect in a house with a small child."

"I don't believe it. You saw the video. Can we, maybe, go inside?"

"Ms. Carson, we have no reason to bother this family. Maybe it's a different house, further up or down the road. You made a mistake. Easy enough to do."

I checked across the street and saw the pull-off where I had parked. The entrance to the path I'd walked down when I first saw Earl's drone. Same gate. Same keypad. Same house. There was no possible way I was wrong.

"This is the house. No mistake. You need to go in. Check the basement. They've got to be hiding something."

"I'll give you a ride home," he said instead. He opened my door, and I climbed in reluctantly. For a fleeting moment, he glanced at me through the car window with a puzzled expression on his face. "Ms. Carson, it's easy to mix up houses, addresses. With everything you've been through in the past few days, it would be understandable."

I wanted to scream "don't patronize me" but I managed to keep my mouth shut. "This is the house. I'm sure of it."

Then he walked to the driver's side, slid in and started up the car. We turned around and headed back over the hill to Earl's. The trip took no longer than fifteen minutes, but it felt like an eternity. I sat in silence the whole way, my arms crossed, lips pursed, listening to the chatter on the police radio and trying to figure out how Burk had managed it.

When we pulled up at Earl's, the cop leaned over and said, "We're not giving up, Ms. Carson. We'll just have to approach this another way."

"This is insane. I was there. In that house. With him," I said, through clenched teeth. I started to shake. I didn't know how to make him believe me.

I climbed out of the cop car and headed for the front steps. I turned one last time toward the policeman. "He lives or works there. I know it," I almost yelled.

"You were drugged, Ms. Carson."

"Not before. After."

"We will find him," the cop said as he drove off.

I clomped up the steps.

"I know what I saw," I muttered to myself. The drug might have messed with my memory, but the video ... that didn't lie."

Dad sat on the deck, enjoying a cup of coffee.

"You really think that Earl and Tyler are spying on that house?" he asked.

"I was sure of it. But based on what I just saw ... I don't know, Dad. The cop didn't even ask to go in. I know he thinks I'm looney tunes."

"To be fair, Trisha, if I heard this story from anyone else, I wouldn't believe it, either. You said before that Earl was in some kind of danger. Did you mention that to the detective? Tell him what you know?"

"No. I didn't. Didn't want Tyler or Earl getting in trouble before I can figure out what's happening. And anyway, can you imagine what he would have thought if I started to spout off about bottle caps, corporate espionage and ransomware? That Earl was in danger? I have no proof. I don't even know who these people are!"

"You have a point," Dad acknowledged. "Just to make it clear, Earl hasn't said anything to me about Tyler."

I flopped down in a chair next to him and it slid back about a foot.

"Trish—"

"I was just there ... what? A day or two ago? I know what I saw then and I know what I saw when I walked behind that house."

"You walked where?"

"It was nothing."

"Trisha."

"One night last week, while walking The Babe, we climbed up a trail from the canyon. We happened to go right by the house. A whole lot of activity going on, men walking in and out, and I saw one of Earl's quadcopters hovering around. I'm sure of it."

Dad took a long sip of his coffee, glanced out at La Cruz Canyon and shook his head.

"You just happened to find yourself behind this house while walking the dog."

I bit my lip and nodded.

"I can always tell when you're lying."

"I'm not lying."

"You hide your hands. Sometimes in pockets, sometimes when you cross your arms and sometimes, like now, you hide them behind your back."

I unclasped my hands from behind my back and rested them on my hips.

"I do not."

Dad shook his head. "Girl, I don't want you to get hurt. That's all I'm saying. I've been around you enough to know you'll go back there and check the house out again by yourself. Right?"

I wanted to say no. But I couldn't.

"I guess," I said.

"Trisha, do you know what the word 'dangerous' means? It means harmful. Risky. Not a good idea."

"I understand. I do. But this man, Burk, stalked me, tried to seduce me, and when that didn't work, he drugged me. I need to know why,

Dad. I need to figure it out. Because something bad is going to happen if I don't."

My phone pinged when I walked through the doorway of my room. I picked it up.

"I don't believe it." A text message from Burk.

R u ok? Tried to follow but u and car disappeared.

I wanted to respond with the first thought that came to mind, but I stopped myself. Even the Devil didn't use that much profanity in his texts. So, what to say? It had been two days since I'd seen him. I wondered why he'd waited to contact me.

Took you long enough to check.

You drove off.

Was sick.

Tried to help. Water, food, remember?

I didn't respond.

Try again?

Was this guy for real?

NO.

Second chance?

I turned off the ringer and stuck the phone beneath a pillow on the bed. I pulled it out again and clicked on my emails. The 'unknown user' message was back. So much for the hard restart. I noticed that my co-phone mate had a name. When he or she signed on, the name 'Null' appeared at the top of the page. I signed Null out and called into the customer service line for my cell phone carrier. Someone had either hacked into my email or my internet account. I waited … and waited … and waited some more, listening to tinny background music. Twenty minutes passed and the line went dead. I resisted the urge to toss the phone against the wall.

I walked over to my PC and glowered at it. Even with Null watching over my shoulder. I decided to do another search on Burk. A week ago, my probe left me with nothing to read, no photos to inspect. On the login page, I typed in my password, clicked enter, but an error message popped up, telling me it was incorrect. Had I hit the wrong keys? I typed in my password a second time. Same message again. I tried a third time, watching my fingers. A fourth time. It didn't work. A fifth. The error message again. I was locked out. My computer and my phone were not my own.

"Dad," I yelled down the steps. "What's going on with the internet? Can you get into your account? Email? Websites?"

"Haven't tried, Trishy," he called back. "I mostly use my phone. It's not on the same network that you and Earl use. But he's been having trouble with the house phone. His calls are disappearing."

My mouth went dry. I gaped at the screen, then followed the prompts in slow motion to change my password. I checked that it worked. It did. For the second time in a week, I changed a few other passwords while I was at it: my bank, healthcare, car insurance, a few online stores. Better safe than sorry. The curtain of unease began to subside, and I continued my search for Burk. I could find no digital footprint. No Facebook, Twitter, LinkedIn, Instagram, TikTok or Snapchat accounts, no websites under his name. A digital ghost. Super rare, these days. Maybe Burk wasn't his real name. I didn't want to think about that and pushed the idea out of my mind. I typed in the address from the house over the hill, but nothing came up besides an appraisal.

I signed out of my computer and walked over to the deck. The tall redwoods climbed straight up to a crisp blue sky, but I barely saw their quiet beauty. My mind swirled, searching for the bits and pieces that would put this whole thing together. Getting an idea, I went back to the computer and attempted to sign on. But in that short bit of time, my password had been changed again. I couldn't believe what I was seeing.

I clicked on the 'forgot my password' button, responded to the email and then created a new password so I could log on again. My stomach tied itself in knots. Who controlled my computer? Not me, that's for sure. Ten minutes later, the screen blinked and went black for a nano-second. When the sign-in page popped back up, I put in the new-new password. It didn't work. Then I signed off and shut the computer down. Unplugged everything from the wall, including the modem, which I reset. Then I waited, pacing around the bedroom for five minutes. I stopped in front of the refrigerator.

"You're not behind this are you, Frida?"

"There is nothing behind me," answered Frida.

"Technology sucks. Hey, Earl," I yelled out from my room.

"What's up?" he called back from downstairs.

"I'm pretty sure I have a hacker on my computer. He keeps changing my password. What do I do?"

"Run a malware scan. Should get rid of any interlopers. I'll send you a link for a free one."

"I'm having trouble with my phone, too. Someone named "Null" keeps signing off my emails and then using it for his messages. Do you think it's someone from the cable company? My email both on the cell and my computer, plus the internet goes through them."

"Couldn't tell you for sure, but they're probably connected, Trish. Will send a link to get rid of them on your mobile. Change your password."

"That's what I've been doing for the last hour."

Back at the computer, I began attaching and plugging everything back in. I turned it on, held my breath, and tried to sign into my account. It worked! I threw my head back and let out a yelp. Trisha-one. Null-zero, if it was Null.

"Goodbye, Null," I chuckled as I clicked on the link Earl had sent me. The malware scans would now destroy any gremlins my hacker had placed in the underpinnings of my phone and computer.

CHAPTER 27

I wanted to meet Lena and baby T at the reservoir for a swim, but I didn't think that made sense. There was a good chance Burk would find us. And, if truth be told, the idea had triggered my open water anxiety. The mere thought bumped up my heartbeat and blood pressure. I didn't need that hassle, so I changed the location to the pool. We'd take turns swimming and watching the baby. Even Little T got his water fix in the baby pool, which he loved.

I sat on the edge of the pool, dangling my feet in the water. The sun warmed my back and blotted out my worries.

"Cookie, you're becoming a regular these days," said the gray-hair octogenarian who paddled back and forth. "Come. Swim with me. We'll share the lane."

It was an invitation I couldn't resist. Adults had been given the pool for the next hour. Then, the kids would be back for family time and there wouldn't be room to swim laps. My silver-haired friend stayed on his side of the wide lane while I hugged the lane line and stayed out of his way. What a sweetheart he was. Always watching out for me, always encouraging me to stay longer, swim a few more laps.

I stopped at the other end and stood in waist-deep water, my head back, enjoying the sun sinking into every line and crease on my face.

"Won't be long now," my partner said as he swam up next to me.

"Won't be long for what?"

"Till you go off and join that Masters swim group with your sister. I know it."

"I don't think so. This is fine for me. I'm not interested in competing."

"Didn't you swim in an open water race not so long ago?"

"How did you hear that?"

He shrugged. "Pool gossip."

"Well, I did. But it was only a mile. And I was scared the whole time."

"But you did it?"

"I did."

"So, you're going to go off and join that Masters swim group. That's what I think."

"Not in my future. Maybe you should join?" I skimmed my hands over the top of the water and splashed him.

"Now you stop that," he grumbled as I pushed off and swam to the other end. Watching the arms and legs of swimmers underwater always amused me. So many different strokes, different kicks, but they all moved the swimmer down the pool. My thirty minutes flew by.

"Lena," I yelled, waving to her as she sat by the edge of the children's pool. She waved back. "You're next." I pointed to the locker room. "Going to change."

Out of my wet swimsuit and in dry clothes, I strolled over to Lena who squinted into the sun as she looked up at me.

"He's all yours," she said as she grabbed her black cap and amber-tinted goggles. "Oh, and he's getting tired. Good luck." She took the shortest route toward a middle lane.

A little girl about eighteen months old managed to splash T and send him into a very vocal tailspin. I picked him up, wrapped him in a towel and set him in his stroller. We walked to a small picnic table in the shade. He fell asleep as soon as the stroller moved.

I pulled out my phone. Null was back. The malware scan on my phone didn't work and his emails remained annoyingly private. Since I paid the bills, I didn't need permission to see what he wrote. I signed the shadowy user out. Then I waited. Fifteen minutes later, the ghost in my phone returned.

Null knew when I signed him off and as abruptly as Null appeared, he disappeared. Then two messages popped up from my savings bank. I kept the small inheritance my mother left me in this bank. One alerted me that the user made a purchase from a cell phone and asked if I knew about it. The second thanked me for signing up for bill pay. I'd never done that. In fact, all I ever did in this account was deposit money. Null had stepped over the line. No one had the right to touch what little money I had.

I called the bank immediately and told them what was happening.

They bumped me up to the head security honcho who instantly shut down the whole account. Now, a highly secure verbal password would be needed to access the account. Passwords and accounts. I'd changed half a dozen usernames and passwords on several important accounts just a few hours before. Using my computer. Null had to know when those changes happened, had to have seen them happening. It dawned on me that nothing I did on my computer was safe. My hacker knew all about my accounts and my private information. Someone was watching me and everything I did on both my computer and cell phone.

I dug into Timmy's baby bag tucked into a basket on the back of the stroller and pulled out Lena's laptop. I went to my cable account, typed in my latest new password, and held my breath. Not surprisingly, it didn't work.

I tried to keep my panic at bay. But I almost lost it when the sign-in page materialized in Spanish. Null must have changed the language preference. Heat rose through my chest into my neck and face. My stomach began to cramp up. I scurried over to Lena's lane, pushing Timmy, who remained blessedly asleep. When she came to the end of the lane, I stopped her.

"You have to get out. We need to leave right now. My computer, my cell phone, all my accounts have been compromised. I have to go see Uly."

My gray-haired swimmer friend stopped when he heard my panic. "Cookie, until this is figured out, call or go to the websites of the major credit agencies and put a freeze on your accounts."

"Can't this wait?" my sister asked. "This is my water time."

"Please."

Lena sighed. "Let me swim a few more laps. By the time you contact the credit card people, I'll be out."

I made the calls and the panic subsided as each entity assured me they'd put a hold on any activity until they heard differently from me. I studied the computer, trying to see the corrupt monster inside. Nervously, I began to type anyway. My latest sign-in information stayed unchanged. I let out a huge breath.

I went to the general cable settings and browsed through the house account. When I clicked on the phone icon, I realized that all calls were being forwarded to a strange phone number. I tried calling it, wondering what I would say if someone picked up, but it went to a mailbox that didn't take messages. I unclicked the forwarding icon and deleted the phone number. Maybe Earl would start getting his calls again.

I touched the envelope icon. My hacker had forwarded all my emails to a Gmail account that definitely wasn't mine. I wrote the address down and unclicked the forwarding button. I sat back and glancing at the pool, not seeing it, trying to figure out what I should do. After a moment, I had it. I knew how to jam the jammer. Just needed to rely on my ineptitude with technology of any kind. All it took were three attempts of putting in phony passwords and the Gmail account slammed shut.

Score another point for me.

CHAPTER 28

"You owe me for this," Lena said as we cruised down the highway toward Uly's office. "Timmy was having a good time. I was having a good time. Could it continue? Noooo. You have something important to do. You're on a mission. How about running a malware scan?"

"I did. I ran one on my phone and computer. Didn't work."

"Did it ever cross your mind that maybe the same freak that drugged you is behind this hacking?"

"Of course. But why involve me? I've got nothing to do with this scheme."

"Well, someone might think you're valuable. Maybe they think you know something and want to know what you know."

"Which is nothing," I said. "I'm hoping Uly can help, if this isn't beneath him, that is."

Lena sat there with her arms crossed, slumped down in the seat. Timmy had drifted off to la-la land in his car seat behind us.

"Sorry to drag you guys with me, but I don't think Uly likes me very much. That's why you have to be there."

"He doesn't like anybody."

"He trusts you. And you talk his language."

"No, I don't. He's in another orbit when it comes to computers and coding and hacking. He has done some things in the past that, if they weren't outright illegal, were, maybe, at best, marginally legal. I'm an amateur in comparison. In fact, now that I think about it, just drive me and Tim home and you can go on your way."

"I need you with me. It will only take a few minutes."

"Turn the car around."

"Please."

"I want to go back to the pool."

"I thought you wanted to go home. It won't be long. I promise."

"After this is over, you have to buy me and Timmy some ice cream."

My phone rang. My health care provider had a message for me in Spanish. I groaned.

"Someone hacked into your health care account? Yeah, maybe we should go to Uly's," agreed Lena.

Silence filled the car as we careened down the highway.

"Slow down," cautioned Lena.

"Hey, I forgot to tell you something about Burk."

"Burk, the drugger? You already told me. The police didn't find him where you said he would be."

"They didn't search hard enough. He's there. I know it."

"Do you think he's hacking your accounts?" asked Lena.

"It's crossed my mind. But why would he? I don't know what he could be trying to find."

I took the exit off the freeway and headed for East Francisco Drive. We passed one car dealership after another.

"So, what's this juicy news that you forgot to tell me?"

"He texted me this morning."

"Seriously?" There was a pause. Then, "What did he say?"

"He asked if I was okay and said that he tried to help me, but I drove off. Which is true. The 'drove off' part, not the 'try to help' part."

"Please tell me you're not taking the blame for your own drugging. Don't you read any of these articles about how abusive people blame the people they're abusing? Convincing them it's all their fault?"

"I'm not taking the blame for anything. Anyway, it sounds like he wants to get together again. I'm thinking yes. It will help me find out what he and his pals are up to."

Lena's eye widened to the size of saucers. She began to sputter.

"That's it. I always knew it. You are crazy. No, with a capital N and a capital O. You were in the hospital… let's see… was it a month ago, a week? No. That nutcase drugged you …"

Her voice reached a crescendo on the word 'nutcase' and woke Timmy who started to fuss.

"See what you did," said Lena.

"Me? You're the one shrieking. It's not my fault this time."

Lena turned in her seat to check on her son who had quieted down and was studying the passing buildings.

"We're here," I said, pulling into a parking spot across the street from

Uly's office.

"I'll stay in the car."

"Lennnaaaaa."

"Oh, all right. Let's get this over with," she agreed reluctantly.

She climbed out of the vehicle and released Timmy from the safety seat while I unpacked his stroller. She fitted him in and hooked him up. Then, we scampered across the street and she pressed the button to Uly's apartment and waved at the security camera.

"It's me… us," she said, waving an arm to indicate Timmy and me. The door unlocked and we walked in.

"I'm back." I nodded to Uly who was standing in the small hallway with the faded rock 'n roll posters. His eyes drooped more than I remembered. His hair hung limp around his shoulders again.

"You're here all the time," I said with a smile.

"I haven't figured out the address for the fake FBI guy yet, if that's what you want," he said.

"No. Something else. I have a hacker. And yes, I ran a malware scan."

"Sometimes they're not powerful enough to destroy whatever's eating away at your electronics," he said.

Uly didn't blow me off. Instead, he sat down at his computer and asked what accounts had been hacked. I directed him to my cable account, and he plugged in my new, new, new, new password. It worked.

"I don't believe it. Null has always changed my password within ten minutes of me coming up with a new super-duper unhackable one."

"The last time you changed it, were you on your own computer?" Uly asked.

"No. On Lena's laptop."

"Well, there you go."

"What does that mean?" I asked.

"Your computer is infected, not the network. More than likely, you clicked on some spyware and it downloaded all its vicious little code to your computer. Once it was in, infecting email on your phone was a piece of cake. They found the email address on your computer," he explained wiggling all ten of his fingers in the air. "They can see everything you're doing. It knows every single little stroke you make."

"And I'm feeding him the information."

Lena sat there, nodding her head.

Uly continued to click around my account on his computer.

"My advice. Go home. Shut down your computer. Unhook the

modem and do all your password changing and online banking from somewhere else. For right now, don't touch your computer."

"That's it?"

"Yep. And change each username and password so that they're all different."

I groaned again.

"Let me tell you something, spyware that infects computers, laptops, tablets, even phones, love names that are all the same. I'm guessing you used the same sign-in names and passwords for all your accounts."

"Pretty much."

"So, if this spyware can decode or find one of your usernames and passwords, it scans your computer. Guess what pops up? All the rest of your accounts with the same information. And you are cooked."

"I get it."

"That's what I do. Always," said Lena. "Or I use an encrypted password developed by my system."

"Whoever is doing the hacking… he's very sophisticated. He knows to act fast because you will figure it out eventually and turn the money spigot off," added Uly.

"Money spigot? What's that?" I asked.

"Your bank accounts, your store credit cards. Maybe Social Security. Should I go on?"

"No. I get it," I said.

Lena and exchanged glances. He had never spoken more than three sentences to us before.

"Thanks, Uly. We can go now."

I glanced at Lena. "I hope you have an extra laptop I can use."

"No, I don't," said Lena.

Uly walked over to his cupboard and pulled out a laptop.

"Here. Use this." He handed it to me. Then, he tilted his head. "I live here," he said.

"What?"

"I'm here all the time because I live here."

"Oh, that's nice," I said.

Lena rolled her eyes and tried not to smile.

Uly sat down and turned back to his monitors, slipped on an expensive pair of earphones and started to nod his head to whatever he was hearing. We took it as our cue to leave.

We crossed the hallway and let ourselves out.

"He might not have liked you before, but I think he does now."

"Come on. Don't start this again."

"He gave you one of his souped-up laptops. He also told you where he lives."

"He told us."

"No, he told you. He likes you and he likes coming to your rescue. I bet he wouldn't do that for anyone else."

"You're being ridiculous," I said, putting the car in gear and heading for the freeway. My phone rang. A Spanish language message from my health care provider had a nutrition tip for me.

Lena gasped and put her hands over her mouth. "Maybe you'd better —"

"Call my doctor first? That's the plan."

CHAPTER 29

I stood in the doorway of my room and scowled at my PC.

"Worthless piece of junk," I hissed at the inanimate object sitting on the table. "I'll never use you again. You're dead to me."

I walked over to the computer and unhooked everything; the keyboard, the mouse, the speakers, the modem, the monitor, the printer and the surge protector. Then I put it in the closet in one messy pile. Overkill, for sure, but I wasn't taking any chances. Uly's laptop was now front and center on my desk.

Just in case the loaner laptop with all my new passwords didn't clean up my cell phone, I called network security again and this time, made it to a live person. After a quick diagnostic of my cell, the support staff found an app that told my hacker whenever I signed on and off. They deleted it and my cell became my own again.

"Better. Much better. Frida, what do I have to drink?"

"Trisha, you have orange juice and milk."

"That's all?"

"Yes. That is all."

"One more thing before you sign off. Have you been talking to anyone?"

"I talk to you," answered the robot.

"Anyone else?"

"I talk to Earl."

"Anyone else?"

"No."

"That's all," I said, and Frida turned herself off.

Would Frida know if a different voice claiming to be me tried to activate her?

In the tiniest, highest voice I could muster, I squeaked, "Frida, who am I?"

"You are Trisha."

"But I don't sound like Trisha," I continued in my baby voice.

"I can see you and I can hear you."

"What? Please repeat that?" I said in my normal voice.

"I can see you and I can hear you."

"That's all Frida." And the robot shut down.

"Earl," I yelled frantically.

"In my office," he called back.

"I know she can hear me, and talk back, but can Frida see me?" I shouted.

"She shouldn't be able to." I heard Earl moving down the hallway to my room.

"What do you mean 'shouldn't be able to'?"

"Well, the cam feature that looks inside the refrigerator can also look out toward the room."

"What? In my bedroom? Why would you do that?"

"Wait. Slow down. I never activated that function. The camera is on downstairs and outside for safety reasons. But I would never use it in your bedroom."

"Frida just said she could see me."

"Can't happen."

"It did. Watch this. Frida," I said in my high-pitched baby voice. "Who am I?"

"You are Trisha."

"But I don't sound like Trisha."

"You are Trisha."

"Can you see me?"

"Yes."

"Are you sure?"

"Yes."

"Can you see anyone else?"

"Yes, I see Earl."

"That's all Frida."

"Told ya," I said to Earl.

Earl went over to the fridge and pushed a few buttons on the console. He took the cover off exposing the silver circuit boards and the tiny camera.

"The video cam feature that controls your room is turned off. There is no way Frida could see you. Must be a malfunction. I've been having some problems with the whole unit. I took it apart the other day. Might be a glitch somewhere."

I stared at the control panel, trying to make sense of the small rectangular board.

"This is AI, right, artificial intelligence? It can't go rogue and turn on other features by itself?"

"It's not that sophisticated. Frida is programmed to do what I tell her. I control her features and I have the room-facing video cam turned off. Come here, I'll show you."

We moved to Earl's study. He walked over to the computer, didn't bother sitting down, leaned over his chair and started typing. He brought up the control panel for the different AI units in the house. He clicked on 'Guest Bedroom' and the robot's main settings for voice and video came up. Earl had clearly toggled the switch to "on."

"No. That's not possible. I turned it off." He sat down and clicked on a few more keys, pulling up the video monitor settings throughout the house. One cam in the downstairs storage room was deactivated.

"That is odd," he mused. "When I check the system, all downstairs monitors were on. Upstairs monitors in the bedrooms were off. Including here, my office and my bedroom. And your bedroom, of course."

"Did you double-check?"

"No, but I clearly made a mistake. I'm so sorry, Trisha."

"Can you tell if the video cams have been turned on and then off again?" I asked.

"Not easily. I would have to do some research, and it would take some time. I know a few people I could talk to, though."

"Would you, please? Could someone—"

Earl held a finger up to his lips. I stopped talking. Whatever was happening in my bedroom, maybe in the house itself, wasn't good. I knew it and so did Earl.

"I'm going to take The Babe for a walk. Want to go with us?" suggested Earl.

"A walk? All right."

"Hey, Babe," Earl called as he left the office and leaned over the staircase. "Walk?"

The Babe paced in circles next to the front door as Earl and I moved down the stairs. Not until we cleared the driveway and headed in the opposite direction of the house over the hill did Earl say anything.

"I'm so sorry you got involved with all … this."

"All what, exactly?"

"This spying business. It's gotten out of hand. Bernard tried to warn me. But it was too late."

"Right now, I'm more interested in why someone is watching me and listening to me in my room. I thought the hacking of my computer was a violation, but the cameras and audio? That's just creepy—really, *really* creepy."

"I think they're related ... the spying and the voyeurism. That's why we're talking out here. I'm almost certain that the house is bugged, including your room."

"You think so?"

"Almost certainly."

"And my refrigerator is doing the looking and the listening?"

"I'm afraid so. But I'm almost positive that whoever is on the other end is interested in me, not you. Well, interested in what I know," clarified Earl.

"Which is what, Earl? You originally said that some high-tech company decided to check out their opponents. But they're really keeping tabs on their own employees, aren't they? Seeing if anyone is fraternizing with the enemy?"

"Exactly. And I'm almost positive they are."

"Is Burk involved?"

"Probably."

We strolled down the path. The afternoon sun filtered through the trees and left shadows on the hard brown dirt. Little white wildflowers reached out from the brush.

"Why are they spying on their employees?"

"I have some thoughts about that."

"Are you going to share?"

Earl turned away.

"You know I'm in danger. I've been drugged because of something you're involved with. Why me? I'm not letting this go. You know I'll figure it out eventually. Can you at least tell me about Tyler's involvement? He's afraid to come home because he thinks he will be followed and that it will be dangerous for you. You're not that hard to find, Earl. If someone can hack into the house's AI system, they obviously know where you are."

"Tyler's been taken advantage of and he feels responsible for what could happen to me. He's trying his hardest to remedy the situation."

"He asked me to get information from that house. But he's been so vague. I'm supposed to locate a sheet of numbers that's inside the house over the hill. Does that mean anything to you?"

"It does."

Earl sat down on a wooden bench that overlooked La Cruz Canyon. He patted the seat next to him. The Babe jumped up and gave him a big lick.

"No, Babe. Down. I want Trisha to sit here." If a dog could mope, then The Babe was moping as he jumped down and sat on Earl's feet.

"Earl. Why is my refrigerator watching me?"

"I want to think on that for a while before I tell you my theory."

"Tyler is worried about you," I said.

Earl smiled and stood up. "He's a good boy but he's in way over his head. Let's walk back to the house. From now on, watch what you say when you're in any of the rooms, but especially your bedroom."

"Will do, but Earl, I have to leave. So sorry. The Babe will keep you company," I said.

I jogged back, ran up to my room for my backpack and studied my refrigerator. A dark shiny lens stared blankly back at me. Since Earl hadn't switched the camera in my bedroom to off, I had to assume that someone was watching. It took all my self-control not to stick my fingers in my ears and stick out my tongue at the camera. I left the open refrigerator console for Earl to deal with.

"Now where did I put my swim bag?"

My plans had nothing to do with swimming, but Frida didn't need to know that. I wanted to research AI without that big white box peering over my shoulder and listening to me talk to myself.

CHAPTER 30

No prob. House is yours, my sister texted when I asked her about stopping by. I didn't mention using her laptop because the response would have been 'forget it.' Her laptop was her moneymaker.

I walked into an empty house. Dr. T and Lena had decided to drive down to the Peninsula, visit his parents and show off the baby. Lena's bedroom with her laptop and three monitors gave the impression of being slightly neater than usual. She'd made the bed. When I stopped to think about it, it was probably Dr. T. Lena wasn't one for tidying up.

I made myself as comfortable as possible between the piles of dirty baby clothes and then did a search on hacking. More than 850 billion posts popped up. *Whoa! Overwhelming. Need to pare it down.* I searched for ransomware attacks. A mere 13 billion posts waited for me to click on them. I wondered if cybercriminals had attacked San Francisco. I typed in ransomware attacks, San Francisco. Only 723,000 results popped up, each more fascinating than the next. Who knew the City by the Bay attracted hackers worldwide? The University of San Francisco Medical School servers had the distinction of being the most recent victim. The hospital paid hackers $1.14 million in bitcoin for a decryption tool to unlock the data. There had been cyberattacks on the San Francisco public transit authority, on NPR, one of the country's largest public media companies, and on an esteemed well-funded art museum. I scrolled through pages and pages of successful attacks. But one in particular stood out because it had brought the city of San Francisco to its knees. Around ten years ago, a disgruntled computer network engineer walked off the job with all the computer codes for the city's network and wouldn't give them back. The government had ground to a standstill. No emails, no access to legal documents, no payroll. Nothing. It had cost

San Francisco millions in lost revenue. I found enough detailed reading material about the incident to keep me busy for the rest of the day.

From what I could tell, Nicholas Eroe Popolare had been a skilled network engineer and administrator who'd been contracted to build a system for the city. He devoted himself to the project and worked tirelessly, making it as perfect as possible by upgrading the equipment, installing new hardware and adding firewalls. As the protector of his creation, he had secure control of the username, password and special code needed to access the system. When the people in charge realized Popolare had locked everyone else out, they demanded his login information. Eroe Popolare walked off the job and disappeared for a few days. He reappeared via a lawyer who negotiated with the city: a hefty settlement for the code. According to the lawyer, the engineer was concerned that the more people who had access to the workings of the system, the greater the chance they would screw it up. He couldn't let that happen. He had to safeguard his system, his grand design. The lawyer proposed the following: The city would not prosecute him, and he would hand over the code pieced together with one hundred and forty-nine letters, numbers and symbols. They jumped at the settlement. They soon found out there was a catch. The city would receive the correct numbers, letters, and symbols, but their order was scrambled.

Three days later, the city fathers hadn't heard back from Popolare or his lawyer. Frantic, they marched in a cadre of Silicon Valley whizz kids to save the day. The complex algorithms they developed didn't work. Eventually, via his lawyer, Eroe Popolare demanded a million dollars for each digit of the code in the correct sequence. The city would deposit the money in an overseas bank, and he would unscramble the code, one piece at a time. He figured through the process of elimination they would come up with the correct order by the time he had about thirty to forty million dollars; enough to disappear forever.

While the city continued to manipulate multiple numbers, letters, and symbols in search of the answer, Eroe Popolare skipped town. His need for peace and quiet led him to the Ligurian or sunny Italian Riviera near Porto Venere where his family lived. While hundreds of posts detailed this outlandish and successful theft, not much personal information about the computer guru appeared. I only learned that he was in his fifties, walked with a slight limp as the result of a cycling accident, and was small in stature. Surprisingly, there were a limited number of photographs of him as an adult.

I wondered if Popolare ever came back to the United States. He had to be a legend in the hacking world. I bet Uly, as well as the guys in the house over the hill, knew all about him. For sure, Earl knew who he was. I went back and scoured the ransomware attack posts, trying to see if there was anything about a refrigerator being hacked. After hours of reading, taking notes and thinking, I thought I'd figured out the technique used, but got no further. I hated to acknowledge it, but my only real connection to that house pointed to Burk. I would have to see him again.

I closed my sister's laptop and headed out the door to my car. What normal person would seek out someone who drugged her? How could I possibly make my interest sound authentic? Inside the car, I sat for a moment and wished I could talk it out with Jon. Along with having a fine logical mind, he would never drug me. He cared about me. Maybe I'd been wrong and everyone else had been right. I pulled out my cell and before I could talk myself out of it, texted him.

Hi. I'm sorry. I miss you. Talk?

I started the car and headed back to Earl's house, thinking about Burk and my next move. But in my mind, all I could see was Jon. I could hear him, "Go to the police." *Well, Jon, I did, and nothing happened.* Maybe I shouldn't have texted him.

"Oooh. This is so confusing," I groaned to the empty car. Then, I stepped on the accelerator and flew down the street.

CHAPTER 31

To me, the privacy and warmth of Earl's house had vanished. Now I lived in a house made of glass. Everything I did or said might be seen or recorded. I dragged myself up the stairs and into my bedroom. Earl had been there and had closed Frida's console on the refrigerator.

Just to make sure, I took one of T's baby photos and anchored it to the fridge, covering the lens. Whoever peered into the other end of that camera couldn't see me. At least for the moment.

I moved out to the deck and sat down. Was it possible Earl had installed some other hidden cameras that he hadn't mentioned? Could there be a bug or tiny cam somewhere else in the room? Paranoia began to take over. I had to find out. I explored the deck, inch by inch. Then I went back into the doorway and my eyes moved across the ceiling, down the walls, past the windowsills. I stepped closer to the few pieces of art that Earl had hung on the wall, took them down and examined the frames. Nothing there. Next, my desk. I opened the drawers and ran my fingers in and under them. Nothing. I turned the wooden chair upside down and felt for something, anything unusual. But it was just a wooden chair. I spent the next three hours taking apart the rest of my room, the small kitchen, the bathroom. When Dad walked in, carrying a plate of ice cream for me, he stopped at the doorway.

"What in the Sam Hill are you doing? Did you lose something?"

"Yes, one of mom's diamond earrings. You know, those little studs you gave me after she died."

"Trisha, how could you be so careless? Your mom and I didn't have much, and those earrings were precious to her. When did you see them last?"

I motioned for Dad to come over to my desk. I grabbed a notebook, tore out a page and wrote, "Room is bugged."

"What? No."

Then I wrote, "Act normal."

"You want me to—"

"Dad, thanks for the ice cream. I remember where I left the earrings. They're in the side pocket of my swim bag. I took them off before I went in the water today."

I shifted toward the closet, pulled out the bag, unzipped a pocket, reached in and pulled out a leaking sample-size shampoo packet. "See, here they are."

Dad tilted his head to one side the way The Babe did when Earl talked to him. Then he straightened up and nodded.

"Don't scare me like that. You must take better care of those. Maybe leave them here when you go swimming."

"You're right. Want to help me clean up?"

Dad picked up the mattress and placed it back on the frame. What took hours to destroy only took about forty-five minutes to put back together since I had help and a plate of chocolate chip ice cream for encouragement. To his credit, Dad didn't say a word. He just crooned Bob Marley's reggae classic, *I Shot the Sheriff*, under his breath as he picked up chairs, put the silverware back in the kitchen drawer and made my bed.

"Okay, we're finished. Headin' downstairs," he said, walking out of my room toward the staircase. My search had yielded nothing. No listening devices, no mini spy cameras. I accepted, in a semi-confident way, that the bedroom was clean. But would I ever feel comfortable here again?

My unflappable refrigerator stood silent in the corner. Since Frida couldn't see me, I picked up my phone, clicked on 'talk' and pretended to call Lena and have a conversation with her, pausing at all the right places.

"Hey, Lee, I need to discuss something with you."

Pause.

"The phone is fine. I want your take on something."

Another pause.

"Not sure you're going to like this, but I'm thinking of calling Burk."

Long pause.

"I know."

Short pause.

"I know. But listen."

Short pause.

"He said he was trying to help me, but I drove away."

Pause.

"I don't know why I called you in the first place."

Short pause.

"Lena? Lena? What a jerk! She hung up."

I grinned at my masterful performance, put the phone in my pocket and walked out to find Dad, now humming a Beatles tune, interspersed with a few "Yeah, yeah, yeahs."

"I want to show you something. My trusty automobile ..." I let the words trail off while I headed for the front door, my father padding after me. Stopping at my car, I opened the hood and stuck my head underneath. He moved next to me, his hands propped up on the transmission.

"What in the world is going on?"

I gave him the short version about my peeping Tom refrigerator and my conversation with Earl. He pulled his head out from under the hood, his hands pushing against his lower back.

"Can't stay like that too long. Kills my back." He spoke quietly. "So, you're saying that our house's AI system is bugged?"

"Yes, according to Earl."

"This is getting way out of hand. You're drugged. Your computer and phone are hacked. And Burk is the connecting link. I don't like it. Call the police."

"I did. Remember? They couldn't find him. Some family was in the house. It wasn't even twenty-four hours later and he and everyone else disappeared."

"How about you and I do a little daylight surveillance to see what we can find?"

"I was going to do that anyway."

"I figured as much. Didn't want you going alone. Let's get The Babe. If nothing else, he might pretend to protect us."

We approached the house from the downside of the hill. Bees buzzed around the flowers that we passed, the warm afternoon a nice change from the frigid nights we'd been having. I stopped Dad at the locked gate. My watch camera had picked up the numbers when Burk punched them in, but I wondered about the soundness of using them. Not to mention the legality. We inched toward the gate and looked at the yard on the other side. All was quiet.

"Let's come up on the house from the back. That's what I did the other day."

Dad nodded. We moved along the road until the path showed itself, off to the right, just across from the pullout. Deer had created this narrow byway when they walked up from the canyon floor. We started down the hill.

"There. That's it." I pointed at the back of the low fence surrounding the home. "When I was here that night, Earl had Black Betty hovering around the house, on this side, watching people come and go. The garage was packed with servers."

We moved off the trail to the right, hidden by trees and large shrubs. After hiking through the dense underbrush, the house appeared directly in front of us. Instead of the stylish mountain bikes that had been parked there during my first visit, a healthy collection of children's toys, a short plastic basketball hoop, and a little blue plastic wading pool littered the yard. The windows on the lower level had the blackout curtains closed and the garage had a heavy-duty padlock and chain securing it.

Right then, the downstairs door opened and out walked Burk with his bike. I hit Dad in the arm and pointed. We watched as he walked the bicycle to the front of the house, then we heard the gate slide open. Through the brush, I watched him pedal down the other side of the hill.

A minute later, a small boy, about three years old, stuck his head out of the door. I heard a female voice say, "Come back, now." The boy protested and sprung out into the backyard, picked up a small basketball and headed inside. The door shut and locked.

The house grew quiet after that.

Dad motioned for us to head for the path.

"Uh … maybe your boyfriend has some other connection to that house. Is he married?"

"I don't know. He never said so. And he's not my boyfriend, Dad."

The underbrush grabbed at my legs and a twig cut into my skin. When we reached the actual trail, Dad noticed the scratch. "What happened to you?"

"It's nothing." The deep red blood trickled down my leg and settled inside my shoe. *Did Burk have a son? A wife?* He had lied to me about everything else, why not a family? It shouldn't matter, but it did. I'd been betrayed by someone who drugged me. And for some senseless reason, it bothered me.

"Let's go home," I said. Dad reached around in his pocket and came up with a napkin.

"Here. Try to clean your leg up."

"I don't need it," I said, brushing his hand away.

"You're bleeding. This will help."

"I'll be okay." A cloud passed over the sun and the path turned dark, like my mood.

Earl leaned against the doorway as we walked up the steps.

"Trisha, are you bleeding? Can I help?"

"No, thanks," I muttered. "Do you have a screwdriver I can borrow?"

"Sure thing," said Earl. "Something needs fixing?"

"I'm sorry. I didn't mean to snap at you. Just tell me where it is. I'll get it."

I made a quick trip to the garage and picked up two screwdrivers, a Philips and a flathead.

"Let me know if you need help," Earl called out as I jogged up the staircase.

"Thank you," I yelled. "I'll be fine."

I stood in the middle of my bedroom, hands on hips and said, imitating Dr's T's pronunciation, "The Trisha Carson show is o...ver. And there will be no return engagement."

I strode toward the refrigerator and began unscrewing the bolts to the video console. The outside cover came off easily. Then, I unplugged the refrigerator, opened the door and saw the dark little eye that kept a watch on my food. I couldn't quite figure out how to remove it, so I rested the blade of the screwdriver on it and pounded the handle with a small can of olives. Pieces of tiny black glass sprinkled all over the inside of the fridge. In case that didn't work, I taped a small sticky note over the shattered opening, then cleaned out the glass and shut the door.

I stuck the flat-edged screwdriver into the edges of the small panel on the front and pushed on it until it loosened. I did it on each side until with one final push, the whole console popped out. A few wires connected the console to the home security system. I rummaged around in the kitchen drawer until I found a pair of scissors. Hopefully, with the power off, I wouldn't electrocute myself. I made three little snips and the console fell into my hands.

My last step was to plug Frida back in. I put Timmy's photo back over the prominent gaping hole on the fridge door just in case Earl chose to visit.

"That's so much better," I commented to the room. now clear of the camera and its listening device.

My phone vibrated on my bedside table. A text from Burk.

Why am I not surprised? As I'd hoped, he must have overheard my fake phone call to my sister. He wanted to get together … any place I chose. He wanted to make it up to me.

Of course he did.

Willing to try. Want to meet this evening? @7 Around the Corner?

Not a chance. That's where I almost passed out a day or two ago.

No. Jack's Brewing Company, Larkspur Landing.

About as public a place as I could think of.

 C U there.

CHAPTER 32

The rambling brewery edged up against the Marin side of San Francisco Bay, across from the ferry terminal. Boats pulled in and left from the wide wooden docks. Ghostly, gray fog concealed the sun, and the wind blew cool and blustery. I arrived thirty minutes before I'd told Burk I'd be there. I wanted to be at the table early so I could protect any drink I might have.

The waiter stopped by and asked what I wanted to drink.

"Do you ever serve beers that are locally made?"

"All the time," he said.

"My friends are developing a beer they call Coyote Ridge. I've been told it makes your mouth pucker."

The waiter laughed. "Once they get a brew that you consider tasty, bring it by. Give us a crack at selling it."

"I'll pass that along, but you may have a long wait."

"That's okay. You can't rush great taste," he advised. "How about a pale ale?"

"Lemonade will be fine."

My table by the window overlooked the main dining floor and had a perfect view of the front door. Each time it opened I held my breath. The lemonade came. I sipped it and watched the clock, and the front door. 6:45pm, 7:00pm, 7:15pm. No Burk.

The waiter stopped by again. "Would you like to order?"

I was starving. By now, I didn't care if Burk showed up or not. I ordered fish and chips. At 7:30, happily eating with no dining companion in sight, the waiter stopped by again.

"Are you on your own tonight?"

"I guess so."

He cleared away the other silverware. "Anyone that would stand you up is a fool," he grinned and walked away.

That made me smile. A few years ago, my life skidded and almost came to a complete stop. I changed everything about me that I could. Things started moving again. Now life was better. Not great, but better. I glanced out of the window toward the ferry terminal. The moody sky had turned battleship gray. I watched as a tall man stood next to his bicycle and chatted with a slight man wearing a gray hoodie, holding the handle of a small bag, like carry-on luggage. No mistaking. The taller of the two was Burk. Like two mimes having an animated silent conversation, the men gestured and talked. Burk shook his head no. The other man stiffened and stepped back. He almost tripped and fell. I pulled out my phone and took a picture. Then I zoomed in on his face. So familiar, but I couldn't place him. The shorter man leaned in from the waist and said something. Burk stayed firm, still shaking his head emphatically. The other man threw up his hands and walked away with a slight limp toward the terminal. He stopped to buy a ticket and disappeared into the waiting area. I watched as Burk pulled out his phone.

A second later, my phone pinged.

Sorry. Stuck in the city. Can't make it. 🌹

I watched from the comfort of the brewery as he placed the phone in his pocket and walked his bike into the terminal, picked up a ticket and moved into the waiting area.

Truth be told, I didn't want to see him either. But I did want to get back into his house. Now maybe was the best time. I called over my waiter and asked for the check.

"Everything okay? Don't let some idiot drag you down."

"I'm not. Not at all." I paid the bill and headed for the door.

Parked outside Burk's house in the pullout, I wondered what to do next. Walk around to the back? Climb over the fence? Press the button on the gate and see if anyone answered? I wanted to use the gate code and walk straight up to the front door. I had grown tired of the "Who's there? Who's not there?" game consuming my life.

Minutes ticked by. It didn't make sense to announce myself. Instead, I walked down the path to the trail and the small hill covered by brush behind the house.

No one passed by. No cyclists, no dog walkers, no kids walking home bouncing a basketball in the fading light. Muted sounds of splashing and squeals signaled a pool party not far away. That's where I wanted to be. Lounging on a floatie, sunglasses on, enjoying life. Instead, here I was, standing in underbrush spying on a house where I thought my drugger lived. *How do you get yourself into this shit, Trisha?* I turned to leave when I heard the front door open. I walked further to one side, squatted behind a bush, and caught a glimpse of the front door. Out walked the woman, the little boy trailing behind her and in tears. They blended into the dim shadows of the evening, but I could hear them clearly.

"I want Daddy."

"Daddy had to go on a trip. We'll see him soon."

"But I want to stay here," whined the little boy. He sat down on the front step.

"We can't. Nobody can. We're all moving," said his mom.

"Uncle Burk?"

"Yes."

"Uncle Sergei?"

"Yes, everyone." Standing in the somber shadows, she knelt beside him and said something I couldn't hear.

"You promise?" said the boy, standing up and taking his mother's hand.

"Of course." She led him to the car parked in the driveway.

"Wait, Mommy. I have to go pee."

"Now?"

"Right now."

She jogged back to the house and unlocked the front door. "When you're done, be sure to wash your hands, then meet me at the car."

The little boy dashed into the dark house. A light turned on inside.

Not long after, he skipped down the front steps and ran over to his mother leaning against the automobile. She carefully lifted him up, put him in the car, buckled him in his car seat and then slipped into the driver's seat. The front gate slid open and they headed down the hill in the opposite direction from my car parked across the street.

I waited for about ten minutes and listened. The car didn't return. If I heard correctly, the house was going to be deserted … if it wasn't already. They were all leaving.

The faint shadow of deer appeared in the woods below, halfway to the reservoir. A family of four moving, almost silently, then stopping to munch on something tasty. I stayed behind the hedges and walked toward the back, parallel to the fence that surrounded the house. At one end, a wooden gate led to the backyard. I quietly lifted the latch, inched through the opening and stood with my back flat against the fence. Blackness covered the corners of the yard and heavy shadows hovered over the rest of the grass close to the house. I pulled a stone out of my pocket that I'd picked up on the trail and threw it at one of the black shaded windows. As it bounced off, I thought belatedly about alarms. *Too late to take back the rock.* I held my breath and listened intently. All I heard was the clink of the rock against the window and the muffled plop when it hit the grass. No alarms. So, I threw another one. Nothing. No one glanced out from behind a curtain or opened a door to check. If someone came, I'd be exposed with no place to hide. But no one did.

I hustled to the side and tried the handle to the backdoor. Locked. Each window? Secured. The story repeated itself on the other side where the bicycles were parked that first night. I made my way around to the front and took a quick look up the steps at the front door. The boy had run inside and then back out to the car. He'd shut the door but hadn't locked it. In the mom's hurry to pack her boy up and leave, she'd forgotten to check. Quietly, I moved up the steps, gave the door a slight push and it opened. No alarms went off. No laser beams zapped across the floor. Nothing.

What little had been there—the couch, the metal folding chairs, and the large TV on the wall—had been removed. My footsteps echoed while I walked through the vacant dining room and into the kitchen. Systematically, I opened each cupboard. Bare. Same with the drawers. Even the trash can. The doors to the three rooms off the hall stood ajar. Not a good sign. I peeked into the space that doubled as a storage center. Each carefully marked piece of tech had been removed.

I took a quick glance out of the window while moving back into the kitchen toward the door to the lower part of the house. Darkness stretched across the road and covered my Honda parked outside. Then the hill behind my car suddenly turned bright. A vehicle raced up the incline, toward the house. Instinctively, I moved a distance from the window and inhaled deeply. But the car didn't slow down. The light grew brighter and then gradually fainter as it moved on and the road sunk into blackness again. I exhaled and my breathing settled down to normal.

I pulled out my cell phone and clicked on the flashlight. The small but bright white beam shone directly on the door in the kitchen. It opened easily. I shone the light down the steps and tried a tentative, "Hello?" in case someone was standing there, waiting for me in the dark.

I inched down the steps, stopping to shine the light in all directions. The stairs creaked on the bottom two steps and I jumped sideways from the sound. My heart rate pumped into overdrive as I reached the bottom and shone the light from one side of the room to the other. More blackout curtains covered the small windows and protected the empty room. I walked over to the wall and flipped the switch. The glaring light hurt my eyes and I squinted at the worktables in front of me. Computer cables and surge protectors snaked across the floor to empty long tables. Dust marks revealed where the computers once sat. I found a few chip bags in the corner, along with fast-food cartons and empty soda cups.

"Slobs," but I scooped up the refuse and went through it anyway, hoping for what, I couldn't say.

The bottom floor stretched from one end of the house to the other. A corridor off the main room connected four small bedrooms to the hallway, two on one side, two on the other. The first had a queen-sized bed that took up most of the space. No space even for a dresser.

The next room must have belonged to the little boy. It had a junior-sized bed, a wooden dresser painted blue, and a bedside table. A little lamp with a cowboy riding a horse around the tan shade rested on the table. I sat down on the bed and let my hand drift along the small mattress.

If I wanted to hide something, I'd put it where most people wouldn't think to look, like my child's room. I reached over and lifted the mattress. Nothing there. Then I pulled up the box spring. No rips or tears. I flipped it over and found two big thick pieces of gray duct tape parallel to each other. I grabbed at the edges and began pulling the tape off, taking part of the fabric covering the springs with it. A large legal-size envelope was stuffed deep inside. Interesting filing system. I carefully pulled it out, opened it, and found two file folders; one held receipts for computer equipment and supplies, a few phone bills, and bids from a security company. A vaguely familiar set of initials, NEP, were scrawled across the bottom of each receipt. I did a search on my phone for *NEP*. Nothing that made sense to me. Then, *NEP computer.* The name Popolare popped up, and so did San Francisco. When I typed in *NEPopolare, San Francisco,* pages and pages of search results surfaced. I clicked on one news article from the San Francisco Tribune. And there it was. The whole story about the San Francisco shutdown and the infamous Nicholas Eroe Popolare. So the notorious computer genius had been my neighbor.

The other folder held several sheets of long yellow paper. On one was a handwritten table with a complicated set of numbers and letters and a list of small towns in California, Idaho, Arizona, and Nevada. The other sheet listed names and telephone numbers.

Were these the numbers Tyler wanted me to retrieve? I couldn't study them, not here. I stuck everything back in the envelope and put it in my backpack. Then my phone pinged. It shouted like a fire alarm in the deserted house. I looked down at the text message. It was from Dad.

Call me NOW.

I tapped his phone number, wondering what had triggered him this time.

"Trish?"

"Yeah. What's going on, Dad?"

"It's Earl's friend."

"The guy from Oregon? Bernard?"

"Yes."

"What about him?"

"He's dead, Trisha. His body was found floating off Ocean Beach in San Francisco."

CHAPTER 33

Dad was waiting on the deck of Earl's house when I got home. He tried to explain what happened, or what he thought had happened.

"I came home, and Tyler called … you're right, he's not missing … and said that Bernard's body was found in the ocean and that Earl needed to come immediately."

"Tyler called?"

"He gave him specific directions. Earl was frantic when he got off the phone. I could hardly get any information from him. First thing he did was run up to his office. Then he ran out of here."

"You mean the police weren't the ones to tell him?"

Dad shook his head.

"Did Earl call the police to check it out?"

Dad shrugged his shoulders. "Don't think so."

"This could be a trap, Dad. Nothing more than a trap."

"Tyler wouldn't lie to him."

"Maybe he had no choice. Where did he say he was going?"

"He didn't say. Probably to find Tyler."

"Can't you be more specific than that?"

"I'll call him." Looking worried, Dad took out his phone, pressed a few buttons. Earl picked up.

"Buddy, Trisha is here. She says this is a trap. You have to come back home."

I couldn't hear what he was saying, but Dad's eyes grew large and he sat down.

"Really." He paused.

"Really," he repeated.

"Ask for a location," I almost shouted in his ear. But Dad hung up.

"He said that he knows it's a trap and that Tyler is the bait. He said The Babe is with him."

"This is a disaster. It's dark out and Ocean Beach is about three and half miles long. Where is he going?"

"Trish, he knows what he's doing."

"I don't think so. I'm calling SFPD."

I tapped the cell phone number for Inspector Burrell.

"Inspector Burrell, it's Trisha Carson. I'm fine. Well, not so fine. Have you heard anything about a body found in or off Ocean Beach?" I asked. "Hmm … nothing? Thanks for checking. Let know if anything changes, okay? I'd appreciate it. Bye."

I said, "She hasn't heard of a body found along the beach. She even put me on hold and checked with the Park Service."

Dad ran his hands over his face and pushed back his hair. "You think he's in danger?"

"Of course, he is. His grandson calls to tell him that his good friend is dead. And the police have no record of a body found in or near Ocean Beach? It's a setup. Can't you see? Even Earl knows it, and he's going anyway. This spying thing has gone south. He's dealing with big-time hackers and criminals. We have to find them or who knows what will happen. These cyber snakes could turn into actual killers if they decide Earl and Tyler are disposable. How could Earl get involved with something like this?"

"Maybe he was bored. Or missed the action," said Dad.

I was about to run out the door to my car when I stopped. "Did he take his gun?"

"What gun?"

"The one he keeps—oh, never mind." I ran up the steps to Earl's office. The fake book, the one with the big blue marble and the manilla envelope, lay open on his desk. The gun was gone. I ran out of the room and launched myself down the stairs.

"It's not there. It's not there," I yelled to Dad standing at the foot of the staircase. "We have to find him and stop him before he uses it."

"What gun, Trish?"

"He had one hidden in his office. You didn't know?"

"No. He never volunteered the info."

"You said he missed the action. This kind of action? Has he been a spy all this time?" I asked.

"I couldn't tell ya, Trisha."

CHAPTER 34

"Where're we going?" Dad asked as he settled into the passenger's seat.

"I'm not sure."

A wall of thick fog engulfed us as we drove down Highway 101 toward the Golden Gate Bridge. I switched on my headlights. Husky drops of moisture clung to the windshield like glue.

"You're going to need your wipers," advised Dad.

"Not sure that will help." But I turned them on anyway. The flip, flip, flip of the windshield wipers moving from side to side smeared the ever-present dirt and dust already there.

"Geez, Trisha. I can't see a thing. When was the last time you washed your car?"

"I don't always have time."

I pressed the windshield washer knob and a stream of water joined the fog drizzle. The grime only smeared more.

"Press it again."

"Okay, okay." I pressed the button a few more times until the grime started to subside. Not that it made any difference. Dense fog forced me to slow down dramatically. The gloom even erased the brake lights of the cars in front of us.

"This is as bad as I've seen it," observed Dad.

I strained to watch the road ahead. Traffic moved on to the Golden Gate Bridge, the large russet-orange bridge towers invisible even as we crossed.

"You know, they painted the towers International Orange because you could see it in the fog," said Dad.

"Well, it's not working. I don't see anything."

We were driving in a three-lane cocoon. Occasionally, a shadow of a car passed me in the next lane but disappeared before it cleared the front bumper. The hazy lights of the toll plaza glowed through the cotton ball that surrounded us. We breezed through and headed for the curve in the road that took us to 19th Avenue. I stepped on the accelerator and my weary Honda took off. I slipped into the other lane.

"Slow down, young lady," instructed Dad. "You're going to get us killed."

I grumbled to myself and lifted my foot off the accelerator.

"Dad, grab my backpack. There are a couple of folders in there. Take a look and tell me what you think."

He pulled out the files and scanned each page.

"I see numbers and some receipts. The numbers follow a pattern, but they don't mean anything to me. Then, there are a list of cities and contacts. What is this?"

"I have an idea, but I need to study them."

"Do I want to know where they came from?"

"No."

"But it has to do with Earl and everything else?"

"Pretty sure." The traffic lights now glowed green for blocks ahead.

"Have you figured out where we're going?" Dad asked.

"The pseudo-brewery."

"Well, a little advice. Don't park in front of the house. Cruise by and see what you can see."

"I don't plan on parking."

"You sure you're thinking things through?"

"I'm driving in a heavy fog."

"You were. Now, it's about gone. Slow down! You're doing almost twice the speed limit. You continue like this, one of your many police friends will show up. It's time you think about what you're going to do."

The light turned red, and I stopped, trying to keep my composure.

"I know what I'm going to do," I said, crisply pronouncing each syllable of each word.

"How about letting me in on your plans."

The light turned green and we took off, gradually this time. "Well, ah... first..."

"You don't know."

"I do. Kind of. We'll drive around the neighborhood until we find Earl's car. I won't stop at the brewery house, but just drive by to see if there are any lights on. It might be good to drive down the Great

Highway."

I turned right at Fulton Street, which borders Golden Gate Park. With the park on one side and apartments on the other, we headed in silence for the beach. The closer we got to the ocean, the more the fog returned. I turned left on the Great Highway. Waves that had crossed 6,000 miles of Pacific Ocean slammed into the beach, but the fog made it impossible to see them. I drove on the deserted road, breathing in the damp salt-tinged air.

"Got a chill to it," Dad said.

"Yeah, but it smells good."

We passed the two-story Beach Chalet, a popular restaurant with great views of the ocean when the fog stayed out at sea. Shimmering lights from their big plate glass windows glowed through the murkiness.

On the other side of Golden Gate Park, I turned left on Lincoln and went up a few blocks, driving through the Outer Richmond neighborhood with its side-by-side family homes. Deserted parked cars hugged the curbs. I drove past the spot where Tyler had appeared on this bike. No Tyler this time. I continued down a narrow side street that paralleled the ocean. We crept past each vacant car.

"Waste of time," I muttered.

Then up ahead of us, to the right and almost on the next block, sat Earl's vehicle. "Dad, over there."

"I see it."

I parked behind Earl's deserted car.

"Let me check this out," said Dad. He walked over to the abandoned vehicle and pulled on the door handle. Locked. He moved to the other side, trying each door and the trunk but they were secure. Dad shook his head as he walked back to my car and climbed in.

"Not gonna help us."

"Well, I'm going to pay a visit to the beer maker."

"How do you propose to do that?"

"Walk up his front path and knock on the door."

"What if he answers?"

"I'll ask about Earl. If he's seen him."

"And when he says 'no', because he will say 'no,' then what?"

"I'll push my way in."

"You certainly will not."

"Oh, wait. He knows me as Arabella Stockman," I said.

"As who?"

"A potential investor. Never mind. My idea won't work. What would you do?"

"Well, first, I'd avoid the front door, Arabella. Go around to the back. Listen. Check the surroundings. But that's all. I wouldn't go in."

"I could get arrested for that."

"You asked me what I would do. I told you. Walk by the house. Glance at it. That's all."

"Okay."

"Promise?"

"Promise."

"Dear girl, if your lips are movin', you're lyin'."

"I don't know why you have trouble trusting me," I said.

Sliding out of the car, I pulled my sweatshirt close. The northwest wind whipped the tall shrubs around and the air temperature had dropped almost thirty degrees from Earl's house in Marin. Dad sat in the car, pointing at me, and shaking his finger. Not sure what any of that meant. I kept on going, past the spot where Tyler had disappeared and through the tall green shrubs to the other side of the Great Highway. I shivered in the chilly damp air. Behind me, I heard footsteps; they moved faster as they drew nearer.

I picked up my pace. When the footsteps did, too, I broke into a jog.

"Slow down, will you?" called Dad. "I can't let you do this by yourself."

Our little sprint left him out of breath.

"You scared me," I said, staring at him.

"You don't know anything about being safe on a street at night. I need to teach you a few things."

"Later. Now we're only a father and daughter out for a night stroll. No unneeded conversation."

We continued walking along the street. A woman came toward us from the other way, walking a mixed-breed terrier. She stepped into the street giving us a wide berth, when Dad, being Dad, couldn't help himself. He had to say something.

"If that isn't the cutest dog ever," he gushed. The woman beamed and launched into a story, a long story, about how she had rescued him and how skinny he was. The local appeared to be in her Ocean Beach best: a down jacket, scarf wrapped around her neck, and gloves.

I smiled and began to tug at Dad's arm. "We have to go now."

"Trisha, don't be impolite."

Dad instantly forgot about me, like I had melted into the fog. He remained completely attentive to the wrapped up lady and her little dog who sniffed at his shoes. I dropped his arm and walked a few feet away. I could see the house ahead of me.

I stopped one yard away. No lights shone in the windows. No car parked in the driveway. No signs of life inside at all. I walked up to the door and knocked, then tried the door handle. Locked. I glanced down the street and Dad had knelt next to the little dog to pet him. I turned toward the side walkway and slipped into the backyard. One trash can overflowed with debris from the beer making experiment: yeast containers and empty sugar bags. The other two sat empty. I climbed up the stairs and put my face against the window, straining to see past the kitchen into the dining room. I pulled out my cell phone, turned on its flashlight and shone it into the house.

The furniture I remembered was gone. I wouldn't be surprised if the occupants from this house had joined the occupants from the house in Marin. But where did they go?

A curtain moved in a bedroom window from the house next door. I waved at the nosey neighbor peering down at me.

"Just checking on my friends," I called out. The woman retreated abruptly, and the curtain fell back into place.

"Trisha? Trisha?" Dad's voice was blown into the backyard by the wind.

I darted down the steps and made my way to the side walkway.

"Over here," I said, walking out to meet my father. He stood with his hands stuffed deep in his pockets and his collar turned up.

"This has to be where Tyler told Earl to come. Only nobody's here. It's empty."

"I could have told you that," said Dad. "It pays to talk to people. That nice lady with the dog—who invited me for dinner next week, by the way—said they moved out a couple of days ago. The owner was the quiet type, according to her. He had a few conversations with her, mostly about keeping that sweet dog of hers off his lawn."

"They? Who else lived there?"

"She saw a young man with a lot of hair coming and going. That could be Tyler, don't you think?"

My zip up Giants hoodie did little to keep me warm and keep the shivering at bay. The thick drizzle from the fog had started to seep through and goosebumps covered my arms. I couldn't wait to get back to the car and turn on the heater. Dad walked next to me in silence.

"I'm thinking Jason Chang from this house is with the Marin group from over the hill."

"Any idea where they might be?"

"Not a clue."

I unlocked my car and Dad and I slipped in.

"Put on that heater," said Dad.

I turned the key in the ignition and the engine fired up. The heater switched on and a blast of damp, cool air flooded the front seat.

"Uggh! Turn it off until it warms up," said Dad.

Earl's car sat in front of us, still deserted.

"Before we go home, I want to drive by the beach," I said.

Dad nodded. "Maybe we'll find The Babe."

I turned along the windswept road that paralleled the ocean and pulled over to the side. I grabbed the flashlight from the glove compartment.

"Be right back." I climbed out of the car and was almost blown off my feet. Trotting down to the beach, I shielded my eyes from the blowing sand. No one walked the bleak oceanfront tonight. Head bowed, I shouldered against the wind. The flashlight created a puny glow three feet ahead of me. Not enough light to even see the Pacific.

"Earl," I yelled. "Babe. Come, Babe. Earl."

The pounding surf drowned out my voice.

Dad leaned against the car, watching me as I jogged back up to the street.

Grim faced, I shook my head. "Let's go."

The car's heater blasted away, warming the interior. "I'm going to call him again." Dad punched in Earl's cell phone number. It rang a few times and went to voicemail. He shrugged.

"Don't know what else to do," he said.

I pulled out and we started home. The Beach Chalet, moored to the edge of Golden Gate Park, floated like a ghostly ship behind the fog. A chill seeped into my bones. Earl wouldn't be driving home any time tonight. I could only hope he was safe. Somewhere.

CHAPTER 35

The phone started to ring as we walked in the front door. Dad answered. It was the San Francisco Humane Society. Someone had found The Babe, running around Ocean Beach.

"Yes, I'll pick him up tomorrow." Pause. "Don't know how he got there." Another pause. "Yes, thanks."

"Well," Dad said, "We know The Babe isn't with Earl."

"Wherever he is," I added.

"I am bone tired," I said as I pulled myself up the steps to my room. My stomach growled and like a switch flipped on, I wanted food. Immediately. A pint of ice cream cooled in the freezer of my non-seeing refrigerator. I crumbled up some graham crackers and dropped them into the ice cream container. That would do. I climbed back onto the bed, pulled up my backpack, unzipped it and shuffled through the folders I'd taken from the house. *What kind of person would use their child's bed as a hiding place? So callous.*

I organized everything: the receipts for equipment in one pile, the list of cities and contacts in another, the papers filled with numbers in the third. With a start, I remembered I'd seen them before. I slipped out of bed, taking the sheet of numbers with me to Earl's suite. I had left the hollow book open on his desk. The gun might be gone, but the papers with the numbers and letters remained. I compared them to those in my hand. Identical. My heart sank. Earl must be part of this spy network. With his background, he could easily be one of its leaders. This confirmed it. I scurried back to my room. Even at this late hour, I had to talk to Uly. If anyone could tell me what I had in my hand, Uly could. I gave him a call.

"What?"

"Don't you say 'hello'?"

"You want something, or you wouldn't be calling me."

"That's true. I have papers with letters and numbers and city names. I think I know what they are, but I want you to check them out."

There was a long pause.

"Now?"

"Yes, please."

I heard a slight groan. "Come over, then. Bring pizza and a six pack."

I plugged in a thumb drive to my loaner laptop and downloaded the newspaper story about Nicholas Eroe Popolare, the man who ran away with the proverbial keys to the city of San Francisco. I added the photos I took from the restaurant of Burk and the man he met at the Larkspur Ferry. I examined the grainy headshot in the article and then back at my pictures. Were they the same guy?

I did a quick search for Popolare's biography. Nothing I found mentioned that he'd returned to the United States or lived in Marin. Still. I put the papers back in the envelope and into my backpack.

"Hey, Dad, I'm going out."

"Now? It's almost midnight."

"Gotta go." Not waiting to hear his argument, I left, stopping first to pick up the pizza, then the beer, before heading to meet Uly.

CHAPTER 36

Even near midnight, San Rafael's warm weather lingered. I found a place to park near Uly's bunker and walked across the dark, deserted street to his front door. I never had time to press the doorbell. I heard a click and the front door opened by itself. Uly stood there in a pair of gray sweats and his Ramones tee shirt. I think that's all he ever wore.

I watched, amused, as the aroma of melted cheese, tomato sauce and pepperoni reached out and grabbed him. He pulled the box out of my hands, opened it, took a slice, and stuffed it in his mouth. Then he turned and walked down the hall, leaving me standing there with his fading rock posters, the beer and the door open behind me.

"Did you drop by just to deliver a pizza or do you need help?" he asked from the other room.

"I need help."

Instead of sitting by his computers, he stood at the other side of the room next to a small card table.

"Want some?" He held the box out to me. I shook my head 'no' and he put it on the table. "Beer?"

I handed him the six pack. He grabbed a bottle, flipped off the cap using the side of his table, and took a swig.

"Laptop working ok?"

"Yes, I haven't used it much, but it's fine. I want your opinion about some papers I found. I'm not sure what they mean."

He held out a greasy hand. It took me a minute to unzip the backpack and get him the envelope. He clicked on a little desk lamp. I stood there, not sure what to do. Hesitantly, I walked over to the chair in front of the computer and started to drag it toward him and the table.

"Don't move that chair."

I stiffened and then pushed it back. "Is this one okay?" I asked, pointing to the straight back chair next to the room for the servers.

"Yeah." He glanced up briefly. "Why did you give me a file with receipts?"

"See the initials? NEP. Do they mean anything to you?"

Uly scanned through the receipts, putting his finger on the initials each time he saw them.

"Nope."

"What if I told you the initials stood for Nicholas Eroe Popolare. You know who that is, don't you? The guy who walked out with the codes to the San Francisco city system?"

"I know who he is. Everyone knows who he is. He's a legend."

"I think these papers belonged to him," I said. I explained to Uly about my search and what I had found. Then I showed him the photos I took of him and Burk.

"Is this him?" I asked. I enlarged the small photo as much as possible.

"Could be. It's too grainy to say for certain."

"I'm guessing that he lived in the house over the hill from me. Maybe these other papers can tell what he was up to."

"He lives next door to you?" Uly was starstruck.

"He did. Or I think he did. He left. Can you help?"

"He's not there anymore?"

"He disappeared. He and his wife and little boy and his employees."

"He went off the grid a while back. Italy, from what I heard," said Uly.

"Well, he was my neighbor."

"You sure it was him."

"Call it an educated guess."

For the next fifteen minutes, Uly didn't say a thing, just studied the files. At one point, he shuffled over to his computer, plugged in some of the numbers. He shook his head. "Nothing is coming up. But that doesn't mean—"

I cut him off. "The other pages with the city names …"

Uly didn't turn around. He kept tapping on his computer. He started to laugh.

"What's so funny?"

"So, say he plans on attacking the networks of these towns. What a come down, right? From San Francisco to Fresno?" He laughed again.

I was stunned. "You think he might try and shut down these systems, blackmail all of these towns?"

"Dunno."

"It makes a weird kind of sense. After all, he's done it before. Maybe he ran out of money," I said.

"Have you talked to the police about this?"

"No. Not yet. I found these papers this afternoon, stuck in the box springs of his kid's bed. Who would do something like that? Use his kid's furniture as a shield?"

He turned and looked at me, incredulous. "Uh … ok. Well, I know someone who knows someone who might be able to help. You gotta move back. No peeking over my shoulder."

"Okay, okay." But I continued to peer at the screen, waiting for him to start typing. Couldn't seem to help it.

"I said move back. Better yet, turn around. Face the door."

I did as I was told, but stood there, my arms crossed, tapping my foot.

"I'm putting in my encryption key. It's just a one-time thing. Just stay where you are."

"Okay. I get it. I won't move." *As if I even know what an encryption key is.*

"Now you can turn around. But stay there. Please?"

Uly started typing and I moved a little closer. He was in the zone and no longer thinking about me. The messages zipped back and forth for a few minutes. Then stopped.

"We're on hold, so to speak."

"Someone else has these codes and city names," I said.

"What do you mean?"

I pulled out my phone and went to the photo folder. I found the pictures I took when I was in Earl's study. The numbers were the same.

"Where were they?" he asked.

"I can't tell you, but it breaks my heart that he's involved … so much more involved than I thought."

"While we're waiting, I want to show you something." He moved to another monitor. "You know that video watch I loaned you?"

"Yeah?"

"Well, you're not much of a videographer, but I found something interesting. The guy whose house you live in? Earl? The computer genius. I think he and Popolare must have known each other."

On the screen were my videos of the interior of the house when I visited it, the day Burk drugged me.

"How did you get this? I have the watch. Not you."

"I can see what's being filmed when it's turned on," he said with a lopsided, silly grin.

"You've been spying on me? What kind of person does that? I wear that watch almost all the time. In my bedroom. Everywhere."

"Hold on," he said. "I just said I can only see what you're shooting. If the video cam isn't activated, I can't see anything. Remember to turn it off. By the way, I liked your Norma Desmond impersonation."

"Still, you could've told me. There's not much to see. Empty rooms. That was about it."

The camera panned the equipment room and all the spare computer parts. There was a quick shot of the books on the bottom shelf. That's when Uly stopped the video. "What do you see?"

"It's a little blurry but I see books. Blurry books."

Uly stopped the video. The freeze frame in front of me was super sharp.

"Next to the books."

I squinted at the spine of a thick dark blue textbook. A magazine called "Cybercrime Economics" leaned against it. The lead article headlined on the cover announced a story about municipal ransomware, co-authored by leading experts in the field, Earl Cunningham and Nicholas Eroe Popolare.

"When I first saw the cover, I thought of you, since Cunningham is your landlord. Not all that surprised Cunningham was connected to Popolare. Talk about a dynamic duo," said Uly. "Those numbers on your phone? They're from Cunningham, aren't they?"

"I can't talk about it."

"He's doing something illegal?"

"I …" and I stopped. I refused to incriminate Earl.

An awkward lull hung in the air. It took fifteen minutes before Uly's contact responded.

"Fuck yeah! My hunch was right. Sanita Harbor is being held hostage. Classic. Totally classic attack. They got into the system, downloaded a shit load of data, encrypted it and left a sweet little ransom note. Their city grid was shut down completely, maybe a few hours ago. My friend wondered how I knew since it wasn't out in the media yet."

I sat there, stunned. "This is a disaster. Sanita Harbor isn't some large city. They can't afford this."

"These goons are very greedy cybercriminals. They don't care who they hurt."

"Do you know how to do this?" I asked.

"I don't do this kind of stuff. Don't want to go to jail. But it's a lively underground industry. And it's not that hard for a newcomer to get a foot in the door. No need to create your own ransomware or buy it on the dark web. You can lease it. Rent-a-Ransomware, kinda thing."

"So, I'm guessing this page of numbers is valuable." I ran my hands through my hair, trying not to panic.

"I'm guessing the rest of the numbers are for these other cities. They're next in line."

"How does this work?"

"Well, ransomware gets into a computer network, just like that hacker broke into your PC. Someone clicks on something they shouldn't. Maybe a fake site, bogus email, weird attachment. Then a code travels throughout the network. Sometimes, it only locks everything up. In this case, it digs itself in deep, under all the other code. It fills an empty space, a hole in the code, so to speak. It just sits there, not doing a thing, playing dead. It's dead code until someone says 'go.' I think you found the activation codes. The ones that will shut everything down."

"You mean this code was already in these systems?"

"Hell yeah. Just waiting for the attack command. Like a sleeper agent, waiting for the code word."

I walked back to Uly, reached over and grabbed the papers I'd given him, stuffed them back into the file and put it in my backpack.

"What are you going to do with those?" asked Uly.

"Not sure yet." The adrenaline rushing through my brain didn't help. My head expanded like a balloon with each breath. I needed to calm my thoughts and figure out the next step.

"Thanks, Uly."

The man with the bags under his eyes held one of the last pieces of pizza in his hand.

"You goin'?" His southern drawl was more pronounced.

I nodded. "One more thing. Why would this guy, Popolare, computer genius extraordinaire, write everything down? Why not store it on a file somewhere on his computer or a thumb drive?"

"Easy. Paper is hack proof."

"Old school is better?"

"For some things. You wanna stay? Have some pizza?"

I took a step back.

"It's late. And I'm not hungry. You're not talking about pizza, are you?"

He turned around to face his bank of monitors. I barely heard him say, "No."

"I'm flattered, Uly. But I have a boyfriend."

"No, you don't."

Technically, that was true. But Jon had never texted me back. "How do you know that?"

He grinned and held out the last piece of pizza and shrugged. "Sure you don't want a piece of pizza?"

"No."

As I walked back to the door, he said "By the way, I think I found your guy."

"What guy?"

"Your hacker, the one who broke into your computer."

"You did! Where? Who is it?"

"Need to do a little more digging before I say anything. See ya."

"That's it?"

He nodded but refused to say anything else. His attempt to sway me with a piece of pizza had failed. So I left.

Once outside, I jogged across the street to my car. A few twenty-year-olds hanging out on the corner never glanced in my direction. I started the car and moved onto Francisco Blvd as fast as my car could accelerate anyway.

How did Uly know about Jon and me? Lena must have said something. She never could keep her mouth shut. Just like Dad. I pulled over to the curb and texted her.

You up?

Yes. Crying baby.

Sick?

No. Just being a baby.

???

What?

Did u tell Uly about me and Jon?"

No. Y?

Sure?

No reason to. Y?!!

He knew Jon and I split.

Y would he care?

He made a move tonight. I think.

NO WAY

And he found my personal hacker. Maybe.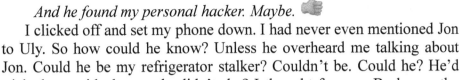

I clicked off and set my phone down. I had never even mentioned Jon to Uly. So how could he know? Unless he overheard me talking about Jon. Could he be my refrigerator stalker? Couldn't be. Could he? He'd tricked me with the watch, didn't he? I thought for sure Burk was the eavesdropper. Maybe even Earl. Smart, gentle Earl. My father's friend. My landlord. I thought I knew the man. Earl. Uly. Burk. My hacker could be any one of these three.

Earl was the biggest surprise. Now I find that he is connected with a criminal like Popolare? Dad would be crushed when he learned that his friend and his hacker buddies planned to cripple the networks of a dozen or more small towns. I drove down the quiet street and past the car dealerships. Anger swirled and knotted up my stomach.

Before I went to bed, I texted Burk.

Did u forget some papers at the house?

Then I turned off the phone and to make sure I wouldn't be bothered, I stuck it in the refrigerator next to the eggs.

CHAPTER 37

I slept in. When I woke, streaks of sun shooting through the fir trees stretched across my bed. For a minute, I closed my eyes and thought about falling back to sleep. Then I heard a door slam.

"Trisha?" My sister had entered the house.

"Don't tell me you're asleep?" I heard her say as she walked up the steps, headed toward my bedroom.

"Dad? Are you here?" After a pause, I heard her mumble to herself. "Where is everybody? Trisha, you better be in your room. I had to get a babysitter for Timmy so I could get over here this morning."

She stood in the doorway wearing black workout capris and a tee shirt which showed the letter 'e' in at least fifty different fonts. She was a graphic artist down to her clothes.

"Why are you standing in my room?"

"Dad let me know about your adventure last night. Now Earl is missing along with Tyler and the dog was found wandering around Ocean Beach which is like, thirty miles away!"

She came over and sat on the edge of my bed.

"Then you text me in the middle of the night saying that Uly hit on you. I figured your life, and this house was falling apart. Ad that I'd better do something before you disappeared, too."

I threw back the covers and walked into the bathroom, shut the door and turned on the shower. Just as I stepped into the steaming water, Lena opened the door and leaned against the sink.

"What's going on?"

"Can I take a shower in peace? Please?"

"Not until you tell me what's up."

Water flowed through my hair, down my face. I wanted to ignore her, but she deserved an answer. "It has something to do with techie-types hacking their way into city governments. And Earl … yes, our Earl … is involved. And not in a good way. Happy now?"

"Yes. Now get out while I finish up in here."

Surprisingly, Lena turned around and left. But she didn't close the door. I took a deep breath and continued soaping myself up. When I strolled out, rubbing the towel over my hair, I discovered Lena staring into the refrigerator.

"That's why you didn't answer any of my texts." She pulled out the chilly cell phone and tossed it on my bed.

"What happened to the inside of your refrigerator? Did someone attack it with a pickaxe?"

"Something like that."

"You?"

"My refrigerator was spying on me."

"Of course it was."

"No, I mean it. Someone hacked into its system and was watching and listening to me."

"Who would want to do that?"

"I first thought it was Burk. Maybe Earl. Then I thought it was Uly. How else would he know about Jon and me?"

I pulled on a pair of lightweight Levi's and a crop top with a Giants logo across the chest, the one I use when jogging.

Lena scanned me up and down.

"Stand up."

"Why?"

"Just stand up."

I did.

"Turn around."

I did. Then I put my hands on my hips. "What?"

"Not bad."

"Thank you, sister. I'm trying, but it isn't easy. Now, what did you do with my phone?"

She pointed over to the bed. I picked it up and smiled.

Before Lena could start with her questions, I pulled her into the bathroom and turned the shower back on.

"What are you doing?" she asked.

"Earl thinks the house may be bugged," I said.

"Seriously?" asked Lena.

"Just listen," I said. Then, I embarked on the story of the day before.

My dinner with Burk (which never happened), my visit to the house on the other side of the hill, the discovery of the papers stuffed into the box springs of a child's bed, papers whose list of numbers matched those hidden in Earl's office.

"That's a lot for one day," said Lena. She perched on the bathroom vanity.

"Oh, I'm not done," I continued, telling her about Earl's disappearance and our trip into the Outer Richmond to find him.

"Did you?" she asked. I shook my head and reported on my visit with Uly.

"His theory—well, actually, more than a theory now—is that the hackers over the hill are planning to invade the computer networks of several small towns around the west. I think the main guy behind it is Nicholas Eroe Popolare."

"I know that name," said Lena. "Why?"

"You mean I know something about computer history that you don't?"

Lena rolled her eyes. "Talk."

"He's the guy that developed the computer system for the city of San Francisco and then walked off with all the passwords," I said.

"Oh, yeah. I remember now. He left for Italy with millions of the city's dollars."

"That's the guy. Anyway, he came back to California and has been living in that house over the hill. Apparently preparing to shut down some other municipalities. And his partner is my landlord."

"I don't believe it," said Lena.

"Which part?"

"That someone as well known as Popolare was living in Marin without anyone noticing. And that Earl is involved with the whole thing. There has to be an explanation."

"Okay. Tell me what's wrong with this theory."

Instead, Lena changed the subject.

"Why choose small towns to hit with the ransomware? Go for the big cities."

"I have been thinking about that. Maybe this is a test run, an opportunity to work out the kinks. Then it's onward to bigger fish."

"So, what happens next?"

"I've reached out to Burk. He's the connection. He'll make the next move if he wants those papers back."

"And what do you want?" asked Lena.

"Earl and Tyler. And I need to find them soon. They're in danger."
With that I reached over and turned off the shower.

Lena called the babysitter and arranged for her to stay until Dr. T came home so she had time to help me come up with a plan. First, we laid all the papers out on the bed. My sister took a picture of each one, sending it to my email, to her own email, and even to Dad's email. Once they came through, she downloaded the pages onto a thumb drive.

"Insurance," she said.

Burk had responded immediately after I stuffed my phone in the fridge. First, there was the casual approach.

What papers?

When I didn't answer, things became a little more aggressive.

What do u have?

Trisha, r u there?

Answer me!

His texting stopped at 3 a.m., only to start up again two hours later.

I need those back.

Now!!!

Five hours had passed since his last text. Time I responded.

I don't think so.

Make a deal?

How about a swap?

I showed my text to Lena before I dramatically pressed the send button.

"Where's Dad?" she asked.

"He was going over to the city to pick up The Babe and meet the people who found him wandering. He's hoping it'll lead to some clue about Earl."

"That makes me nervous. What if they're part of this whole 'hacker thing' and want him as a hostage, too?"

"Dad doesn't know anything about anything. You should have heard him last night. He met some lady while we were walking, and she invited him over for dinner."

"So?"

"He said 'yes.' He doesn't even know her. They talked for like, ten minutes. Nobody goes to somebody's house they don't know."

"You want him to be happy, don't you?"

"With a stranger?"

"Everybody's a stranger until you meet them. Never mind. This is beyond your comprehension," said Lena.

My phone pinged. It was from Burk.

What do u have in mind?

Earl and Tyler for the papers.

I grinned at Lena like the Cheshire Cat from *Alice in Wonderland* when I hit send.

CHAPTER 38

Dad and The Babe were home, and the big dog was sleeping with his head on our father's lap. The snoring pup didn't even open his eyes when I walked over to pet him.

"What happened to you?" I asked The Babe. He whimpered, rolled over and stuck his face as close to Dad's stomach as he could.

"Is he okay?" asked Lena.

"Definitely showing signs of anxiety," said Dad.

I sat down next to him. "Where did they find him?"

"Not that far from where we were last night. Over the hedges across the Great Highway, running up and down the beach, never getting too far away from that spot."

"Who found him?" asked Lena.

"A ranger. Guy works for Golden Gate National Parks. He sometimes doubles as a lifeguard at Ocean Beach. He was out walking his dog and saw The Babe running around, frantic."

"We're so glad you're safe," I said, patting his large square head.

Lena and I walked into the kitchen, searching for something to eat. My cell phone rang. I answered and put it on speakerphone as I continued my journey through Earl's refrigerator.

"Trish, where are you?" It was the driver of my carpool for work. "We've been waiting for you for fifteen minutes. Aren't you working today?"

"Oh, crap, I completely forgot. Sorry. Things are falling apart over here. Go ahead. Drive in without me."

"Okay," said the woman on the phone. "Think you'll make it before the game starts?"

"I have no idea."

My next call was to my supervisor. I left a message that I would be late but didn't give a reason.

"I work tonight! I completely forgot. Have to go get ready," I said to Lena.

She grabbed two sodas, walked out to the living room, sat down next to Dad and to petted the dog. "Poor Babe," I heard her say as I sprinted up the steps to my bedroom. I dove into the closet. No uniform. On the chair by my desk? Nope. There was only one place left to check. I rummaged through my dirty clothes hamper and found everything I needed, from pants to shirt to vest. Even my knee-high black socks. The wrinkles gave them a lived-in flair, not quite up to the professional standards of my employer. I walked into the bathroom and struggled to straighten out my shirt collar. It would have to do. I grabbed my badge hanging on the doorknob and slipped it around my neck.

"Ready."

Lena needed to get back home to Little T, so she and I walked outside and down the front steps together in silence. Dad came out and watched us leave.

"Tell them you had dog problems," he called after me.

When we were far enough from the house, I asked Lena for a favor.

"Can you do a check on something for me?"

"What do you need?"

"I want to find the year when Popolare and Earl started working together. It was at least a decade ago. Maybe you can dig up when they met and where. Also, do a search on the publication *Cybersecurity Economics*. They co-authored an article for it."

"Why is that important?"

"I've been thinking about why they teamed up again. To me, it's got to be somewhere between random and planned."

"I'll do a search and see when their names appear together. I can't promise anything."

"Thanks. You're a good sister," and I leaned over and gave her a kiss on the cheek.

My start time for work came and went during the drive to the ballpark. I pictured all the Guest Services employees in their assigned sections, waiting for the gates to open.

I was thirty minutes late. Instead of moving toward my assigned spot, I headed in the opposite direction... to the radio broadcast booth. I wanted to find Jan. She sat there, staring at a wide monitor, the red light that indicated that she was on the air unlit. I knocked on the window. Startled, she came to the door. Her purple hair had mutated to a brilliant green and was cropped above her ears. "What's up?" she asked.

"That's what I want to know. Have you heard from Tyler?"

She shook her head.

"It's not just him anymore. It's his grandfather, too."

She shook her head again.

"Thought I'd check. Just in case."

"Gotta go."

She moved back into the booth and locked the door. Tyler had picked an excellent person to confide in. If she knew where he was, she wasn't saying. I walked back down the hallway swarming with fans in orange and black, carrying blankets, and wearing warm beanies. I passed by the Giants clubhouse into the employees-only hall and the crowds disappeared. Ahead was my supervisor.

"Sorry about being so late. I had a problem with—"

He cut me off. "They need you at the Marina Gate. Go help with the giveaways."

"Sure thing," I said, relieved that the conversation was so short.

Stacked cardboard boxes of orange and black tote bags with the SF Giants logo printed across the front and back, reached shoulder high.

"Things have been slow so far, but the ferries are on their way. We're going to be slammed. That line is yours," said one of the giveaway employees as I walked up.

I walked over to my mountain of boxes, ripped off the top, grabbed an armful of totes and waited. The fans approached me in a flood, their hands outstretched, reaching for the tote bags. The job moved fast and everyone laughed and joked with me. If this giveaway was like all the others, when we ran out, our guests became a little testy.

The brisk wind raced off the Bay and blew through the gates. Between fans, I wrapped a scarf around my neck and zipped up my jacket. I was on automatic: "Here you go. Thank you for coming. This is for you. Enjoy the game." I repeated the words over and over with a smile. I'd said the same thing hundreds of times, and I normally meant it. This time, my smile was stiff and artificial. My mind stayed on Earl, Tyler and my missing neighbors. The more I worried, the faster I handed out the tote bags, the fake smile fading with my mental health.

"Could I have a bag for my brother?" requested a woman wearing an orange and black fright wig.

"Sorry, only one per ticket."

"He's coming, but he'll be late. He really wants one of these."

"I'm sorry. I hope he gets here before we run out."

Clearly dissatisfied with my answer, the woman repeated her demand and stepped closer, but my supervisor, standing behind me, smiled and firmly explained our giveaway policy. The guest gave me a nasty look and walked past me, mumbling to herself.

Another ferry moved slowly next to the pier. Fans stood on both its upper and lower decks, ready to be released into Seal's Plaza and make a dash into the ballpark. The deckhands tied up the boat and the crowds zigzagged down the gangway. I grabbed another armload of totes in anticipation of the crush when I sensed a presence behind me.

I turned to find Burk standing there. He leaned over and whispered in my ear. "I want those papers."

"Well, I want my friends back. You and your hacker buddies get nothing until Earl and Tyler are safe."

The fans crowded the plaza and started streaming through the gates. Burk didn't leave. "You don't know the trouble you're in."

"Go away. I'm working," I said in a loud voice. My supervisor was at my side immediately.

"Is there a problem?"

"No problem," said Burk. "Misunderstanding, that's all," and he walked away.

"You okay?" asked the supervisor.

"I need a minute."

"Sure. I'll take over. You go." He slid easily into my spot and handed out the totes.

I walked along with the crowds, scanning for Burk. Fans packed the wide entrance hall, but he had disappeared. A deep red flash of heat crept up my neck to my face. I wanted to find Burk and throttle him. I walked into the Garden with its vegetables, herbs, and sweet smelling fruits and pre-game fans. No Burk there, either.

I glanced up at the bleachers that butt against the Garden. Five guys, ranging from around ten to forty, stretched across the barrier, reaching for every ball hit during batting practice. Burk stood off to one side, staring not out at the field, but down at me. I turned around and jogged out of the Garden, then up the ramp to the stands where I had seen him.

He stepped behind the cable car parked at the Arcade. I darted after him. As I passed in front, he grabbed my arm and forced me to walk me to the railing overlooking McCovey Cove. He glanced out at the Cove, a narrow body of water crowded with anchored boats and kayaks manned by fans eager for a home run ball. These guys were the die-hards. Burk held me tightly with one hand; in the other was the paper ticket he'd used to enter the ballpark. He crumpled it up and tossed it into the Bay.

"Where are they?" I asked. "If you don't tell me, I'm going to the police."

"I wouldn't do that if I were you. Get me the papers. This is the last time I'll ask you," he demanded. With that, he turned to walk away. I reached for his arm.

"Or what? What are you going to do? By the way, I know what's on them, you hacking scumbag. You want them? Give me back my friends!"

His eyes narrowed as he scowled at me. He carefully took my hand off his sleeve and bent it backward. I winced with pain and my knees buckled. The fans walking on either side of us began to blur. I closed my eyes and bright blue streaks of light flashed behind my eyelids. Four hands grabbed my other arm before I dropped to the concrete deck and Burk let go. When I opened my eyes, two teenagers dressed in Giants hoodies struggled to keep me standing. Burk was gone.

"Bro, that's not okay," the chubby teen with a mouthful of braces yelled after him.

"Are you all right?" asked the taller boy, a sixteen-year-old with jet black hair and a bad case of acne.

"I think so."

"The guy went that way," he said, pointing into the crowd flowing along the walkway. I tried to concentrate on the people moving around me, but I couldn't. He had disappeared.

"Want us to call someone? The police, maybe?" asked the chubby one.

"Thanks for your help. I'll get Security."

They walked away, occasionally looking back at me before they turned into the bleachers.

The fans rolling by, bumping into me on either side, didn't help my spinning head. I tried to drown out the noise of the fans behind me while I shook my hand and wiggled my fingers until they began to feel normal. It took a good five minutes before my breathe in—breathe out mantra took effect.

My head centered, my heart rate somewhat close to normal, I headed back down to the Marina Gate. For some unknown reason, I couldn't force myself to seek out ballpark security. At least, not yet.

"Better?" my supervisor asked. Before I could answer, he scooted past me through the gates to help with the last ferry coming into the pier.

"No," I said under my breath. "Not the least bit."

CHAPTER 39

I grabbed my last armload of totes and they flew out of my arms. Fifteen totes left, twelve, eight. When I was down to five totes, my supervisor closed the gates in front of me. Handing a co-worker the rest of my giveaways, I walked back to the designated meeting spot for the Marina Gate employees.

The supervisor gave me my assignment for the rest of the game and told me to take my break. As I headed down the walkway underneath the bleachers, I saw two of San Francisco's finest.

"Hey, is Officer Kalaw here today?" Officer Natalie Kalaw and I had met the year before at the ballpark. An indisputably decent human being, she was always there to lend a helping hand and offer calm advice.

"No," said one. The other police officer stood silently, staring at me. "She's at the station," meaning the San Francisco Police Headquarters, just across from the ballpark parking lot.

"Thanks. Maybe I'll stop by after the game."

"Anything we can help you with, Ma'am?" asked one officer.

"No, thanks though. She's a friend of mine. Just wanted to say hello."

He nodded and the officers continued walking underneath the bleachers. I saw the taller policeman reach around and rub his lower back. *That's what wearing thirty-five pounds of gear does to the body*, I thought. I caught up with them and tapped one on the arm. "Hey, it's me again."

He smiled. "Need directions to the station?"

"No, but I do have a question. If someone was up behind Section 150, you know, by the cable car across from McCovey Cove?"

They were both listening now.

"And they wanted to get out of the ballpark as fast as they could,

209

would the Lefty O'Doul gate by the Third Street Bridge be the fastest way out?"

"That's the most direct way," said Officer Number Two.

"Strange question. Why? What's going on?" asked the other.

I didn't want to get into the whole story, so I made up a tale about making a fan unhappy when I told him he couldn't smoke in the ballpark.

"He grabbed my hand and bent it back. I saw stars," I said. "A couple of teenagers chased him away."

I now had their full attention. They asked for a description, but besides being tall with blue eyes, sandy hair and wearing a black sweatshirt, there wasn't much I could tell them.

"Any writing or logo on the sweatshirt?"

"No."

"When was this?"

I was embarrassed to tell them. "About an hour ago."

"Next time, don't wait. Contact one of us immediately," said the taller cop.

"Was he drunk?"

"No."

"Nothing about him stood out? Tattoos? Facial hair?"

"Afraid not."

"We'll walk over to that entrance, see if there is anyone outside the gates who is smoking and fits that description."

"Thanks."

"You okay?"

"Unnerved, but ok."

"We'll find him. But in the future, yell for security or police if you ever feel threatened. Especially if they lay hands on you."

I nodded and watched them walk away. My supervisor walked up to me. "What's going on?"

I gave him the edited version of what had happened.

"It was that guy that bothered you at the gate, wasn't it?"

I nodded.

"I'm going to check with the command post. They have cameras everywhere, especially at the gates. They may be able to check the video and find him."

"He's gone by now." I regretted talking to the cops. What if they did manage to pinpoint Burk in the reams of ballpark videos? What if they could see me talking to him? They wouldn't see a cigarette. The police would know I lied. Worse yet, what if he hadn't left and they found him? Took him to jail? Would I ever see Earl and Tyler again? I hadn't thought this through.

"Come on. Let's go," my supervisor said, tugging me toward Security.

"I don't know."

"Come on." He wasn't going to let it go so I followed him up the stairs to the office by the large jumbotron and walked into a room where two men were watching a bank of monitors.

"Hey, Trisha," grinned one. "What's up?"

I stumbled through my semi-truthful story. He listened and nodded.

"Did you call security or the police?"

"No. Not at the time. I did talk to the police later."

"Close to an hour later," my supervisor admonished.

"Do that first next time. Or at least find another employee with a radio as soon as you're able. We can direct the different cameras in and around the ballpark and zoom in on anything."

He took some notes about the approximate time Burk talked to me at the gate and where he went after that.

"The last time I saw him was by the cable car."

"Okay. We'll check and get back to you."

I walked out of the door and down the steps, followed closely by my supervisor.

"I'm going to take my break now, if that's ok."

"No matter who this guy is to you, don't let anyone hurt you," he said.

"It's not like that."

"You knew him, didn't you?"

I said nothing.

"Ok, ok, none of my business. Go take your break."

I examined my throbbing wrist. A large black and blue bruise had bloomed and was growing darker by the minute. *An unwanted bracelet I can't take off*, I thought as I walked away.

The game sped by. Not many fans hung out in the Garden. At the end of the seventh inning, the bar, like the ones on the promenade, closed. The few people sitting on the wooden benches either left or hunkered down to watch the last few innings on the nearby televisions.

My supervisor walked past at the bottom of the ninth. "They want to see you in the command center."

"What about … " and I pointed to the Garden.

"Not to worry. I'll cover for you."

When I climbed the stairs again to the office above the field, the two officers I'd spoken to earlier were standing behind the command post employees. No one turned around as I walked in. They stayed fixed on the screens in front of them.

"We found him."

"You did?"

"On the video. I want to show this to you."

On the monitor appeared a grainy image of me handing out tote bags at the gate and Burk standing behind with his face close to my ear.

"Is that him?"

I nodded. "Yeah."

Then they fast forwarded until they came to my interchange with Burk near McCovey Cove. He had his back to the camera. His hand flicked toward the Cove.

"I don't see a cigarette," said an officer.

"I think he tossed it into the Bay. Just there. See?" I hoped that they bought my lie.

The officer nodded slightly.

Later, the video picked him up at the Lefty O'Doul gate where he left the ballpark and turned right.

"We found him again passing in front of the Giants Dugout, then in front of the Willie Mays gate on Third and King. You can see him walking toward Second Street. That's when he moves out of range." He fast forwarded to an image of Burk walking across the wide four-laned street and disappearing up Second past MoMo's, a popular watering hole across from the ballpark.

"We know what he looks like now. We'll pass out a photo of him to all security and gate personnel. He won't be back here to bother you," said one of the men.

"Thank you."

"Did you park in Lot A?"

I nodded.

"We'll have an officer meet you at the Marina Gate and walk you to your car."

"Thank you. That makes me feel better," I said, and I smiled as I left the office. But it didn't make me feel better. Not at all.

As I pulled out of the nearly deserted ballpark parking lot, the two officers who walked me to my car nodded. I waved back. Plenty of traffic clogged the streets around the park even though it was close to midnight. I drove over the ungainly Third Street with its huge concrete counterweight and turned right onto King Street where the traffic cops picked up the last of the orange cone-shaped barriers. Then it was left on Second, the street that Burk had walked up. I pulled into a parking spot. Across the street at MoMo's, fans spilled out onto the patio, celebrating the Giants' win. Noisy groups of people walked by, passing in and out of dark shadows, laughing and chatting about the game.

I climbed out of the car and joined a group of five guys who waited at the corner for the light to change. One turned and saw my Giants parka and ballcap.

"Good game tonight," he said as the others turned to see who he was talking to.

"Great game," I said. "Hope you had fun." I didn't follow them as they walked across the street. I stood there, pretending to wait for someone. In the dim light, I tried to scan the faces of those strolling up the Second Street hill, leaning in against the wind. Some fans disappeared into noisy bars; others continued up the hill.

It was a stupid idea. There was no way Burk would be hanging out at a bar three hours after he saw me. Unless he'd waited for me, of course. Not a pleasant thought. I scuttled back across the street and headed for the car and Marin. A few long blocks from the Golden Gate Bridge, I talked to my phone.

"Text Lena."

"What do you want to say?" answered my phone.

"Driving. If you're up, call me."

"Ready to send?"

"Send."

I put the phone down and switched on the radio. The Giants game was being replayed.

My phone rang.

"Why do you text so late?"

"You're up anyway. It's not like I woke you. Did I?"

"No. I was having a conversation with little T. He wants to play, not sleep."

"Remember how you found me when I was drugged?"

"Yeah."

"It was an app on my phone, right?"

"Yeah."

"Can you show me?"

"Sure. But not now. Bye."

"No, wait. Can you come by tomorrow, please? In the morning? I need something delivered."

"Not a chance." Lena clicked off.

Knowing Lena, that didn't always mean "No." The codes would get to Inspector Burrell. Then I would use Lena's tracking powers to find Burk.

At the last moment, before the entrance to the bridge, I turned off on an exit that would take me to Marina Boulevard. The only thing lit up at this time of night was a huge grocery store glittering in the darkness. I headed for the parking lot at Fort Mason. I didn't expect to see any cars this late at night but there were a few Park Service vans huddled against the side of their headquarters.

I pulled between two parking lines, turned off the car and waited. This is where Jon and I had met. The coffeeshop where he said goodbye was less than a mile west on the edge of Crissy Field. I climbed out of the car, careful not to put any weight on my hand which was throbbing.

The fog had rolled west into the Pacific Ocean, leaving the sky over San Francisco Bay surprisingly clear for a summer night. I walked toward one of the buildings, heading for the pier beyond, when a Park Service patrol car pulled up beside me.

"Ma'am, can I help you?"

It wasn't Jon.

"No. Just got off work. The Giants game. Needed a little quiet time before I headed home."

"I get that," he said, "But you'll have to leave. The parking lot closed at 10 p.m."

"Sure. One thing. Is Jon Angel working tonight?"

"You know Jon?"

"I do."

"He just clocked out. Not sure if he left yet."

"That's okay."

"Let me check."

"No. It's fine." I started walking back to my car.

He clicked on his mic and I heard him mention Jon's name. I walked faster in the opposite direction. *This was a dumb idea.* Before I could climb into the car, I watched a figure move out of the darkness and jog directly toward me.

"Hey, wait," Jon called.

I stood frozen, not sure what to do.

"Trisha," he said, coming to a stop right in front of me.

I couldn't help myself. I threw my arms around his neck. "I'm sorry. Really sorry. I didn't want to miss you, but I did."

He gently put his hands around my waist.

"You didn't answer my text," I said.

"Very true," he said, gazing into my eyes.

He reached out to take my hands and grabbed my wrist by mistake. I gasped and pulled my hands away. "What's wrong?"

"Not sure I should tell you."

I wanted to tell him. I wanted to trust him, but I didn't know how to ask for help. Or even how to accept it. I'd been hurt so many times. AA taught me one small step at a time. Maybe this was my small step. I took a deep breath, and the words started to come out. "Someone was trying to scare me tonight at work. He twisted my wrist."

"A fan?" The muscles tighten in his face.

"No."

"Then who?"

I shook my head and looked down at the dark pavement.

Jon took a step back. "Did you tell Security or ballpark police?"

"Yes."

"And?"

"They found him on video and are circulating his photo so he can't come back in the ballpark."

The anger faded from his eyes. "Are you still trying to find the missing grandson?"

"It's so much more than that now. Earl has been kidnapped. I'm sure of it. If he and Tyler aren't found soon … well, it could get serious, fast. And there's more. I was drugged. I ended up in the hospital."

"You were drugged? Are you okay?"

I nodded.

"Who did this to you?"

"This guy. Same one who grabbed my wrist. I'm pretty sure he's involved with the people that took Earl."

"You contacted the police, right?"

"I told them what happened. A version of it, anyway. But I don't think they believed me. Jon, I'm tired; my feet hurt and my wrist is killing me. It's been an awful few days."

"Tell ya what," said Jon, opening my car door. "You go home. Get some rest. Tomorrow, we'll talk this through. I'm going to make a few calls."

My whole body relaxed. *It's going to be ok.* Jon leaned over to kiss me. I inhaled the scent of his skin, the leather of his jacket and the cool night air. Maybe asking for help wasn't the worst thing in the world.

CHAPTER 40

I woke up the next morning thinking about Jon and wondering if I could fully let him into my life. A scary proposition for me. But I wanted to try. My family had it right; he was a keeper. I rolled over and opened my eyes; there was The Babe, snoring softly on the floor next to my bed.

"Hey, pooch. I bet you miss your hoo-man."

The big dog wheezed. I grabbed the robe thrown across the bottom of the bed and slipped it on. My refrigerator still had the photo of Timmy at the reservoir covering the gaping hole in the door. Emboldened, I stood up, stripped off my robe, tee shirt and PJ bottoms and stood in front of the fridge stark naked, hands on my hips.

"Hey, anyone who happens to be listening or trying to check out my room, I'm standing here nude." Like a model on a fashion runway, I strutted in front of the fridge.

"You're missing all this, you perverts!" With one more swish of my hips for good measure, I grabbed my clothes for the day and walked into the bathroom, slamming the door behind me.

Dad had left me a message propped up against a cereal box in the kitchen. "Have gone to China Camp to get my mind off Earl. Let me know if you hear from him."

I poured out a bowl of cereal, threw in a handful of blueberries and a few raspberries, and headed for the deck off the living room. A muffled snore came from the couch as I passed. There was my sister, asleep, hands curled under her chin. I decided at once to keep my midnight meeting with Jon a secret, until I knew more about our future. But wouldn't Lena be surprised?

"Lee?" I whispered.

She didn't move.

"Lee." I tried again a little louder.

Not wanting to wake her, I stood there for a minute. The Babe, who had followed me down the steps and into the kitchen and living room, had no such hesitation. He stretched his neck across my sleeping sister. Then the big gentle dog licked her. Once. Twice. An eye opened. "Dog, you have bad breath."

The Babe took that as an invitation to join her and he jumped up on the couch near Lena's feet. She groaned and sat up.

"What are you doing here?" I asked.

"You said you wanted me to come over. So here I am, complete with dog slobber on my face. What's this all about?"

"You can help me?"

"I don't know how to answer that until you tell me what you want help with. Is there anything to eat?"

Lena walked with me back into the kitchen. "I saw Dad before he left. He was all worked up about Earl and Tyler. Are you any closer to finding them?"

"Let's go for a nice, relaxing walk. I found a new trail that I've been meaning to show you."

"Now?" Lena thought I was crazy. I grabbed her arm and hauled her through the front door.

"Trisha, what are you doing?"

With a push, she bounced down the front steps, me by her side. We walked arm in arm to the end of the empty road and found a winding trail that led us the back way into La Cruz Canyon. I leaned toward her and whispered, "Don't talk."

"I'm not taking another step until you tell me what's happening," demanded Lena in a whisper.

"Just a few more yards," I said quietly. Eventually, we entered a clearing and I walked over to log and sat down.

"I told you the whole house, even my room, may be bugged," I said. "I can't trust talking there." Lena opened her mouth to say something, but I stopped her again. "Burk was at the ballpark last night."

"Seriously? What did he say?"

"Not much, but he almost broke my wrist. He can be a scary guy."

Lena took my hand and gently ran her figure over the bruise.

"Do you think it's broken?" she asked.

"No," but I winced when I turned my wrist in a circle.

"We should go to the hospital."

I shook my head.

"T could examine it."

"No! Don't you dare tell him about this," I said. "I have to find Burk. He might be the only way to get Earl and Tyler back."

I pulled out my phone and handed it to my sister. "How did you track me when I fell asleep in the parking lot?"

"Trish, this isn't a good idea. You could get hurt. Much worse than a bruised wrist," she said quietly.

"But I'm getting close. Show me."

"What's the password for your phone?"

"*Strike3*," I said.

"Of course, it is," she said.

Lena typed in my password, then navigated to the location sharing tool she had downloaded to my phone.

"I used this to find you. And I had your permission to do it. But Burk hasn't agreed to be tracked, so this won't work for him."

"Is there a way to track his phone?"

"It's illegal," said Lena.

"That's not what I asked you. Can I track his phone?"

"Uly did show me how. It's what the police use to track the bad guys."

"Show me."

"I don't want to."

"Please."

"You're not going to leave me alone until I do, are you?"

"Afraid not."

"Okay. But I had nothing to do with it if you get caught."

"Agreed."

Lena navigated to a website and signed me on. I plugged in Burk's cell phone number.

"There," she said.

"Where?" I asked, not sure what to look at.

"In the East Bay, Oakland. Near Jack London Square."

A little map with a blue blinking dot suggested his location.

"This is only accurate if he has his phone on him. If he gave it to someone else, or left it somewhere, then it's anyone's guess," said Lena.

"Then that's where I'll go."

"And do what? Yell at him? Threaten him? Go to the police first."

"That's step two, and where you come in. You and the police."

I grabbed my phone back and punched in Inspector Burrell's number. She picked up.

"Inspector Carolina Burrell."

"Hi. It's Trisha. Trisha Carson."

"Well, if it isn't my favorite Giants employee." There was a smile in her voice. "What have you gotten yourself into this time?"

"Well," I started.

"Wait a minute. I'm gonna get a cup of coffee. I have a feeling I'm going to need it," she said.

I didn't know where to start. I told her about Burk, the ballpark encounter, the missing landlord and his grandson, the bugged house and my theory that a group of cybercriminals with plans to hack small city governments were neighbors.

"Where is this Burk now?"

"In the East Bay, I think. Maybe around Jack London Square."

"Why is he bothering you?"

"After they moved out of the house, I may have … uh … mmm … stopped by …"

"You broke in? No. Don't answer that."

"They were hiding computer codes there. Codes that can—will—lock up the computer network of a city. Had them stuffed into the back of a mattress that belonged to the little boy who was living there," I said.

"What little boy? There's a child involved? Do you think he's in danger?"

"No, I don't think so. His mother is with him, and he seemed perfectly safe to me. I want to give you the codes. You can get them to the officials of the targeted cities. I want them out of my hands."

Inspector Burrell questioned me at length, digging for more information about the boy and his mother. I mentioned what little I knew. Then she asked detailed questions about the codes.

"My sister, Lena Shriver, is going to drop them off in a few hours. These networks may already be infected. This ransomware hides in a space or a hole in the system to be activated whenever the hackers choose. I'm not sure how easy it will be to find and destroy it, but I've got to believe these codes will help."

"All right. I'll be waiting," replied Inspector Burrell.

"Where am I going?" asked Lena.

"San Francisco Police Headquarters. By the ballpark. Ask for

Inspector Burrell. Don't give them to anyone but her, ok?"

"And you?"

"To find Burk."

"Bad idea, Trish. Really bad idea."

CHAPTER 41

I took the low-slung Richmond-San Rafael Bridge across the San Francisco Bay. Below me, the small Red Rock Island, less than six acres around and only 135 feet below the bridge, had a huge wake off one side. It appeared to be steaming full speed ahead in the strong ebb tide. The port and Jack London Square in Oakland made sense. Mammoth container ships docked there. Vast marine terminals with locked doors and empty containers large enough to hide two men were easily obtained.

As I approached the port, the towering white cranes used for loading and unloading container ships came into view. Big, boxy warehouses lined the empty side streets. My hands tingled as I checked the phone. Burk had shifted from his initial location and was closer than I expected him to be, edging nearer with each passing second. When I arrived at Jack London Square, I found a parking garage and drove in. I sat there, in the dark, eyes glued to the screen on my phone, watching the blinking blue dot as it headed toward me. When it showed Burk's car approaching the entrance to the garage, it suddenly made sense.

I wasn't following him. He was following me.

My heart vaulted into overdrive. My mouth went dry. Heat bolted up to my cheeks. I'd fooled myself into thinking I was in control. But Burk had the upper hand. If I stayed in the garage, I'd be trapped. I climbed out of the car and ran toward a side entrance, turning into a dark staircase that led up to the street. Burk had to be using the same illegal location finder that I was or maybe he'd done something to my phone directly. It would explain all the "coincidental" meetings. *But how was that possible? He never had ... oh no!* I remembered the night of the tech party at Oracle Park. Burk had my phone when I went off with my supervisor. He had more than enough time to download anything he wanted to my cell. That had to be it. However he'd done it, Burk had been following an electronic trail of breadcrumbs that led right to me. And I had been the one leaving them for him to find.

I wanted to find Burk, but on my own terms. Preferably out in the open, somewhere with people. Then I could set up a swap, the computer codes for Earl and Tyler. Time was ticking. How much longer would they hold on to them before deciding they were more trouble than they were worth?

When I pushed open the parking garage door, I found myself on a wooden boardwalk surrounded by restaurants that bordered the Alameda Channel. This would be a good place for my conversation with Burk. Plenty of people around. Constantly refreshing my phone, the app showed that Burk had turned before he reached Jack London Square.

A sense of relief rippled through my body. I had a few more minutes to go over my plan; maybe alert Inspector Burrell. I watched the phone to see which way he was heading. There was a chance I'd need to follow him. The little map indicated that he hadn't moved. A wave of disappointment slipped over me.

If Burk didn't show, my chances of finding Earl and Tyler would evaporate. I had no idea where to start hunting. I walked across the boardwalk into the adjacent marina and wandered along the piers past the large power boats with names like *Tally Ho*, *Wanderer* and *My Retirement*.

I glanced over to the entrance of the garage. Burk stood there, staring at me. His eyes never left mine.

This was it. My heart pounded in my ears. I walked deliberately toward him, then stopped in the middle of the boardwalk. He responded with a few purposeful steps in my direction, stopped for a moment, then continued until he was close enough to touch me.

"I want the original papers with the codes. Now," he said.

I shook my head no and took a step back.

"First Tyler and Earl. No deal without them," I ordered.

He reached out and tried to grab my arm. But I sidestepped and bumped into a couple strolling down the boardwalk.

"Hey, watch out," exclaimed the man.

"Sorry," I said. I inched closer to Burk. "Don't ever touch me again."

"Miss, is this guy bothering you?" questioned the man, his eyes blazing at Burk.

For a second, he paused. *Did I have the upper hand?*

"We're all good here," Burk said. "A misunderstanding. That's all."

The man and woman walked over to a bench on the edge of the boardwalk, sat down and continued to watch us. *I had backup.*

"I'll give you what you want," he said. "But even you aren't that stupid. Those computer codes are useless now. They've all been changed."

"Then what do you want them for?"

"We need the originals. Can't leave anything behind. Next step is for you to follow me."

"Where did Popolare go?" I asked. "I'm sure the city of San Francisco would be interested in his return to the States."

"Do you want your friends or not?" asked Burk. "Get in your car and pull out of the garage. I'll be in my car waiting for you."

This is too easy. I jogged to the entrance of the garage. *Way too easy.* But I had to find my friends. I threw open the door that led to the steps and stumbled into the stairwell. Blackness surrounded me. I lost my bearings and almost lost my balance. I paused and listened. No one was following me. I spun around and almost tumbled down the first flight of stairs. A man waited at the bottom of the stairwell.

"Careful, lady. Slow down. You almost fell."

He reached up to grab my arm. Then, the door opened behind me. At the top of the stairs appeared an imposing dark silhouette.

"Burk," I said.

"Now," he said.

Everything went black.

My head slammed against something hard and I began to open my eyes. I was trapped inside the trunk of a moving car. Pitch black. Dark. Too dark. I tried to reach out, but zip ties held my arms together at the wrists in front of me. I was lying on a rough carpet, my knees slammed up against my chest, the top of the trunk just inches above my body.

My head throbbed from where I'd been hit and each time we went over a bump, it bounced against the car, sending waves of pain through my skull. My whole body trembled uncontrollably as panic took hold. *Need to get out of here. Need air. Can't breathe.* Muffled voices filtered through under the rumble of the engine.

"Hey," I yelled. "Let me out."

I kicked the back seat of the car again and again, but it didn't move. The muted voices quieted for a second. I paused and listened, then screamed and pounded the seats again, striking as hard as possible. No response.

The trunk of the car began to shrink, the top and the sides inching closer as I struggled. *Can't die. Not here.* I buried my head into the carpet and closed my eyes. *Calm,* I repeated to myself. *Just stay calm.* I focused on my breathing. *Slow (in). Down (out).* I repeated the little mantra until my mind and body began to unwind.

In the blackness, I rummaged around as best I could. No backpack. Bet it was upfront with Burk and friend. Underneath me, something small and metal jammed painfully into my back. Probably the fastener that opened the compartment to the spare tire. Inside would be a tire jack and maybe other tools I could use as weapons. But reaching them seemed impossible.

The car rattled and jolted, the speed steady and fast. We must be on a highway. The pitch of the engine soared up a notch as we passed other cars.

"Help me. Help me. Get me out," I yelled. But the passing cars continued by. I was on my own.

I had no idea how long it had been since the parking garage. An hour? Two? I heard muffled laughter. The car swerved hard to the right and my head slammed against metal. I passed out. Again.

When I came to, the car's speed had dropped. We must have exited the freeway. The car turned right and slowed down even more, the road switching from smooth to rocky and rough. Was it dirt? Gravel?

Think, Trisha. Think now! The trunk latch. There had to be a trunk latch. I struggled to turn over, hitting my head repeatedly and seeing bright streaks of light with each slam against the side of the trunk. Inch by inch, I twisted and flexed my body, pushing against the car until I'd rolled over and faced the rear of the vehicle. Sweat trickled down my forehead from the exertion and my tee shirt grew damp and rank. But there in front of me, glowing beautifully in the darkness, was the trunk lock release.

I reached up to pull it and stopped, hesitating. If the latch opened, a red light would pop up on the dashboard. If I jumped out, they would stop the car, grab me and just throw me back in. With escape now only a latch-pull away, I calmed down. *Think it through.* They had my backpack, but they didn't have my phone. I'd tucked it into the waist of my jeans. *Why did it have to be on the other side?* I squirmed onto my back and pulled my knees against my chest, the uncomfortable bolt digging into my skin, then rammed my shoulders against the side of the trunk and violently jerked into a tight ball. The cell popped out of my belt.

The men stopped talking. Had they heard me? I started to yell and kick again. Over and over. My legs weighed more than bags of cement, but I kept at it while I moved the phone across the rough rug with my zip tied hands. As long as they thought I was protesting in general, they shouldn't be too concerned about my movements. I held the phone in one hand and managed to unlock it with the other. I said quietly, "Text Lena." The little black rectangle responded with, "What do you want to say?"

"Locked in trunk of car. Locate me through phone."

"Ready to send?"

"Yes," I whispered loudly.

"Sent."

"Turn on GPS."

"Location tracking enabled."

I pushed the phone to a corner of the trunk and waited.

We drove along the bumpy road for maybe another ten minutes, and I didn't move. The sound of other automobiles had disappeared altogether. About thirty minutes passed and the car came to a complete stop. I strained to hear what was happening. Two car doors opened and then slammed shut. If they came for me, I was prepared. My feet and very tired legs shook with fatigue, but I coiled into a tight ball, ready to strike. I turned back around and grasped the trunk release with my zip tied hands. My one and only card to play was surprise.

I never got a chance to play it. Their muted footsteps grew fainter, until they disappeared.

I waited a few more moments, then pulled the lever. The trunk popped open and I vaulted out, the blinding sun making it impossible to see anything. Then my knees buckled beneath me and I slammed into the ground. I boosted myself to a sitting position, leaned back against the car and closed my eyes for a minute. I opened them again and the landscape came into focus. I could make out a well-cared for vineyard bordering a winding road. Where was I? Napa? Sonoma? Maybe Livermore? Certainly, nowhere in the city.

The zip ties dug into my wrists. I suddenly remembered a video I'd seen while doing a search on women's safety. Pushing myself to a standing position, I raised my hands over my head and slammed them down against my stomach, sticking my elbows out. Miraculously, the zip ties snapped apart. *Freedom!*

I lowered the top of the trunk quietly and pushed it so it would shut. The click of the lock sounded like an explosion to me, but not even the birds in the trees turned to locate the sound. I scanned my surroundings. The beautiful vineyard climbed over rolling golden hills pressed against the horizon. It seemed too pretty to be the site of something so criminal. I ducked around to the other side of the car. I had to find a secure spot to hide. A house and a few outbuildings skirted the edge of the vineyard. Two large containers, the kind normally used for storing furniture, sat on the other side.

My legs wobbled as I darted from the car toward the containers. I ducked behind the first and surveyed the backyard of the small home. Toys, the same toys I'd seen at the house over the hill, lay scattered on the front lawn. As if on cue, the same small boy came out with his mother trailing behind him. Burk poked his head through the doorway and said something to the woman. She nodded and went back inside, pulling her son in after her. A few mountain bikes, a late model BMW and a black SUV sat off to one side of the yard.

I reached for my phone. Then I remembered. I'd left it in the trunk of the car. To retrieve it, I'd have to run across the path again, completely exposed. Even that possibility vanished when the front door of the house opened and Burk and the man from the stairwell walked out.

After a brief discussion, the other man said something about "the girl in the trunk." Then, they both climbed into the car and began to drive away. Where were they taking me? What did they plan to do with me? And what would happen when they realized I had escaped?

Pressing my back against the container, I slid down to the ground, grateful I had enough air to breathe. Suddenly very tired, I laid my head against the cool exterior of the pod and closed my eyes.

What was that?

I bolted up. Voices, coming from inside the pod. Then a shout.

"Let us out! We'll do whatever you want."

Tyler!

"Don't say that," Earl reprimanded. "I'm not going to do anything they want. And neither are you."

"I want out of here. It's so hot."

A third weaker voice began to mumble.

I knocked on the side.

"Hello? Earl? Tyler?"

Dead silence.

"Who's out there?" asked Earl.

"Me. It's Trisha."

"Trisha," yelled Tyler. "Get us out of here! Hard to breathe. I'm so thirsty."

"I'll try. How long have you been locked in here?"

"A few days," said Earl. "Bernard is here, too. Hurry, please. Bernie isn't doing so well. Are the police here?"

"Not yet. But they will be." Hopefully, I was right. "Hang on. I need to find some tools."

Tyler yelled, "Don't go. Don't leave."

"I'm not leaving. I promise."

With Burk and buddy out of the picture, I took the chance to move across the path to the side of the house. I inched closer to a window. The sounds of a television and a child singing along to animated characters drifted outdoors, but I saw no one inside. I went to the next window and glanced in. No one. The woman and child remained out of sight, which meant I was, too. For the moment.

I darted over to the large tool shed by the pod and the vineyard. The pungent smell of manure hit me when I opened the door. The tools were perfectly organized, some hanging from pegboards, others lined up against the wall. I scanned them but didn't see anything like a bolt cutter. But I did see a sledgehammer. It would have to do.

I picked up the heavy hammer with two hands and walked toward the pod.

"Stay away from the door. I'm going to break the lock with a hammer. I hope."

The sound would surely alert the woman and child and anyone else inside. They would call for Burk. Burk would come back. Or would he? Either way, I had to hurry.

I slammed the hammer against the lock. The sound of metal-on-metal rang out in the quiet landscape. I swung again, but I kept missing the lock.

"Hurry," cried Tyler. He banged on the inside of the door and the lock clanked against the metal frame on the outside.

I aimed for the lock and swung again. Another miss.

"I can't breathe in here. Please, Trisha. It's so hot. I can't see," said Tyler.

"Same here," I said, as sweat dripped down my forehead, stinging my eyes.

"Ty, she's trying her best," I heard Earl say.

"Change of plans," I said. "I'm going to hit the container directly."

I started hammering on the door frame next to the lock. After three hits, it began to cave in.

The woman ran out of the house.

"Who are you? What are you doing?" she shrieked. She stopped in her tracks. The little boy had followed her into the front yard.

"Go back in the house and stay there," I yelled. She scooped up the child.

"I'm calling the police," she yelled as she darted back into the house.

"Do that," I nodded. "Yes, please, call the police."

I swung and banged a few more times. The metal crumpled again, but only slightly. There was just enough space for me to see Earl's bright red face.

"Thank you, Trisha," he said.

Ten minutes later, I heard the police sirens.

CHAPTER 42

The vineyard and the container holding Earl, Tyler, and Bernard prisoner weren't in Napa or Sonoma, but the small town of Petaluma, about thirty-five minutes north of Earl's house. As the Sonoma County police pulled up, I was still battering away at the container with the heavy sledgehammer. The deafening clang of metal against metal resounded through the tranquil vineyard. Cries from the three men inside the pod added to the confusion and the lady with the small boy in her arms was hollering, "That's her. That's her." About that time, the small boy began to wail.

The police bolted from their cars, guns pulled and yelled, "Drop the hammer."

I pushed the hair out of my eyes. "You mean me?"

An officer responded, "Drop it now."

"No problem," I said, letting the sledgehammer fall from my hands. I leaned against the container, breathing heavily, my hair and tee shirt drenched in sweat. "Please, finish the job and get those guys out of there."

Within fifteen minutes, Earl, Bernard and Tyler were free and gulping down cold water. Tyler waved at me.

"Thank you for finding us," he said as he guzzled the cool liquid. Then he grabbed another bottle and dumped it over his head. Tyler's face bloomed tomato red and his wiry black hair dripped with water and sweat.

"Yes, thank you," said Earl with a weak wave.

Paramedics loaded Bernard onto a gurney and into an ambulance for transport to the hospital. While other EMTs scurried about Earl and Tyler, I wasn't as lucky. I sat on the ground, arms behind me, handcuffs circling my wrists. I pleaded with the officers to call Inspector Burrell. Even Earl's and Tyler's protests that I wasn't to blame were ignored. The woman and the boy were now back in the house, no doubt weaving an incredible story about the crazy lady attacking their storage pod.

Two cars approached the strange scene on the dirt road. One was driven by my sister, the other by Inspector Burrell.

"Hey, Trish, love your new bracelets," greeted Lena with too big a smile for my taste.

Inspector Burrell looked at me, shook her head with a sigh, and walked over to the local police. A few words later, they moved to my side, hauled me to my feet and unlocked the handcuffs.

"Let's start from the beginning," said one. "Please tell me your name."

It took a while to explain what had happened. Inspector Burrell stood a few feet away from the local police, listening. Her radio went off and she tilted her head to hear better.

"Good," she said. "Okay. Thanks." She kept talking but one of the policemen moved over and blocked my view of her.

"Ma'am, tell me again how you got here."

"For the third time … in the trunk of a car. My phone is still there, so you should be able to track it if they haven't found it already."

Inspector Burrell stepped closer.

"The car was stopped. Like you said, your phone was in the trunk and your backpack on the floor of the car. Both men are in custody."

Over the years, Inspector Carolina Burrell had become my friend and bailed me out of weirder situations than this. The local police and Inspector Burrell walked away from me, talking. In a few minutes, the officer came back and said, "You're free to go, but we might have some more questions later."

He handed me his card.

"Another one for your collection," said Lena. "How many cards from different officers do you have now? Ten? Twenty?"

"Now is not the time for sarcasm. I have just been locked in the trunk of a car. I'm recovering from a traumatic experience. I'm soaking wet, my arms and legs feel like they're going to fall off, and I bet I have a concussion. And anyway, you're wrong. It's only five. Maybe six."

I shook out my wrists, painfully sore from the handcuffs and the zip ties. My biceps ached from fighting with the furniture container and my legs and back throbbed from kicking the inside of the trunk. I asked the police if I could go in the house and use the restroom. Lena and one of the cops came with me. In the living room, the mom and little boy were speaking with an officer. I heard her say her husband was out of the country and two of his friends had moved them to this spot the day before.

"Daddy's gone," the little boy stated. The policeman nodded.

Lena walked closer to the living room where the woman answered questions, while I disappeared down the hall. In a few minutes, we moved out to the yard in silence and stood close to her car.

"I heard her say she didn't know anyone was inside the container. She's been here less than a day," my sister said.

"Did she say that her husband is the Popolare guy?"

"I think so. But he's out of the country."

"Back to Italy. That's my guess."

"And that she and her son were only there on a temporary basis. They were leaving next week," said Lena. "Why did they abandon the Marin house? Why is everyone disappearing?"

"They must have known that they were being watched. So they launched the first code and took off. I bet they planned on leaving them in that pod to roast to death."

Inspector Burrell sat in her car, talking on the radio. She held up a finger as Lena and I moved in her direction. She said a few more words and signed off. "You're free to go, you know. You don't have to hang around here any longer."

I smiled. "Thank you for believing me."

She turned to Lena. "Are you working with her now?"

My sister paled. "Absolutely not."

"Well, you have intercepted a scheme that would have taken down the entire networks of at least six small to midsize cities. You should be proud."

"I had a feeling."

"Well, once again your feelings panned out. Good work," said Inspector Burrell.

"Can Earl and Tyler go home now?"

"Tyler's the missing person you told me about a few weeks ago, isn't he?"

"Yes."

"The police want to continue talking to him. Not a big deal. But they're going to take him in for questioning."

I took a step back and let out a small gasp. "He's just a dumb kid," I said.

"He's not a kid. He's a person of interest," said Inspector Burrell.

"And Earl?"

"He can go," she said.

CHAPTER 43

A strained silence filled the car during the ride from the vineyards of rural Petaluma to Earl's house. Earl sat in the front next to my sister. No one said a word for the first fifteen minutes.

"Earl, are you okay?" Lena asked while she kept her eyes on the road.

"Tired. And worried about Tyler."

"Did he say anything to you when the three of you were locked up?" I asked.

"Only that he'd made a mistake. Being in that pod was like being in an oven. The heat was fierce," said Earl. "It was hard on Ty, but harder on Bernard." He stared out the window, signaling the end of the conversation. But I couldn't keep quiet.

"They were going to leave all of you there. In that pod. In this heat. Did you know that? You could have died. But for some reason, you decided to work with them. These criminals."

"It's not what you think," he said.

"Then enlighten me." He stayed silent. "You and that Popolare guy. You were trying to cripple a dozen city governments. Inspector Burrell knows it. I know it. What were you going to do? Ask for money? Threaten to put all their data online? I don't know why you aren't in custody."

"As I said, it's not what you think."

No one spoke as we drove into Marin and up the winding hills of Earl's neighborhood, past Burk's former "home." Lena had texted Dad when we left Sonoma County and he waited on the front steps with The Babe. The dog ran up to the car, his little stump of a tail snapping back and forth. When Earl stepped out, he jumped up on him hard, almost knocking him back into the car.

"You coming in?" he asked, peering back at me.

"My car is at Jack London Square. Can you give me a lift over there?" I asked my sister.

"Oh, why not. This day is shot anyway."

Earl gave me an odd look as I climbed out of the back seat and slid into the passenger seat. Dad came to his side and took his arm, and he let himself be led away like a child. Earl stooped over as he shuffled away, his shoulders sagging. He had the energy of a deflated balloon. Lena turned the car around and started down the hill.

"I have a small request," I said. "Don't tell T all of this. Let's stop your narrative at Inspector Burrell's office, okay?"

"I've been thinking of the best way to frame this," she said.

"Don't frame it at all. It never happened. Okay?"

She nodded.

We joined the heavy traffic going to the East Bay. On the Richmond-San Rafael Bridge, traffic slowed to a complete standstill. I glanced out at the water beneath me and tried to find the small sandy cove on the east side.

"Are you going to swim the open water event at Keller Cove, that beach at Pt. Richmond, this year?" I asked.

"If I find a babysitter, I will." Lena replied. "You should do it."

I shook my head. "No. No more open water races for me."

I fiddled with my seatbelt strap. I smoothed down my damp tee shirt and pulled back my hair, scanning Lena's car for a scrunchie. I held my hair for a few seconds, then let it go.

"Will you stop fidgeting," appealed Lena, giving me a light slap on the arm.

"I'm tired and I stink," I said sniffing under my arm. I rolled down the window. "I can't figure out why they kept Tyler but not Earl. Unless —" I stopped.

"Unless?"

"Of course. I've been so stupid. What if he's been working with the police or some government hush-hush agency to infiltrate this cybercriminal network? What if that's why he was free to go?"

"That would make sense," agreed Lena.

"That must be it."

We crawled off the bridge and the traffic picked up as we moved into four lanes. Once we were past East Bay Downs, a local horse racetrack near the Berkeley exit, traffic slowed down again. Two windsurfers flitted across the greenish-brown water of San Francisco Bay to our right. *If only my life could be so carefree.*

"Burk. Yet another creep for your memoirs," said Lena shaking her head. "Jon is the best guy you've been with for what, two, three years? I don't understand what your problem is. You must know by now that your husband is long gone. He's never coming back. Why won't you allow yourself some happiness?"

"Lee, please."

If I could've moved further away from her, I would have, but I was already plastered against the passenger side door. There was nothing I wanted to say until I got the chance to work things out with Jon. And that's what I wanted to do.

"Do you know that I pray for you? Well, not pray, pray, but ask someone, something, to push you in the right direction."

"You've never prayed a day in your life," I said with a grin.

My sister glanced at the traffic in front of us. "Nothing else has worked. You've always been stubborn, but these days, you're like a brick wall."

"Lee, it's been a long day. I know you mean well, but … " I could hardly get the words out. A thick weariness hung over each inch of my body.

"I appreciate you driving me, I do. I just want to get to my car, go home, and take a shower."

We rode for the next forty-five minutes in silence. She dropped me off in front of the garage at Jack London Square.

"You need to think about your life," my sister said as she put the car in drive.

I laid my hand gently on her arm.

"That's what I'm doing. That's all I've been doing."

CHAPTER 44

A few days later, I found myself alone in the big house. Dad had a lunch date with the woman he'd met while we were scouting for our roommate. And Earl? He was already back to his old routine, volunteering at China Camp. But he'd also had several visits from a bunch of suits who never smiled. Whenever they showed up, they just disappeared into his office like a clutch of Armani-clad robots.

I relaxed on the deck, eyes closed, head lifted to the sun when the front door opened. Tyler had stopped by to take The Babe for a walk.

"You plan on coming back this time?" I asked with a smile.

"Ha ha. Funny. Come on, pup." He picked up the dog's leash, then walked over to the deck and sat on the rail.

"I can't thank you enough. I was a total jerk for getting involved with that shit, those people. I don't know what I was thinking."

"I hope the money was good while it lasted," I said.

"Not enough to put Grandpa and his friend—"

"And you ..."

"And me, in danger," he said.

"You did this for the money?"

"I wanted to buy a new car."

"Seriously? All this for a car?"

"Well ..."

"Your grandfather would have loaned you the money, I'm sure."

"I have no excuse." He spread his arms and shrugged. "The people I worked for were ... um ... very persuasive. And to be honest, they didn't have to push all that hard. They dangled so much money in front of me and it sounded exciting. How did you find us?"

"Modern technology, if you can believe it."

He laughed. "See ya." He waved as he and The Babe headed for the door.

All that upheaval because he'd wanted a car. I was drugged, ended up in the hospital and stuffed into the trunk of a car a so he could ride around in some hot wheels. Unbelievable.

I had a chance to speak with Earl the next afternoon in his office.

"Hey, Trisha. Things back to normal, right?"

"Your opinion. Not mine. You have to tell me what was going on."

"I can't. But on the positive side, Ty is at the radio station and Bernard is in good health and home in Oregon. Where they both belong."

"And Frida the hackable fridge has been replaced with a standard, not-so-smart refrigerator. I know. You've told me. But there is so much more you haven't said," I said.

I sat down on the leather couch across from his desk.

"Earl, I think I deserve an explanation."

He glanced out at the deck for a moment, then walked over and sat down next to me. "There's not much I can tell you," he said. "Legally."

"I wouldn't call that fair, would you? You knew Tyler wasn't missing."

"Well, he was … at least, for a little while."

"I know you and this Popolare guy met years ago. He was your student."

"Something like that. I was more of a mentor. When he came to work for me, I recognized a unique talent. Gifted, I'd say. He wrote the most beautiful code I've ever seen. One evening, he and I were working late, and we began discussing backdoors—a way to bypass a network's security, sneak into a computer system. I had developed a string of methods—I called them parlor tricks—to make a backdoor attack not only possible, but completely invisible. And relatively easy to do, as things go."

"And?"

"He took my parlor tricks and improved them, a hundred-fold. But we disagreed about their application. I thought they should be used to test a system's capability of fending off attacks, use them to identify holes in their security. Popolare had other, less … uh, benevolent ideas, and we had a knockdown, drag-out fight, and went our separate ways. He turned up contracting with the City of San Francisco and creating their computer network. You know the rest, I think."

"When did you reconnect with him?"

"I was asked to keep an eye on him. Find out what he was doing."

"Who did the asking? Tyler? Bernard?"

"Neither. I was in contact with an organization."

"Shadowcorp."

"What?"

"That' what I called them."

Earl smiled. "That's a pretty good name. Anyway, Shadowcorp and I laid the groundwork that brought in Tyler first, then Bernard. At my request. Obviously, they didn't know I was already involved. Remember when Bernard said he'd been assigned to watch a typical suburban family?"

"Yes, the day I tackled him. I remember."

"It was a sham. They were ordinary people. But it gave me some time so I could connect with Popolare and regain his trust."

"And Tyler never knew you were a counterspy?"

"No, he didn't. When he figured out the people in the house over the hill weren't competition, but Shadowcorp's own employees, he thought we were doing something morally wrong. That's when he stopped delivering the Coyote Ridge bottles to Jason."

"Chang? He works for Shadowcorp?"

"Right. Tyler has seen too many spy movies and he became concerned about the reaction from Shadowcorp when they didn't receive their mini microchip. He wasn't worried that much about himself, but what the organization might do to me. Due to my reputation, mostly."

"What I don't get is that, if Popolare thought you were working with him to develop these codes, why the drone? You could have just walked in the front door."

"I did that occasionally. The drone was for surveillance. It saw things that I didn't. I couldn't be there all the time."

"Who or what is Shadowcorp?"

He shook his head.

"Earl, I have to tell you something."

"Okay."

"When I didn't know what was going on, I searched through your office. And I found the activation codes for the ransomware. But I didn't know what they were until later. I gave them to the police."

Earl's face morphed into a mask of stone. Not a twitch. Not an eye blink. "Go on."

"Why didn't you stop the first attack if you knew it was going to happen?"

Earl's face softened. "The Marin group discovered they were compromised."

"How?"

"The mini-chip. It was Burk. He spotted one at Jason's house. Brought it back to Marin and viewed it. That set everything in motion. Didn't take long for them to figure out that Tyler, Bernard and I were connected. Once they did, they pushed the launch date up for the first attack. They kidnapped the three of us, packed up, and left."

"You've been working with the feds or some other agency, haven't you? That's who has been visiting you recently."

"I can't talk about that. But I will say that you're on the right track. Trisha, I'm sorry you became so deeply involved. They wanted to use you to get to me."

"The guys visiting you. Are they Secret Service? National Security? CIA?"

"Trisha."

"I deserve an answer. I was drugged because of you. I was kidnapped and stuffed into a trunk, because of you."

"Them, Trisha. Drugged because of them, not me."

"Did Tyler and Bernard know what you were doing?"

Earl hesitated again. "No," he said.

He moved over to the bookcase and picked up the photo of him at Woodstock. He smiled slightly and placed it back on the shelf.

"I'm not a cybercrime fighter. Or with the FBI or the CIA. I'm retired. I was lucky to be in the right place at the right time when computers were springing to life. That's it. That is who I am."

"But—"

"I still know people—good people—in the industry. I lend a helping hand when I can. Nothing more.

"One last thing," he said. There was a long pause. "Stay out of my office."

He pointed to the door.

Earl left the house not long after our conversation. I walked back to my room, thinking about what he'd said. I had been spinning my wheels, and he had been in charge the whole time. I moved to the deck and stood there alone, watching the sun splash through the redwoods stretching down into the Canyon.

While I'd been hunting down Tyler and Earl, my energy level switched on to ultra power mode, my body and brain fueled by a constant flow of adrenaline. But now, the switch had clicked off and I was tired to my bones. And it didn't feel over. I'd never get the complete story from Earl. So infuriating. I needed to talk to someone who knew what had happened inside the Marin house.

Burk. He would have the answers I wanted. But would he give them to me? He now resided in the Marin County Jail. Before I just showed up and requested visitation, I needed advice. I called Inspector Burrell.

"How are you feeling?" she asked.

"Confused. I need some information and I think the only person who can help me is Burk, but he's in custody, as you know. I'm thinking of visiting him."

There was a long pause. "Trisha, you're a victim. You were kidnapped and drugged by this man. If there is a trial, you will be asked to testify. He has been charged with these crimes against you, as well as half a dozen more for violating the Computer Fraud and Abuse Act. His lawyer may want to talk to you, but it would be highly unusual for you to visit him, especially by yourself. His lawyers could make something of it. I wouldn't advise it."

"I guess I didn't think of that," I said. "Being his victim."

"That's good. I'm glad you're not thinking that way. But promise me you won't go to the jail. And talk to a lawyer before you do anything else."

"Ok. I promise. But I want to know why I was targeted. Only he can tell me that."

"Maybe it'll come out at trial," said Inspector Burrell. "Sorry, but I have to go. Remember, you made a promise." She hung up.

So Burk moved out of the picture. But maybe, Jon would listen. I texted him after we met that night but had kept it light. I promised myself I wouldn't involve him or see him until this case was solved. My phone pinged. It was Uly. He'd sent me a photo of a slender man at the checkout counter of a big box tech store.

This is your guy. Pretty sure he stole your identity.

On my way over.

Uly opened the door before I had a chance to ring the bell. He wore a Dead Kennedys tee shirt. For the first time, his hair, which was pulled up again in a neat man bun, looked clean.

"Come in," he motioned. He put a straight-backed chair by his three monitors.

"How did you find him?"

He smiled. "In-store cameras and such. And I had a little help."

I started to ask another question, but he shook his head. "That's all you need to know."

"If I hear that or something like that one more time, I will scream."

A screenshot of a man at a checkout counter spread across his monitor. Three little children, two boys and a girl, stood next to him.

"That's him? Why does he have to be a father?" I covered my eyes with my hands.

Uly held out a piece of paper with the screenshot. "I scrubbed all my identifying information. Before you jump to conclusions, I doubt he's the one who hacked your computer. From what I could find out, he's a construction worker. My guess is he bought a couple of fake credit cards, had his name put on them, but your account information was embedded."

"So, someone sold my identity to him?"

"That's my guess," Uly said. "You've had a few credit card hacks, right?"

"Yeah."

"This would be from the last one. The guy used the card in the Bay Area. Easier for me to pinpoint the location and when it was used. Can't help you on the first, however."

"Can I ask you a question? It's about something else."

Uly closed his eyes. I guess that meant 'yes.'

I started out awkwardly telling him about meeting Burk at the open water swim, running into him on the trail, at the ballpark, then Coyote Ridge, Earl's drone, my drugging, and Tyler and Earl's kidnappings. By this time, Uly's eyes were open and as big as the owl's I'd seen in La Cruz Canyon. "Is there more?"

"Oh, yes, but you know all about that, already. Popolare and the codes and the ransomware."

"What's the question in all this?" he asked.

"Why me? Why did he choose me as a target?"

"I wouldn't know for sure, but I guess you and your Dad had been thoroughly researched and the Popolare crew decided that you'd be the easiest to manipulate." Uly's comments were littered with 'uhs,' and 'ums' and pauses that went on forever.

"They were wrong about that," I said.

"True. But if he thought he could get in the house through you …"

"Still doesn't make any sense. Earl, and certainly Dad, would have just invited him in," I interrupted.

Uly kept talking. "Maybe get upstairs to your bedroom or into Earl's office, plant some bugs, some cameras. Heavy-duty surveillance, both from afar, and up close. Find out if he was friend or foe."

"Burk came to my rescue at the one-miler to ingratiate himself with me. That's when it started."

"Before that. Bet he's been tracking you for a while," he said.

"Uly," I paused and zeroed in on his expressionless face, "how did you know that my bedroom was upstairs?"

He hesitated. Then, he stood up, walked around the room, came back to his chair, closed his eyes and took a deep breath. When he opened his eyes, he tilted his head. "Your refrigerator."

"Frida told you my room was upstairs?"

"Well, there have been some complications with the fridge," he said, changing the subject.

"Oh? Like what?"

"It was hacked by two people, both the audio and video."

"Two people!"

I tried to make sense of what he said. Two people. Uly stood there watching and waiting.

"And you know this, how?"

"I'm sorry," he mumbled.

"No. Uly! You were one of the people spying on me? That's how you knew I lived on the second floor. Why would you do that?"

"When you stabbed the camera and broke the … uh … lens, you didn't disengage the audio at that time. I heard you call me a … uh … uh … perv. Never thought about it like that before. Sorry. It was then I realized that your refrigerator had another stalker."

"Who was it?"

"I couldn't find out. Maybe Burk or one of his co-workers. I wanted to shut it down, but you managed to do that when you cut the wires. I hope this info about your fridge's hacker … hackers … and your credit card hacker … uh …"

"Makes up for you? No, it doesn't. Not at all. You spied on me in my bedroom, while I was on the phone, visiting with my family, playing with my nephew. You watched me getting dressed. Getting undressed. You … you invaded my privacy. I trusted you. How could you?"

I walked over to the hall entrance.

"I trusted you," I said again.

"I made a mistake. I apologize."

"I'll get the wire back to you and here's your video watch." I took it off and threw it at him as hard as I could.

"Friends?"

"You're unbelievable. No. We're not."

I wanted to say something else but Uly turned around, moved over to his computer, sat down and put his headphones in place. Soon his head was bobbing to his music, his fingers flying across the keyboard. He never saw me leave.

Before heading home, I stopped at the San Rafael Police Station to drop off the screen shot that showed the store name and time of purchase to the Cyber Crimes officer. I wrote the case number on the top with my name and phone number. The woman behind the bulletproof glass took the papers and disappeared into the back of the station. I didn't want to talk to another police officer, so I dashed to the glass door and left.

CHAPTER 45

The police officer in charge of Cyber Crimes called back the next day to tell me they had started investigating my information. When he asked who gave me the screenshot, all I said was a friend. Relief flooded through me when he didn't ask who that friend was. He thanked me and then hung up.

A few days later, Lena called and said she had to see me and that she'd like lunch, tuna fish sandwiches to be exact. This meant she had something important to tell me. Maybe she had a new, very influential client. Or she and Dr. T planned to adopt a dog. Or maybe she and Dr. T had set a date to get married. I had a few things to tell her, too.

"Did you make my favorite sandwich?" she asked, walking in with a grin.

"I did. Tuna on a sourdough roll, chips, lemonade and then some gelato."

I handed her a few dishes to put on the table.

"Before you jump into your news, I have something to tell you," I said.

Lena sat down and rested her feet on the chair next to her.

"What?" She was crunching on a rib of celery.

"Well, my computer hacker wasn't the real deal hacker. He bought my information. At first, the police were going to write my case off as another unsolvable white-collar crime. But then I gave them Uly's screenshot."

"Wait. Slow down. You're talking too fast. Hard to understand," said Lena.

I repeated what I'd said, this time painstakingly slow. But the more I talked, the faster the words tumbled out, like a boulder rolling downhill, gathering speed.

"They found the guy and talked with him. He upchucked the name of the person who made these counterfeit credit cards. They paid that guy a visit and found more than 500 credit and debit cards in other people's names. They also collected a stack of medical records from just about every health care organization in the Bay Area and over 10,000 passwords from various social media sites. But it didn't stop there. All that information? He bought it from someone in Russia. On the dark web. With cryptocurrency."

I took a deep breath. "What do you think about that?" I asked.

"Russia? That's impressive."

"They can't get the Russian, but they do have him and his computers. He's in jail now. And I may have to testify."

"You will be running back and forth to the courts, won't you. We need to get you some sophisticated, lawyer-like clothes," Lena remarked.

"Shopping? I hate shopping."

"Not to worry. I just appointed myself your personal shopper. What about the other trial? The one that involves Burk."

"His lawyer wants to talk to me, but the lawyer that Earl set me up with, advised me not to agree to anything."

"I heard Tyler on the radio the other day," said Lena.

"He's back at work. He got involved with this spying because he wanted a car. Guys and cars. I don't get it."

Lena slapped down a local newspaper in front of me. She had circled two stories: one on the ransomware criminals, the other about the East Bay identify theft ring. "Did you see this? You're not mentioned by name but there is a line or two about a tipster. That must be you."

I picked up the paper and read the article.

"It's interesting what they choose to print. There are some gaping holes in this reporting. They didn't say anything about Earl's kidnapping."

"You working tonight?"

"No, I called my supervisor and pleaded for a few days off. She was okay with that. I feel like I've been through the spin cycle."

I paused, then walked around the kitchen, stopping to stare out of the window over the sink. I turned back to Lena. "I've been thinking. Adrenaline rush aside, this hasn't been much of a life. Living in the maid's quarters in my father's friend's house who is some sort of cybercrime fighter. Working at a part-time seasonal job."

"Where did that come from? I thought you loved what you were doing, especially all the intrigue. Something else is bothering you."

"You said in the car the other day something about me picking losers."

"Well, unfortunately, except for the one guy that shall remain nameless because that's the way you want it, that's who you pick."

I didn't respond.

"He called me the other day," Lena and I said together in unison.

"Who?" I asked.

"Jon," she said.

"Why didn't you tell me?" I asked.

"You just said that he called you. Why didn't you tell me?" Lena responded.

"I wasn't sure what was … if we were …" I blurted.

"Trisha!"

"I didn't want to mention Jon in case it didn't work out. I realized I'm kinda like Dad. Not great about 'talking about my feelings,'" I said, making air quotes. "When he called you, what did he want?"

Lena got up and walked over to the refrigerator and pulled out the pitcher of lemonade.

"You. He wants you. He's in love with you, Trisha."

"I know."

"That's all you have to say. 'I know?'"

"I'm thinking about it," I said with a huge smile.

Lena stood there staring at me. "You finally figured out that he's a good guy, didn't you?"

"Yes, I did."

"I wondered if it would ever happen."

She took her glass of lemonade, raised it in a toast. "It's never too late to do the right thing. Here's to the late bloomers." Then she took a sip.

"Wanna hear the rest of my news?" she asked.

"Sure. Why not?"

"You like swimming now, right?"

"I haven't committed either way."

"To further your advancement in this exhilarating water sport—"

"Lena, what did you do?"

"I've signed you up for a two-mile swim at Shelter Lake in the Sierra foothills."

"What? You did what?"

"It's two months away."

"I can't swim that far."

"You have plenty of time to train. Two months. That's eight weeks," my sister said.

"No."

"Yes. And we start today. Get your swimsuit. We're going to the pool."

Acknowledgments

Many thanks to a person I call Mr. X, owner of a software company with experience in computer related security matters, who wishes to remain anonymous. Stacy Robinson, Ana Manwaring, Sabrina Flynn, Sylvia Lacock. Jayne Southern and Aaron Gallagher were my editorial specialists.

Richard Burns and Karen Brigando continue to create the best looking covers around. They managed to include Mt. Tamalpais, a Marin County landmark.

A special thank you to the write-ins sponsored by Northern California Mystery Writers of America and Northern California Sisters in Crime. Both held my feet to the fire, encouraging me to keep writing.

About the Author

If you want to find Glenda Carroll, she'll be in, on, or under water—and writing about it. She understands water sports on a very personal level since she swims, surfs and sails.

Glenda was a long time sports columnist for the Marin Independent Journal, focusing on sailboat racing. During that time, she also wrote for local, national and international sailing publications as well as travel magazines. PacificWaverider.com, a surfing website, asked her to write a twice-weekly column, which she did for more than three years.

She is the author of the Trisha Carson mysteries. They are set in the San Francisco Bay area, including Marin County, the East Bay State Parks and, of course, San Francisco. Her books have a swimming undercurrent, based on her own experience. She has raced in more than 150 open water swim events in Northern California, as well as Hawaii and Perth, Australia. She is listed in Openwaterpedia.com

Glenda tutors first-generation high school and college students in English. She is a member of Mystery Writers of America and Sisters in Crime. She lives in San Rafael, CA with her dog, McCovey.

CPSIA information can be obtained
at www.ICGtesting.com
Printed in the USA
FSHW022319211121
86378FS